About the Author

"YOU CAN'T TOP PHYLLIS A. WHITNEY WHEN SHE BUILDS A ROMANTIC SUS-PENSE NOVEL." —*Columbus Enquirer*

Phyllis A. Whitney has won world-wide success for her masterful romantic suspense best-sellers. Her novels include *The Winter People, Hunter's Green, Silverhill, Columbella, Sea Jade, Black Amber, The Quicksilver Pool, The Trembling Hills,* and *Thunder Heights.*

Miss Whitney, who was born in Yokohama, Japan, of American parents, has spent her working life entirely in the field of books—as bookseller, librarian, reviewer, teacher of writing, and bestselling novelist.

Fawcett Crest Books
by Phyllis A. Whitney:

BLACK AMBER
BLUE FIRE
COLUMBELLA
DOMINO
THE GOLDEN UNICORN
HUNTER'S GREEN
LISTEN FOR THE WHISPERER
THE MOONFLOWER
THE QUICKSILVER POOL
SEVEN TEARS FOR APOLLO
SKYE CAMERON
SPINDRIFT
THE STONE BULL
THUNDER HEIGHTS
THE TREMBLING HILLS
THE TURQUOISE MASK
WINDOW ON THE SQUARE
THE WINTER PEOPLE

LOST ISLAND

Phyllis A. Whitney

FAWCETT CREST • NEW YORK

A Fawcett Crest Book
Published by Ballantine Books
Copyright © 1970 by Phyllis A. Whitney

ISBN 0-449-21099-5

This edition published by arrangement with Doubleday and
Company, Inc.

Selection of the Doubleday Book Club, February 1971

Printed in Canada

First Fawcett Crest Edition: December 1971
First Ballantine Books Edition: November 1985

The interest, kindness and assistance offered me generously by the residents of St. Simons Island, Georgia, have enabled me to collect the background material for this book. I would like to proffer my special thanks to Mrs. Fraser Ledbetter of the St. Simons Public Library, Mrs. Jean Alexander of St. Simons Island Chamber of Commerce, Mrs. May Korb of the Shorebird bookstore, and to Don Everett of the Sailfish Motel.

My imagined island of Hampton is perhaps a miniature St. Simons, since I have borrowed and condensed from that beautiful island for the purpose of my story. There is no Malvern that I know of in Georgia, but perhaps the shadow of Brunswick lies across it. The people of the story are entirely fictional, and so are the happenings.

Lost Island

In my dream I ran along the gray sands of Hampton Island. I was barefoot, and the sand hampered me at every step. Yet I fled in terror, trying to escape my cousin Elise who pursued me. She called my name: "Lacey! Lacey!" and in her hand she carried a flaming torch of driftwood.

I knew that if she caught me she would set my clothes on fire, and I ran on and on, sinking ever deeper in the sand, while Elise relentlessly followed. From somewhere far back I seemed to hear Giles's voice, and knew that he would save me if he could. But he was too far away. When it seemed that fire from burning driftwood would touch my very back, I gave a little cry and wakened myself.

I sat up in bed trembling, and wrapped the sheets about my body, clutching at their smooth surface for reassurance. A pervading sense of evil remained from the dream, though I reminded myself again and again that I was not on the beach, but safely in bed. Nevertheless I was once more on the island—that Southern island which haunted my dreams and had haunted my life. I was in a room at Sea Oaks, Giles Severn's big white house that crowned a slight rise above the silver-gray ocean. The house to which he had brought my cousin Elise when he married her ten years before. The house I had once dreamed of living in, before Elise had stepped between us, before I had run away.

From the windows I could hear the rushing sound of the Atlantic that always filled Sea Oaks, and it was the same sound that I remembered from my childhood. I could listen to it and count my slowing heartbeats. Out there in the moon-

light the island lay shimmering blue in the spring night as it
floated on its supporting waters of river, creek, and sea. From
the mainland of Georgia a causeway ran across marshes to
the bridge over the Malvern River, giving onto the sandy soil
of the island. To the south and north other islands rose as
separate entities, but to those who lived on Hampton they
scarcely existed. The right-of-way of highway and bridge were
out-of-bounds territory, to be used when needed, but ignored
most of the time.

A small island, Hampton, with only a few square miles of
acreage, but an island with a long, stirring history, belonging
to the Hamptons since the days of early English settlers. Once
it had boasted a fort, of which only ruined stones remained—
a defense intended to hold off the Spanish. It had done its task
well and the Spaniards had been beaten back in a famous
battle. Known afterward only to friendly Indians, the island's
few inhabitants had lived in peace. Now, centuries later, it
harbored only two remaining families, joined for more than
ten years in marriage. The island was beautiful and I loved
it. But not possessively like my cousin Elise. The land was
neither good nor evil, though it held all good and evil within
the boundaries of its circling waters, and my dream had
formed out of this knowledge.

But why should I dream of Elise in the role of vengeful
pursuer? I tried to shake myself fully awake. After all, I was
here beneath this roof at her urgent invitation. She feared me
as little as that. I had come knowing that I must face Giles
again, knowing that I must see his son, Richard. I had flown
from New York to Atlanta, and then to Malvern on the mainland this Friday evening. Elise had met my plane and driven
me across the causeway and bridge that made Hampton a
stepping-stone to other, larger islands. I knew she must have
a special reason for this invitation after so long a time, but
she had not yet told me what it was. And I did not particularly care.

My own need to know many things had brought me—
driven me!—here. There was no cause to think that whatever she wanted might harm me. There was no reason to
think of her as a vengeful pursuer. Elise had always had it
all her way. She had Giles and Richard. There was no need
for pursuit—or for my agonized dream flight along a beach.

I reached for the lamp beside my bed and turned it on.
The time was a quarter to twelve, and moonlight pressed
invitingly at my windows. I lay for a few minutes longer

listening to the roar of the Atlantic. The wind rattled through palm branches, but the ocean surf had a more regular rhythm, like the persistent echo of my heart. It called to me.

I slipped out of bed and went to where I could look out toward the only other house left on the island—The Bitterns. The house was not close. The ruins of the old fort and the site of its burying ground lay between, but I could see the twinkle of lights where The Bitterns stood, across this point of land, overlooking not the ocean as Sea Oaks did but a wide stretch of marsh along the river.

From the direction of the stables a horse nickered and stamped a foot. A long-familiar sound on Hampton Island. How I'd dreaded those horses as a child. The only thing I didn't like about the island was the riding—something Aunt Amalie and her two daughters did with that curious cavalier grace and daring that I could never quite emulate.

Judging by lighted windows, Amalie Hampton, my mother's sister, must still be awake. Or perhaps it was my cousin Floria, Elise's sister, reading late at night. I could not be sure of the room from this distance, for all that I knew the house so well.

There was a longing in me to see Aunt Amalie again. Though they had never seemed alike in appearance, there were many ways in which I could see my mother in her, and over the years she had often proved herself my friend and counselor. If what I had heard about Elise was true, I needed counseling now, and I knew she would give it to me generously, even though Elise was her daughter.

Aunt Amalie and my mother, Kitty Ainsley, had grown up together on the mainland in Malvern. Once they had both been in love with Charles Severn, Giles's father, though neither had married him. Amalie had married Judge Gaylord Hampton of Hampton Island, and she had come here to live at The Bitterns, while my mother had married my Yankee father, Larry Ames, and moved to Chicago.

My mother had loved the island she had visited often as a girl, and after I was born we visited Aunt Amalie nearly every year, staying for a month at a time at The Bitterns. Aunt Amalie's younger daughter, Elise, had been close to my age, and as first cousins we were thrown together during these visits to the island. I had wanted someone close to me, I had wanted to love my only cousin, but even then Elise made affection difficult.

The Bitterns was an old plantation house—older than Sea Oaks, but far less beautiful. I had loved its very plainness and reveled in wandering its creaky halls and cool gray gloom. Aunt Amalie's husband, Judge Hampton, had died years ago, and she had raised her two daughters there—Elise and Floria. Floria was the older by four years, yet oddly enough, one always mentioned Elise first. It seemed as though Elise *was* Hampton Island. Eventually she would inherit it, because that was what her father wished, since Floria had never cared anything about it. Perhaps Elise had grown up destined to marry Giles Severn of Sea Oaks and have everything she coveted—the land that meant more to her than breath, and the stunningly beautiful house.

I could still wince painfully when I thought of Giles. I had not seen him in years, and I was very happy in my work as associate editor at a publishing house in New York. I told myself so, often enough. Yet still—I remembered. How could I not remember so intensely young and hurtful a love? How could I ever forget—for one moment—the terrible consequences of that remembered joy?

I had come back to Hampton on this trip knowing that I would probably see Giles, and dreading the moment when I must meet him face to face. It had been a relief to discover that he was away just now, and no one knew exactly when he would be back. Probably I would be gone before his return and need not see him at all. I was counting on this rather desperately.

As a little girl I had admired my cousin Elise a great deal. I wanted more than anything to be like her. Because she was fair and my hair was only light brown, I wanted to be blond. Because she was beautiful, I wanted a perfect little nose, a smaller mouth, and eyes that were not so large that my face was lost in them. Yet in my childhood fantasies I had left Elise out. In my make-believe *I* was queen of the island, and Giles was king. It's not true that children don't fall in love. There's nothing so achingly painful as childhood longing for something not altogether understood. Even when she teased me about Giles, Elise never guessed the depth of my little-girl love for the tall young boy who was Giles Severn. Oh, I was ready for him by the time I was seventeen!

Yet I could not hate Elise when she came back to the island in all her young beauty to dazzle Giles. She was only being Elise. And it was I who had run away. In my pride I had not wanted to make claims upon him. If he wanted me enough he would follow me, I thought. I had been too young to see that he might think I'd only tired of a game.

I moved from the window, restless now, knowing that I would not sleep. I had not flown here merely obedient to Elise's summons. I had come for desperate purposes of my own. Partly I had come for—what could I call it?—exorcism? To drive out a spirit that was neither good nor evil but relentless. Long ago the island had laid a spell upon me, and I had never escaped. Now I knew I must escape at last. I must be able to live my own life. I must stop gauging every man I met by Giles's measure. I wanted to be free. I wanted to forget that delight of a single month every summer when my life had seemed perfect and complete. A month when I had run wild and unfettered in the island sun, following those playmates I admired more than any I met the rest of the year. And I wanted to get over those bruising summer days when I had been seventeen and had thought so mistakenly that all life was opening up for me.

The island had damaged me. Perhaps irreparably. It had made me unfit for other places, ill-equipped for a world less enclosed, less assured than this. I had sent down psychological roots here, where no roots could thrive, and now I must pull them up forever, however ruthlessly.

Perhaps it would have been different if the severing of island ties had been natural and gradual. It had not been. My mother had died when I was eleven, and my grieving, busy father cared nothing for the soft summers at Hampton Island. Though my Aunt Amalie invited me, the visits abruptly ended and my summers were otherwise spent. The injury went deep. Yet the memory of the young Giles lasted. He had been a gallant figure to my youthful eyes, with an unfailing kindness and consideration that won me to him. I was younger than the others, and sometimes they laughed at me. But Giles had never laughed. He had given me an affection that had a certain sweetness in it. Yet he could be angry at times and quick to bristle when opposed. Gentle with me, but not always with others.

Here I was dreaming again, which was no way to pull up roots and escape so curiously antique a spell. There was a grimmer, far more painful reason which had brought me back to Hampton. I had been hearing rumors about Elise and her escapades, hearing that her marriage to Giles was not all it should be. I told myself that this had no significance for me, except in one all-important sense. I had to know the truth about what was happening to the boy, Richard. I had to know the truth, not because of Giles, but because of his son. And mine. Yes, mine. The son I had never acknowledged, and whom I'd held in my arms so briefly at the beginning of his life. I had given him up so long ago that I had no right to care desperately about him now. Yet there it was—that feeling in me that would not be uprooted, would not be extinguished.

Roaming the room, I went to the closet and looked inside. Vinnie had unpacked for me. Vinnie Taylor, who was my old and dear friend. She had been with Aunt Amalie at The Bitterns when I had visited there as a small girl, and she had come with Elise to Sea Oaks when Elise had married. I found a pair of dark green slacks and a woolly brown pullover and got into them. The spring night would be cool. I slipped low-heeled buckled shoes on my feet and tied a soft green scarf around my short hair. I was ready for the moonlit night outdoors.

The hallway was quiet, with doors closed upon those who slept. All but one door. Across from mine the door stood open and when I went near and looked in, I could hear soft breathing. Moonlight streamed through windows and touched the sleeping boy. I could not see his face—it was turned toward shadow, but I could see the bright gilt of his hair. Light brown like my own, and gilded now by the moon.

There was a longing in my arms. There was an aching I could not stifle. I would have given anything to cross that room and touch him. I would have given anything to bend my head and kiss his cheek lightly. I could not. A taboo lay upon him. Not even Giles, his own father, knew that Richard was not Elise's son, but mine. As always, when I remembered, there was a tightening under my heart.

I was shivering when I turned toward the stairs. The carpeted steps made no sound under my feet as I stole down them, following their lovely curve to the wide hallway below, where a lamp still burned. Near the foot of the stairs stood the familiar glass case which displayed the Hampton-Severn treasures. They belonged to both families, but it had been agreed long ago that Sea Oaks made the best showcase for them.

In the center of the display case stood the golden, jewel-studded pirate goblet which had been unearthed near the burying ground more than a hundred years ago. There were a few Indian artifacts as well, a dagger with a jeweled hilt, and a small jeweled brooch—again pirate treasure. The small brooch

was not the famous Stede Bonnet brooch which had once
rested in this place and in whose disappearance my own
mother had played some mysterious role.

Once the island had been the sole property of the Hamptons—a long-ago royal grant from England when these coastal
lands and sea islands were first occupied in the name of the
crown and given forever to certain loyal followers. At the
same time that Georgia's Darien was being settled by Scots
under the old name of New Inverness, Hamptons were settling
this island, giving it their name. A name that had been pre-
served, retained throughout the years by a strange, proud
custom—until the last Hampton marriage: even when the
bloodline led to a daughter, her husband would adopt the
name according to pre-marriage agreement. Giles had broken
with tradition by refusing to take the name of Hampton. In
this Elise had not had her way. But the child had been named
Richard Hampton Severn, in the hope, perhaps, on Elise's
part, that he would revert to the Hampton name when he
was grown.

The library occupied the front corner of the house across
from the parlor, and from its door a bar of amber light fell
across the polished floor. I looked into the room. Charles
Severn sat in his easy chair reading one of those thick books
of nonfiction with which he spent so many hours. He had
grayed a little since the last time I had seen him, and I knew
that his wife Marian's death more than a year ago must have
been hard for him to grow accustomed to. He was still handsome to an arresting extent. The years had been kind to him.

Giles resembled his father very little. Giles's eyes were
green instead of blue, and his hair was a sooty black. But the
difference went far deeper. There was steel in Giles, and none
in his father. Charles had always been content to sit back and
let Marian run things. Now that he was semi-retired, he went
to his law office in Malvern two or three days a week, working in desultory fashion on those estate matters which were
put into his hands. I think he never understood his son's
drive, or his capabilities. He was gently benign and had lovely
manners. I had always been fond of him.

"Hello, Lacey," he said, looking up from his book. "Can't
you sleep?"

"I'm wide awake," I said. "I thought I'd get up and go for
a walk, pay my respects to the island."

Respects were not what I wanted to pay. My purpose was

to look coldly, to withstand every spell—*not* to respect. But this truth would not serve with Charles.

"You're looking well," he said warmly. "As though New York must agree with you."

That New York should agree with me was, I knew, a mystery to Hampton Island. I laughed softly.

"Vinnie says I'm too skinny. She says she'd like a chance to fatten me up."

Charles chuckled. "Stay a while and give her that chance."

"I wish I could." I moved about the room, looking at objects I remembered.

Upon a desk near a window rested a piece of driftwood. In rough, weathered gray was the form of a graceful little sailing vessel, its prow tilted as if it breasted the waves. I picked it up and turned it about in my hands.

"I found this bit of driftwood on the beach when I was no more than ten," I told Charles. "It reminded me of a ship and I gave it to Giles."

"Then he's kept it all this time," Charles said. "That's Giles's desk, and he has arranged it to suit himself."

So he had not forgotten me altogether. I set the bit of wood down with a slight pang, and moved on to look at pictures I remembered.

Over the mantel was a water color by a local Malvern artist—a glimpse of Malvern marshes when marsh fires were burning. I had always loved that picture as a child. It had the eerie look that early blue dusk can carry, and across the brown grasses and shining patches of water blue smoke drifted from the low, smoldering fires.

But there was another picture I liked even better. It hung between two side windows and I went to stand before it. For generations Hampton Island had been interested in shrimping, and once shrimp boats had sailed out from the island itself. They still operated from the mainland. This picture showed a fleet of boats heading seaward against a faint pink sunrise, their sails plump with wind, and all hands busy on board.

"Those boats still look pretty much the same," Charles said, coming to stand beside me. "Giles owns a fleet of them now, you know. Something, I'm afraid, that never pleased Marian. His mother always wanted him to be a proper lawyer like me."

Giles, as I well remembered, was not given to being "proper" about anything, and the business he had developed had been his inspiration from the first. He had thought of using shrimp and other seafood for some of Vinnie's best family recipes, which were then frozen and marketed as luxury foods. The Sea Oaks brand of specialty items had been successful enough to make Giles a well-to-do man. His mother had never quite forgiven his entry into "trade," nor had she ever stopped raising her proud Southern nose over the smell of shrimp, even though she never visited Giles's freezing plant over in Malvern. Giles was of the new South, his mother belonged to the old.

Charles moved toward his easy chair and gestured me to sit down. "We never see you on Hampton any more," he said regretfully. "How are you, Lacey my dear? I must say you look more and more like your mother every day. You're every bit as pretty, and you have that look of being alive about you that she had. But how are you, really?"

I chose the small rocker Marian Severn had once preferred in this room. I smiled at him affectionately, sensing his fondness for me, and refrained from saying "Haunted." Once Charles Severn had been in love with my mother, Kitty Ainsley. Theirs had been a romantic and not very happy story.

He had been engaged to Amalie, my mother's older sister. Then Kitty had returned to Malvern after a long absence. They had been swept away without meaning to be, and Charles had decided that it was Kitty he must marry. But my mother could not bear to hurt her sister. She went away north to Chicago and married my father a few years later. Charles, however, had not married Amalie, after all. Only a few months after my mother ran away, he had married an old friend, Marian Huntington, and his marriage had apparently been a happy one. Amalie also recovered quickly enough, for she had married Judge Gaylord Hampton, to whom she had been devoted until his death.

I think Charles would never have been the right man for my mother, because she had a taste for strong, dominant men like my father, and she would not want a gentle man whom she could rule, as Marian had more or less ruled Charles. Nevertheless, Charles could hold a grudge and he had never forgiven Kitty for running away. Later, when we visited the island, there was an estrangement between them and my mother saw little of him, not caring to be rebuffed. He had not carried over his resentment to me, however, and I had long given him my affection. In a sense he was part of the island spell for me, and though I wanted to break it, I would not hurt him in answering his question.

"Sometimes I'm not sure how I am," I told him, hesitantly. "Though I know I like my work and I want to feel that I'm contented."

"Life takes surprising turns," Charles said. "It has for me. Has anyone told you that I'm to be congratulated?"

"What do you mean?" I asked.

"After all these years Amalie and I are to be married," he said.

The news was a surprise indeed, and very touching. It was suitable that these two who had once loved each other should come together again when they were older and in need of warm companionship.

I went to him and bent to kiss his cheek. "That's marvelous! I'm happy for you both."

"As you know, we've been the best of friends over the years," he said. "We understand each other. Always did. I've been lonely since I lost Marian, and I know Amalie has spent a good many lonely years at The Bitterns."

Besides which, Amalie's daughter had married Charles's son. I asked the question that came first to my mind.

"How does Elise feel about this?"

He hesitated. "She says all the right words. But I'm not sure she's happy about it. Elise rather enjoys ruling Sea Oaks as Giles's wife, and the reins are likely to be taken out of her hands somewhat when her mother comes here." Then he added with an unusual touch of bitterness, "Perhaps that will be all to the good. Elise needs to be kept in line."

I wondered that Giles could not keep her in line, if that was needed, and Charles seemed to read my mind.

"Giles is busy with his work," he said uneasily. "I think it will be good to have Amalie here."

I told him again how happy I was for him, and moved toward the door. "I believe I'll go outside for a while. I haven't seen the island by moonlight for a long time. Then perhaps I can sleep again."

Charles smiled at me and returned to his book.

The front door was unlocked—who locked doors on Hampton Island?—and I slipped outside. At once the roar of ocean surf filled the night, no longer subdued by the walls of a house. Palm leaves clashed and rattled in the wind, and the whole wild rushing sound was familiar and beautiful to my ears.

Over the little balcony that projected above the door hung a beautiful wrought-iron lamp, lighted now, so that I could

see my way clearly across the portico. The steps ran down
in two spreading arms that curved to enclose a great bank of
azaleas, nearly gone now with the season, and without color
beneath the moon. I ran down the right-hand flight and hesitated for a moment. If I turned left I could take the short
cut to The Bitterns, where someone was still awake and
would welcome me. But at best the burying ground through
which I would pass was a gloomy place by day, and by night
it could be positively eerie. The long way around would be
a pleasanter walk.

I chose the drive of white shell leading between ancient
live oaks which dripped their traditional streamers of Spanish
moss. When I had gone a little distance, I turned and looked
back at the house.

As always, it had the power to move me deeply. I did
not want to react to it now, though its sheer beauty was
breath-catching in a way I could not help. Ever since her
marriage, Elise had been at work restoring the wear of years,
refurbishing with fresh white paint, spending Giles's money
lavishly to make Sea Oaks what it had once been, instead of
the house of rather shabby beauty I remembered from my
childhood. The Bitterns was homely, and sometimes a little
ghostly, but Sea Oaks was all the most beautiful clichés of
the 1830 Southern mansion rolled into one. Such houses were
not typical of the islands, but belonged more commonly to
mainland architecture. One was forever grateful to those
who had built here for not choosing the more usual plantation house.

Where was there anything else in architecture with the
simple dignity of the Doric column? Six such columns rose
in soaring beauty to support the straight symmetry of the
roof. Connecting them on either side of the steps stretched
white balusters, and similar balusters rimmed the suspended
balcony above. "Camelot," Elise had called it when we'd
played our childish King Arthur games, and Camelot it remained to me in memory.

I swallowed unwilling tears that had no explanation, and
turned my back on the house to walk along the white shell
avenue between the great live oaks. Once I reached up and
touched a streamer of dry gray moss with my fingers, remembering that Floria used to call it witches' hair, and
sometimes wore strands of it beneath her Merlin's cap for
our games.

The old sense of island mystery was upon me. I had always

felt it a place of secrets, of hidden motives and unforeseen consequences. How many unforeseen consequences it had held for me! It was as if all my treasures were buried here, waiting for me. On the one hand the island seemed to protect, to enfold, while on the other it opened upon dangerous ground, as unstable beneath the foot as the marshes themselves.

I should not have risked the exterior of Sea Oaks by moonlight. I had come meaning to sneer at all clichés, and I was succumbing to the spell instead, with no will left to resist it. Somewhere from the direction of the stables a horse whinnied, and I wondered if I might go riding tomorrow. I was certainly no devotee, but I could still ride, and perhaps if I did so I could cover more ground and see the island as it was— a tangle of lonely pine barrens and scrub palmetto—thickets for hiding snakes. Hot and sandy, and without appeal for any grown woman in her right senses.

The spring night was lightly cool and I walked on more quickly. There was a scent of blossoms on the air. Lilac was heady, even by moonlight. Yet the perfume was laced by another odor that I recognized with a sense of nostalgia that I tried vainly to stifle—the smell of the marshes drifting over from beyond The Bitterns. There were no marshes close to Sea Oaks, but the smell of them pervaded the island—that damp, slightly tangy odor of wet grasses and mucky earth that spread for miles along the river.

Once you'd breathed that strange scent, you'd recognize it always, even though it was an elusive odor. When you were away altogether you could never recall it accurately. But coming home to the sea islands, every islander breathed it as a welcoming sign of home—and forgot it as he lived with the marshes from day to day.

Suddenly the full sense of the island was about me, enveloping me, shutting me in. I had always felt this as a child. On Hampton I was closed in, safely surrounded, as though no pain or turmoil from the outer world could reach me here. The illusion was deceptive, of course, make-believe, but Hampton, with its reaching arms of water all around, had always made me feel safe and comfortably enclosed. This was the frightening spell I must escape. It must not pull me back and engulf me, now that I was here. It must cease to fill me with longing all the time I was away. For I knew very well it was not the island alone I longed for. It was Giles, who came with the island. Giles and his small son. Who was also my son.

I walked on between the dark streamers of moss, dreaming in spite of myself, remembering old times, happy times. There was a tree . . . Of course! I'd almost forgotten, but I would look for it now. I would remind myself mockingly of those foolish days of childhood. I quickened my steps, glancing about me more carefully, watching for the bend in the driveway that led toward the asphalt road. There it was—the turn. And the old tree was still there—a tall red gum with its markedly imprinted bark.

Moonlight fell dappled through the high branches and when I searched carefully, I could make out the old carving. I reached out with my fingers and traced the space where the bark had been cut away, and crude lettering carved into the trunk of the tree. I touched the top line and then moved below. KING ARTHUR, the lower letters spelled. That had been Giles, carving at Elise's urging, amused with her because he was older and regarded her as a child. Then she had taken his knife and started on GUINEVERE. She had carved her rough "G" above the "Arthur," even though I protested that her name belonged below the king's. Giles did not care. It was only a game to him anyway, and after a while he took the knife from her and helped her finish the name. She did not trouble to carve "Queen" because everyone knew that Guinevere was queen, and of course her name belonged first because she was a Hampton and this was Hampton Island. Or so she pointed out.

When they were through, I borrowed the knife and cut a crude "Lacey" into the bark, considerably below the others, with no sense of being out of place. I wanted my mark on the tree too, even though I was the youngest and did not live on the island like the others.

So the three names had stayed over the years, still marking the tree and giving evidence of the children we once had been, offering proof that Hampton was a small kingdom unto itself. In the misty moonlight around me three children moved and had their being. And I was tied to them. The exorcism I imagined was not going to be as easy as it had seemed in New York. I should be laughing at childish games—and I was not.

Perhaps ours was the game of chivalry the South had always played. It was particularly suited to Hampton Island, which carried on the yearly tradition of an Arthurian ball. The Camelot ball, it was called. Sometimes the ball was held at The Bitterns, sometimes at Sea Oaks, but always it was an event in the area, done with costumes and panoply. Once there had even been tournaments, with riders competing for the rings. This was no more, but the ball was colorful and enormously exciting to children as well as to adults.

In between the real balls we had played at King Arthur, and made up our own fantasies. Elise had been Guinevere, of course. It was her born role to be queen. Giles had been a more reluctant Arthur. His interests were many and broad, and it seemed confining to be a king. Nevertheless, he had performed his destined role. Sea Oaks had been our Camelot, and Hampton Island Arthur's kingdom. As for me, I had taken no role of importance. Mostly I served as lady-in-waiting to the queen, or messenger to Merlin—which was forever Floria Hampton's eerie role. Elise's older sister had always been a little eccentric, and a role in which magic played its part seemed ideal for her. Now and then I pined in a tower as the Lily Maid of Astolat, or floated down from Shalott in a rowboat barge on Malvern River. Once my boat had drifted away and Arthur himself had rescued me, kind and reassuring, casually affectionate. How I had loved Giles that day!

But on the tree I was only Lacey, and Elise had been tolerant and amused by the inconsistency.

We had grown up from those days. Events had swept us apart and broken up our games. My mother had died and the island was lost to me for years. Then, that summer when I was seventeen, Aunt Amalie had invited me back, and I had gone. My father was recently dead, and I had been lonely and restless. Elise was away on a visit to New Orleans, but Giles was there, and we had discovered each other.

Apparently it had surprised him that I was no longer a tousle-headed little girl who brought him gifts of odd shells, and tagged around after him adoringly. I think I was still that adoring child, but he took me for the poised and confident young woman I pretended to be. We went everywhere together. We fell madly in love. Aunt Amalie watched a little aghast, and did not know what to do about either of us.

We were free to make use of the island, and there were hidden beaches, deep little coves. Love-making came naturally, and for me it was a giving of myself forever. Perhaps it might have been for Giles as well, if Elise had not returned to the island and found out what had happened between us. Secretly, I suppose, she had always considered Sea Oaks her home-to-be. When she was ready she had always meant to marry Giles, and it was not in her nature to imagine that he could look elsewhere. She wanted to have her own sort of good time

first, and to fill her life with attractive young men, with
parties and dates, and a wild fling or two of her own that
Giles, of course, would never know about. She was completely
confident that he would be hers easily when the time came.
I was disturbing all her calculations, and she treated me with
a venom I had not seen before. She set out deliberately to
ridicule and belittle my all-too-obvious love for Giles. She
did not dare to make fun of me before him, but she bent
herself to the task of making me believe that it was ludicrous,
and a little stupid as well, to believe that Giles could be
seriously interested in me. At the same time she set out to
dazzle him as she had never troubled to in the past.

Unfortunately, I played into her hands at every turn. If
I had been more mature and a little less dizzily and fearfully
in love, or perhaps if my mother had been there to offer
sensible counsel, the outcome would have been different. But
Aunt Amalie, for all her loving presence, was not my mother,
and her own daughter's happiness was involved. So I took
the wrong road in my every act. In my fright I grew possessive toward Giles. I quarreled with him and made demands
he was not ready to meet. I showed myself not at all the girl
he thought me to be. When I had stirred things to the breaking point between us—with Elise cutting at me cruelly behind
his back, but always sweet and appealing, always helpless and
sympathetic to his face—I found that I was pregnant.

I would not want to live again through that time of miserably young and stubborn pride. I did not tell Giles. I could
not. Now that there was something to ask, I could ask nothing. I ran away, and he let me go. How could he not when
I was behaving so impossibly? In fantasy I saw him following
me, unwilling to give up all we had been to each other. I told
myself that this was the test—if he loved me enough he would
come after me. Fantasy had little relationship to real life.

Giles had been about to go into the Navy. There had been
only a few weeks left for him on the island. Elise was there.
Ever present. He had always known her, and a marriage between them was eminently suitable. Sometimes I tried to give
myself the fake comfort that perhaps there had been a little of
the rebound in what he did. Perhaps I had hurt him more
than I knew—or perhaps he was only relieved to be free of
my importunities, to be free of me. He married Elise, uniting
Hampton Island, took her on a brief honeymoon, and then
went off to sea.

While they were away, I crept helplessly back to Aunt
Amalie, who was my only family, and told her the truth.
Aunt Amalie was a woman of great poise and command, who
had made her peace with life. She had surmounted her own
defeats and she had the courage and enterprise to mend what
was broken. She spent no time blaming me, or being shocked
or reproachful. She saw my predicament more clearly than I
did, and she saw, daringly, a way to save the day.

I will never forget that dark, rainy afternoon I spent with
her at The Bitterns when she formulated her plan. I listened
to her, troubled and uncertain.

"What if Elise won't accept this?" I asked.

Aunt Amalie's face was calm, her manner assured. "I know
Elise. I know she has never told Giles that she can't have a
baby. She is afraid to tell him, because Giles wants a son. If
your baby is a boy, it will be his son in truth."

I remember how I shivered and went to stand looking out
at the rain where it beat a quilted design across the river. This
was not what I wanted. I wanted a miracle I had no right
to ask. I wanted, somehow, to keep Giles's baby. *My* baby.

"There should be an heir to Hampton Island," Aunt Amalie
said. "An heir to Sea Oaks. And your baby could fill the role.
Whether boy or girl, Giles will be the real father. He can
give the child everything—where you can give nothing."

"I could give love. The love of a mother," I said.

Aunt Amalie came to stand beside me at the rain-streaked
window. The smell of the marshes was heavy that day.

"Is this a generous love, darling?" she asked me.

I knew it was not. It was a selfish, possessive love that
wanted something for me, more than for my baby. I was
seventeen years old. I had made a dreadful mistake. At least
my baby should not suffer for it. But oh, how I hated to give
him up.

"What about Giles?" I said. "What about the fraud upon
Giles? Would it be better if he knew the truth?"

Aunt Amalie shook her head. "If you can say that, you
don't know Giles. He would be forever torn between you and
Elise. He would feel a duty toward you, and every time he
looked at his son—"

"I don't want that," I said. "But I want to keep the baby.
I must keep my baby." Suddenly I was determined.

Aunt Amalie was silent for a few moments. Then she put
an arm about me.

"In that case, so you shall, Lacey dear. Don't worry about expenses and what you will live on. I can take care of all that."

"My father wasn't rich," I said, "but he left me enough to manage on for a short time. I'll be all right."

"Yes, of course you will," she said, but her eyes were kind, sad with regret, because she could see what lay ahead of me far better than I could.

It was only after I left her and went back to Chicago that I began to think, that I began to see what I was doing. I was already sure, somehow, that the baby would be a boy, and now I could see what I was taking away from him. His father's love and protection. The safety and enrichment of life at Sea Oaks, where everything he needed would be given him. I was taking away the future that was due my son—as heir to the island and Giles's fortune. In Giles's hands he could grow up to be what he had a right to be. If he stayed with me I would have to hire someone to raise him while I was at work. I could give him so little. Not even a name!

The one great question was Elise. How much would she want him? I would not give him into indifferent hands. I had glimpsed a side of Elise that frightened me. If she resented the child as my son, then this plan would never work.

I wrote to Aunt Amalie, and when Elise came back from her honeymoon, and Giles was gone, they came to see me. Elise talked to me as sweetly and sincerely as I could have wished. She had what she wanted now, and she could afford to be kind to me. She almost made me believe that she had changed toward me, and that I had imagined a ruthless cruelty where none had been intended. Almost, but not quite. I was not so gullible as to think that my cousin held any love toward me, but I could see that this further move was to her advantage, and another way of binding Giles to her. She would never dare be unkind to his son, and perhaps the natural mother instinct which is part of every woman would take over once the baby was in her care. Besides, Aunt Amalie would be nearby to look out for him and to see that her daughter played the role of mother as I would want it to be played. So I listened and weighed, and came to my own decision.

Aunt Amalie's plan was elaborated in detail. It was even conceded that in my position as the baby's "cousin" I could see the child whenever I wished, and that it was not as though I would be parted from it entirely.

When the time agreed upon came, I went to Philadelphia and began visits to a new doctor. I went to him as Elise Severn. When I went into the hospital I was registered as Mrs. Giles Severn. In the meantime Aunt Amalie had brought Elise north too. The doctor who had diagnosed that she could never have a baby was dead, and there was no one to challenge what we were doing. Not even Floria had been told that her sister could have no children, and Floria was away from the island much of that time. The story was given out that Elise's condition was rather precarious and that she needed a particular specialist in attendance. When her pregnancy should have begun to be noticeable she moved away from the Malvern area and came to Philadelphia with her mother.

For a few days after his birth Richard was mine. I held him in my arms every day at the hospital. I loved him fearfully and painfully. Then I was released and Elise took him, delighted and apparently loving. He solved a very great problem for her, and since she was never very perceptive about others, I think she did not fully understand how I felt. Aunt Amalie knew. For a few more days in Philadelphia she was a rock for me to lean on. Then I gathered my resources and what inner strength I had and went back to Chicago. Richard was taken to his new home at Sea Oaks, to await the return of a proud father from his next leave.

I was eighteen and Aunt Amalie insisted that I go on to college. That was wise counseling. School seemed irrelevant at first. But I had to live, I had to make my own life, and there was more strength in me than I knew. I learned quickly, after two or three trips, that I must not keep running back to Hampton Island to play the role of fond cousin. That was too painful, too destructive of the separate life I was trying to build up for the child and for myself. Instead, as Richard grew out of babyhood, I settled for an occasional letter, and gifts for birthdays and Christmas, so that he would not forget me altogether. I treasured pictures of him and watched him growing from a distance. The acute hurting dulled, but the aching emptiness remained. Worst of all, there was, as well, still too much feeling for his father left in me.

Later on whenever Elise invited me to the island, I declined. Until now. I had not changed my mind until letters from old friends hinted at how things were at Sea Oaks, hinted, without knowing the import for me, that perhaps Elise was not being the best mother in the world for her son.

That was when I determined to return and see for myself. And here I was.

I breathed deeply of the quiet night air. I would not disturb them at The Bitterns, after all. In a little while I would go back to bed. It seemed strange that by Sunday night I would be in blustery New York. But before I could step out from beneath the shadowy tree and follow the walk to the house, I heard the sound of running feet, and I paused in surprise, sheltered by hanging moss and trailing vines of wild grape, unseen by the woman who ran past me up the shell drive.

It was Elise, still in the white dress she had worn when she came to meet me, white sandals on her feet, as she ran lightly, swiftly toward the house. I stepped out to call after her, and then hesitated. There was something secret about her running, something furtive that I did not understand. I let her go and waited in silence for a little while. There were no sounds anywhere except for the buzz of insects until I heard the house door open and close.

More slowly than she, puzzled and a little troubled, I started up the driveway, walking through the shimmer of moonlight on the shell road. Why had she been out at this hour? It seemed unlikely that—as was the case with me—Elise Severn would be driven to walk about at midnight by restless, haunting dreams.

As I neared the house I was startled to see that a figure had stepped into the driveway and stood looking up at soaring columns. For an instant I thought I had my answer and that this was the person—a man?—whom Elise had come out to meet. Then the figure turned and I saw it was a woman. I knew who it was, and I hurried my steps.

"Vinnie!" I said. "We all seem to be up late tonight."

She looked at me, guarded and silent.

"I couldn't sleep for thinking about the island," I said. "So I got up to have a look at it. Now I can go back to bed."

"Under the moss there's ghosts out tonight," Vinnie said solemnly.

I nodded at her. "I know. Ghosts of the children we used to be—Elise and Giles and me. Do you suppose my cousin is seeing ghosts tonight too?"

"Miss Elise don' see ghosts," Vinnie said. "Might be better for her if she do. Might be better to remember how come she's where she's at."

I did not attempt to unravel her cryptic meaning. We turned together toward the house.

"I hear there's to be a wedding at Sea Oaks," I said.

Vinnie's face lighted. "That's gonna be a fine day, Miss Lacey."

"I know," I said. "I'm happy for them both."

"And for Miss Elise," Vinnie said. "She need her mama here at Sea Oaks."

This was what Charles had said too.

The steps of the house were before me and I told Vinnie

good night and climbed them, increasingly uneasy. The peace of the night, the sense of nostalgia had been ruffled. When I let myself in the front door, Elise was halfway up the stairs. She turned and looked down at me.

"You're up late, Lacey. I thought we'd tucked you safely into bed some time ago." There seemed an exhilaration about her—a certain wildness.

"I haven't seen the island for so long. I wanted to prove its spell couldn't touch me any more."

"But of course you couldn't do that!" She was assured. "Once the island has you, it keeps you forever."

"I saw Vinnie out there," I said. "She says there are ghosts about tonight."

She stood on the stairs looking down at me, her white dress aglow in the lamplight, her hair a pale gold fall as she wore it shoulder-length in a modified page-boy. The style was coming back, and it became her beautifully. After a curious, still moment, unusual in one so mobile, she smiled at me.

"Vinnie's head is filled with nonsense. Come along, Lacey," she said, and held out her hand, charmingly my hostess and my cousin, yet still with that odd exhilaration about her. "I'll see you to your room again. After a whiff of sea air you'll sleep better, I know. Tomorrow we'll talk. We'll get acquainted again. And there's something you can do for me, if you will."

Her chatter offered me no explanation of why she was up and about. I gave her my hand and we went lightly up the stairs together—affectionate cousins, and friends of old. Or so we would seem to anyone who watched us. Yet I was uneasy about her, unsure.

We were silent in the upper hall, not wanting to wake young Richard. Elise saw me to the door of my room, pausing on its threshold to speak softly.

"I don't know if I mentioned that we have a guest," she said. "He's Hadley Rikers from Connecticut. Giles and I met him when he came down with some friends last year for duck-hunting. You probably know his name—he's famous in racing-car circles."

"I remember vaguely," I said.

She nodded. "You'll meet him in the morning. Sleep well, Lacey dear." She moved away from me and went to the door of Richard's room. There she stood looking in, listening to his soft breathing. It was a small thing, but an assertion of her motherhood. I wondered if it was an act done naturally, or if she meant it as a gesture of possession for my benefit. With Elise I could never be sure.

From across the hall she blew me a light kiss from her fingertips and turned away. I went into my room wondering if marriage and motherhood had changed Elise more than I had realized. Was the mistrust I felt groundless?

At least I was sleepy by this time. It took me only a few moments to get undressed and into bed. I fell asleep at once, lulled by the sound of rushing surf and the soft breeze rattling palm fronds at the window. There were no more dreams of Elise pursuing me, and I slept into the morning.

Vinnie wakened me when she brought a tray to my room. I sat up in bed and smiled at her.

"Such spoiling! You didn't need to do this. I'm perfectly capable of coming downstairs for breakfast."

Vinnie had been a pretty girl in her youth and she was still a fine-looking woman. She carried herself well, and there was a lively intelligence in her eyes. She led a busy life of her own, helping out in various civic and church efforts over in Malvern. She had been married twice and her first husband was dead. George Taylor, her second husband, also worked at Sea Oaks. She had a grown son by her first marriage. A son who had gone North and now occupied himself with movements which Vinnie sometimes regarded with a skeptical eye. Hampton Island was only part of her active existence, but she had known us all for a long time, and she gave us her warm affection, or her disapproving counsel, as the case might be, though she was far from the Mammy cliché of old. Vinnie belonged to the modern South.

"If I'm a mind to spoil you, I will," she told me now. "You hurry and wash your face. Then I fix this tray for you."

I hurried obediently to the bathroom and was back quickly. She plumped up pillows behind me in bed, set the bed table across my knees and the tray upon it. There was buttered toast, with Hampton honey, a small pot of coffee, bacon, a poached egg, and a familiar dish of hominy grits. Lovely! I was awake and rested and hungry. She moved to the windows, opened draperies and flung up sashes to the morning sun.

"It's a beautiful day, Miss Lacey. You get out in it fas' as you can, you heah?"

"That's what I plan to do," I assured her.

She moved on about the room and I watched her as I ate.

"How do you like working at Sea Oaks?" I asked her. "As against The Bitterns, I mean?"

She paused at the dresser, brushing away a speck of imaginary dust, her back to me. "It's all right, Miss Lacey. Maybe I'd rather work for Miss Amalie than Miss Elise. But Miss Elise needs somebody 'round to tell her what's what."

"Doesn't Mr. Giles?"

Vinnie raised her shoulders in an expansive shrug. "Mr. Giles is pretty busy. He got his own hands full. Besides—Miss Elise don' pay him no mind. She don' listen to nobody 'round heah any more. But I can't stand talkin' like this. I gotta get back to my work."

She went off quickly, as though she felt she had said too much. Certainly she had said enough to make me thoughtful. I remembered Elise running so swiftly and secretly down the driveway last night, and wondered about her all the more. Wondered about her marriage to Giles and her relationship to Richard. I had heard unsettling rumors and there seemed a suggestion that they might be true. If they were true, was there any action I could or should take? That was a decision I must eventually face, and I would have to question my own motivations honestly.

I finished breakfast and put on green gabardine slacks and a white blouse. I didn't know what Elise would expect of me this morning, but perhaps I could take a brief walk over to The Bitterns, or down to the beach before I did anything else.

Just as I was ready to leave, there was a rap on my door.

I called, "Come in," and Richard pulled the door open. He stepped full into a band of yellow light from the window and stood looking at me. With his light brown hair and tan skin he seemed like a slim golden figurine of a boy. But for all his golden coloring, he was Giles's son, with the same green eyes and strong chin line.

My heart seemed to stop in my throat, and I longed to open my arms to him. Of course I did not. He was nine years old now, and there was a certain dignity and aloofness about his slender person that held me off as the stranger I was to him. His look appraised me curiously, not giving so much as challenging.

"Hello, Richard," I said softly.

"Hello, Cousin Lacey." He answered me guardedly, and left the band of light to come toward me. "Mother said I should show you this."

I was glad of something to do, some action to keep me from staring at him openly, and I took the enlargement of a snapshot he held out and carried it to a window. I remembered very well the day this picture had been taken, and I could not help a faint wincing.

"Mother said you'd tell me what it's all about." Richard was waiting, and it occurred to me that there was something faintly imperious in his manner. I gave my attention to the picture.

It was like Elise to choose this particular shot with its humiliating memories. The Doric columns of Sea Oaks rose in the background, and the small gathering in the foreground had been grouped on one curving arm of the double steps that ran down from the portico. The picture was a vivid reminder of those King Arthur games we used to play. By the time of this scene we had made something of a pageant of them, and Charles had come outdoors to snap several shots of us in our homemade costumes.

This scene I had reason to remember. In it Floria was thirteen, Giles eleven, Elise a rather grown-up nine, while I was a skinny little eight-year-old. There I was in front of Giles, with my short hair thoroughly mussed because Giles had just rumpled it, trying to tease me back to good humor. Good-humored I was not. I glowered angrily at the camera, with my lower lip stuck out and my eyes defiant and furious. I could still remember the shame that had curled its red-hot little claws inside me. Because of Elise. When we had lined up for the picture I had angled openly for a place beside Giles, and Elise had seen and teased me. "Lacey-loves-Giles!" she had taunted. "Lacey-loves-Giles!"

And I had gone for her furiously. I kicked aside the long skirt of my lady-in-waiting gown made from an old evening dress of my mother's, and flew at Elise in a rage. I managed to rip Queen Guinevere's dress and mash in her cardboard crown before Giles pulled me off and shook me gently into shameful tears. Perhaps it would have been better if he had laughed at me, but he did not. He knew that Elise's words were true, and that I didn't want him to know. So he had been kind, and when we had all pulled ourselves together for the picture, he stood behind me with his hands on my shoulders quieting me, gently affectionate.

"Tell me about the picture," Richard said, calling me back to the present, commanding me.

This was not the way to overcome the Sea Oaks spell. Too often nostalgia seemed to lie in wait for me, ready to engulf me when I least expected it. Because of Richard, I thrust away hurtful memories and went over the figures in the pic-

ture one by one. His mother was Queen Guinevere in a lovely
gown Aunt Amalie had made for her, and with a slightly
squashed golden cardboard crown on her head. The reason
one hand was clasped behind her was so that she could pull
out of sight the rent I'd made in her dress. For the snapshot,
nevertheless, she had managed a beautifully royal smile, and
no one would ever guess I'd had her in the dust moments
before. Elise would never give herself away as I did.

King Arthur was every bit a king, but less glamorously
garbed in the makeshift garments that gave an effect of medieval tunic and robe. His crown was suitably royal, and intact,
as his queen's was not.

Next to Elise stood Floria in her own particular dress.
"Floria was always Merlin," I told Richard. "She was older
than the rest of us, and some of the time she wouldn't play
with us. But when she felt like it she would dress up in that
pointed cardboard cap you can see in the picture, and the
black cape she made for herself, with white paper crescents
and stars pasted all over them. Her long gray beard is Spanish
moss. She made a wonderfully spooky Merlin."

"I know," Richard said. "She still dresses up like that for
the Camelot ball, and she still has that cape. She lets me wear
it sometimes. But who's the boy on the other side of my
father?"

"That's Paul Courtney. He was your father's best friend, in
those days, and he used to come over to the island a lot. You
know him, don't you?"

"Of course." Richard nodded his bright head. "He's coming
for lunch today, I think. He works for my father at the plant
now. But who was he in the pageant?"

I remembered Paul very well. He had been a rather quiet
boy, disinclined toward warlike deeds, and often cast in the
role of Galahad. In the picture he wore layers of cardboard
armor, and carried a wooden shield and sword. His jousting,
however, had been against trees to which we gave the name of
knights. He and I had been good enough friends. He had a
crush on Elise, as I had on Giles, so that threw us together
for mutual support and friendship.

"He was Sir Galahad here," I told Richard.

"Where is Sir Lancelot?" the boy asked.

I shook my head. *"Our* King Arthur had no Lancelot
among his knights. We played all our games in the time before Guinevere and Lancelot fell in love. Your father was too
proud to take second place. Of course he might have been the

brave Sir Lancelot himself, but we had to have a king, so we really had no other choice. Paul took different roles—playing whichever knight we needed. And sometimes I was allowed to be Elaine the Lily Maid. Mostly, though, our extra characters had to be imaginary because there weren't enough of us to go around."

"We still have a Camelot ball on the island overy year," Richard said. "Sometimes they let me stay up late to watch."

"And do you sit on the stairs and look down at the dancing in the hall?" I asked, while old nostalgia and a strong feeling for the boy beside me swept in to take possession. It brought him close to me to know that he did today what I had done in the past.

He looked at me with new interest, as if I had become more real for him. "Did you do that too when you were young?"

"When I was your age—yes," I said, and tried to harden myself against the longing that filled me. A longing to touch Richard with a mother's right and affection—when I had no right. I wanted too much, and coming to the island had opened an old Pandora's box of yearnings.

"You can keep the picture," Richard told me. He studied me thoughtfully for a moment, and then seemed to reach a favorable conclusion. "Will you come to the beach with me later, Cousin Lacey? I must go eat breakfast now."

I was pleased and touched that he wanted me with him, flattered beyond all reason. He was an attractive little boy when he lost that faintly imperious manner.

"I'll try," I promised. "It depends on your mother. I'm going over to The Bitterns now. Would you like to come along?"

"Not now." He paused before he went out of the room. "I forgot to tell you—my father came home early this morning, so he'll be here for the weekend. Maybe we can get him to do something with us."

"That would be lovely," I said, outwardly calm and unshaken, while something within me crumbled.

Richard went away and I sat down on the edge of the bed, trying to face the imminent prospect of seeing Giles. This was what I needed to do. I needed to face him, to look at him quietly and remotely, and recognize that he belonged to another life as far as I was concerned. He was a man I did not really know. Perhaps he had made Elise a very good husband. Perhaps he couldn't be happier than to have Elise as his wife. Or, on the other hand, perhaps he had disappointed and disillusioned her, if anything was wrong with their marriage. All these things I should be able to appraise coolly. I was no longer seventeen. I was a woman grown. I would not remember old love, old quarrels, old pain.

When I was a bit more sure of myself, I got up and went out of my room. As I descended the stairs I could hear voices coming from the dining room, but I did not need to go past the door. I let myself out the front way and ran down the steps into morning sunlight.

The path that led to The Bitterns was well worn. My feet knew the way through the oleander thicket, and pink blooms nodded over my head as I walked toward Hampton Island's oldest house.

The old fort had occupied the bend in the Malvern River, where it turned to meet the sea. At the water's edge on my left rose the stones of the powder magazine which were all that remained of the fort buildings. All around the area were to be found traces of the earthworks which had once surrounded the fort, protecting the little town which had thrived near the rim of the marsh.

The path I followed took me past the fort and into a place of green gloom, where morning sun filtered through the high loblolly pines and sweet gums. From the branches of live oaks and gum trees hung huge wild grape vines, some of them thicker than a man's arm. Underfoot were hundreds of the rough little brown balls that were the seed pods of the sweet gums.

Once this place had been the burying ground for the town, and a few empty tombs were left above ground. I could remember sometimes running through hurriedly as a child on my way from The Bitterns to Sea Oaks, half fearful lest some old settler should step from behind a tree and accost me. Though sometimes I had been brave enough to play here. Now it seemed a peaceful, dreaming place, and there was no need to hurry my steps as I followed the path that led past the edge of the marshes.

The Bitterns had been built wide and comparatively shallow, with a high tabby foundation. A long, deep veranda ran across its entire front, shielding the house from the heat of summer. Two peaked roofs made gables high over the front door, and I remembered that as a child they had always reminded me of a fox's ears, forever pricked to attention. A cat would be too tame and domestic an animal to be compared with The Bitterns.

The same thorny, seldom trimmed hedge I remembered stretched away on either side of a peeling white front gate. Apparently Elise's fever of renewal had not been extended to The Bitterns, and Aunt Amalie was accustomed to the shabbiness and did not care. She was well-to-do and could have spent almost any sum she liked on repairs and refurbishing if she had chosen. Sometimes Southerners made almost a fetish of shabby gentility, I thought affectionately.

Hedge and gate successfully concealed the garden that lay within, though from what The Bitterns seemed to hide I was never sure. The only likely eyes nearby were at Sea Oaks, and the two houses surely had no secrets from each other. Nevertheless, the hedge was there, higher than ever, and it had always added to my feeling as a child that the house wrapped itself in mystery, concealing its life from the island around it. From its upstairs windows it looked out toward river and marsh and mainland, but downstairs it hid, and those who rocked on the deep veranda could see nothing of the world beyond the encircling hedge.

The gate stood unlatched, and I let myself through. I would not be too early for the Hamptons. Aunt Amalie was an early riser, and, as I saw at once, my cousin Floria was already up and out of doors. She knelt, trowel in hand, near a tulip bed, and her colorful garb rivaled the bright morning. She wore slacks of a deep red-orange that nearly matched her hair. A flowered brown blouse topped the slacks, and a wide yellow band held back her red hair. Her taste for vivid hues had not changed since she was young. Now she made a blaze of color there among the tulips. Her flowered blouse was sleeveless and the skin of her arms prickled with flecks of red from the sun. Floria had the redhead's sensitivity to sunlight, but she never did anything about it. She had always had a strange affinity for her antagonist, the sun.

She looked up to see me as I came down the brick path, and sat back on her heels to scrutinize me thoroughly as I came toward her.

I nearly laughed in her face. "Don't tell me I'm too thin and the island had better fatten me up," I said. "I've already been told."

She shook her red head and a thick mass of hair danced over her shoulders, restrained only by the band around her head. "I wasn't thinking that. I was thinking how smart you look. Right off Park Avenue, I suppose. You don't belong to Hampton Island any more."

"Hello, Floria," I said. "It's good to see you haven't changed."

She gave me another long stare out of brown eyes that were flecked with yellow, lending them an almost golden look. "Because I speak my mind, do you mean?"

It was always best to bait Floria quickly, before she baited you. Friendship of a quiet, soothing nature had never been possible with Amalie's eldest daughter. I sometimes felt that she wore some sort of psychic chip on her shoulder that made her always ready for attack. Aunt Amalie, for all her obvious effort, had never been able to help the fact that Elise was her favorite daughter. Since Floria adored her mother, there was likely to be some scarring here.

"Do you still put on your Merlin hat and cape?" I asked her quickly. "Do you still cast spells?"

"Of course," she said. "I'm casting them on these tulips now. Though I've lost the original hat, I still have the cape. I let Richard wear it now and then when he wants to evoke the elements and stir up storms and lightning."

"Does it work?" I asked.

She nodded, giving me her quick flash of a smile that could vanish so quickly. "Always. How are you, Lacey? You're really looking fit enough." She got up from her knees and dusted earth from orange slacks. "I've been wondering if you would come. Elise said she was going to whistle for you, but I wasn't sure you loved her all that much to come running back to Hampton."

"I haven't seen the island in years. So I was happy for the invitation," I said. "As you know, New York is still cold. I must revel in this sunshine while I have it."

I held out my arms and turned around twice with my face lifted to the sun.

Floria started ahead of me toward the house. "I'll call Mother and tell her you're here. Elise will be keeping you busy, so we'd better take you while we can get you."

She went up wide steps to the shadowy veranda, brilliant in her orange pants and flowered blouse, and I remembered her mother's comment one day long ago—"That's Floria in super gorgeous technicolor." But color had always seemed to suit Floria's nature. There was something dramatic and passionate and a little stormy about her that raw, wild colors suited. She lacked her sister's cool, elegant beauty, but she held her own in other ways. One looked first at Elise, and was then drawn by Floria's sheer overemphasis. Sometimes

it was Floria you thought about later, when Elise's charm had
palled a little. Yet of the two Elise was the stronger, the more
stubborn-willed. It was Elise who always won. It was Elise
who always got what she wanted.

I caught a flash on Floria's left hand as she went up the
steps and I ran up beside her and took her hand to study the
shining ring on her engagement finger. This was a surprise.
One somehow never thought of Floria as the marrying sort.
She had too sure a way of frightening men off.

"Who is it?" I asked.

She drew her hand away too quickly. "Paul, of course. Paul
Courtney. Who else would you think?"

This was a further surprise. I would never have thought that
she and Paul Courtney would marry. How Floria had felt
about Paul had been no secret in the past, but in the old
days he in turn had looked toward Elise, even though he had
known he could never compete with Giles.

"That's wonderful," I said gently. "Now there'll be two
weddings coming up on Hampton Island."

She didn't answer me, but went inside, and I heard her
calling her mother. I sat down in the old-fashioned glider
couch on the veranda and let the feeling of the house ab-
sorb me.

They existed at two opposite extremes, these houses of
Hampton Island. Perhaps that was what fascinated me about
each of them. Sea Oaks was an open house. Many of its
windows faced the ocean, and the sound of waves rushed
through every room. The Bitterns stood across the curving
horn of land that projected southward from the island at this
point, and it belonged to river and marsh, as Sea Oaks belonged to the sea. It was a dark house, and sometimes a little
dank. Built in 1720, on the burned-out foundations of an
even earlier Hampton house, it was dark, not only because it
was well shielded from the sun, but dark psychologically because of its memories as well.

For the most part, death had come to Sea Oaks quietly and
decorously. It had its historical past, as any house must that
had stood that long, but for The Bitterns death had often
come violently and left its shadow behind. There was the
ancestor who had shot himself in one of those upstairs gable
rooms. There was the young girl who had pined to death
because of a forbidden lover, and whose headstone in the
small cemetery that had superseded the burying ground told
of her foolish loving. Once a duel had been fought beneath

the live oaks of the other house, and it had been The Bitterns man who had died. He too was buried in the historic little cemetery. There were other dark tales as well—one of madness and suffering, another of dishonor and suicide at sea.

All these had left their shadows, it seemed. As a small child I had sometimes imagined fearfully that I would meet one or another of these dark-fated personages in the hallways of the house, and I had shivered pleasantly, loving it all the more. Not that I was a morbid child. Away from The Bitterns I was cheerful enough. But the house set its spell upon me, and I reveled in its haunting quality. Here where those strange birds which gave the house their name could be heard calling from the marshes, I was ready to fall under the old spell again. I sat in the glider, touching the floor gently with my toe, and looked out from behind the wisteria vine toward a tight little world whose boundary was the unkempt hedge across the front of the yard.

Aunt Amalie came quietly through the screen door behind me. She was dressed for an early morning ride in fawn-colored jodhpurs and a brown jacket, a creamy cravat tied at her throat. Whatever she did, she always managed to look elegant while doing it. Floria got her red hair from her mother, but Amalie's hair had now turned rusty, and she brushed it back from her wide brow and wound it into a soft coil at the nape of her neck, with a wide brown velvet bow pinned above the coil. She was a handsome woman, tall and poised, yet with a gentleness in her, a feminine quality that Southern women often have.

Her lips were smiling, but her brown eyes were grave as she stood watching me. It was always the same when we met. She never rushed at me, but stood back a little and waited for me to come to her. I left the swing and went to put my arms about her, remembering the faint lily-of-the-valley scent she wore.

"Lacey," she said. "Dear Lacey."

I understood her hesitation in welcoming me until I had made the first move. She had told me once that she was always afraid that a time would come when I would blame her because I had given Richard away. I had not, ever. She had counseled me as wisely as she knew how, and I knew very well how loyal and loving a friend she had been to me. More than an aunt. More than my mother's sister. She had been a friend. I had missed being away from her, though we wrote to each other several times a year.

She stepped back and held me away from her, searching my face, searching past the outer surface of my being. Then she glanced quickly over her shoulder toward the house.

"Floria has gone to see about coffee. Lacey, have you seen about him."

him yet? Have you seen what a fine, proud little boy he is? And somehow radiant? There's a look of the island sun

"I saw him this morning," I told her quickly. "He came to show me a picture of our old King Arthur games Elise sent me. He's all you say. Is he happy? Is he contented? Is he growing well?"

Floria came through the screen door. "Susy will have coffee for us shortly. Are you talking about Richard? There's nothing wrong with him that a little more discipline wouldn't cure. And perhaps a little more of the right kind of attention from his mother."

Aunt Amalie went to sit in a porch chair. "Floria! You're always popping off carelessly. Elise is an affectionate mother."

Floria flung her beflowered self down in the swing and patted the cushions beside her. "Come and sit down, Lacey. You're one of the family. We don't have to mince words around you. Elise is affectionate when she thinks about it, but she's not very attentive. His Grandmother Amalie is more of a mother to Richard than she is."

"He doesn't want for mothering," Aunt Amalie said, and it was plain enough that she was annoyed with her elder daughter.

I did not want to talk about Richard in front of Floria. I was too afraid of giving myself away. Besides, these were things I had come to observe for myself. I had no great confidence in Floria's opinions. There was not a great deal of love lost between her and her sister.

"Charles has told me about your coming marriage," I said to Aunt Amalie. "I'm very happy for both of you."

Amalie's face glowed, and I could see her happiness. "Thank you, dear. I'd like to make it a double wedding, with Floria and Paul marrying at the same time."

"That's not for me," Floria said. "I want my own private ceremony. And I want it at the time I choose."

"Which will be when?" Aunt Amalie asked a trifle tartly.

Floria flounced in the seat beside me. "I won't be pushed. I won't be hurried. Paul and I will be sure this is the right step for us when we take it."

This seemed strange. Floria had wanted Paul for most of her life and I could not understand why she was not rushing into marriage with him, now that he was willing.

Susy brought the coffee tray and set it on the low veranda table. There were hot biscuits as well, and blackberry jam. I spread one and bit into Southern succulence, accepted a strong cup of coffee.

"And you, Lacey?" Aunt Amalie asked gently. "It seems such a waste that you haven't found the right man. Marriage would become you, dear."

I shook my head ruefully. "I've told you before. I'm not the marrying type. I'm happy in my work. Happy with my life in New York, my friends there. Being unmarried isn't the most dreadful fate in the world."

Floria said, "In the South it is. But you can afford to be independent in the North. Don't let Mother bully you."

As if Aunt Amalie ever bullied anyone. What she did was far more subtly persuasive, as a rule. She opened up possibilities and choices for you to see, and then she let you choose the wisest course. But I had not come under her influence for a long while. There were men in New York whom I liked, but never enough for marrying. The shadow of Giles lay across my path and I could not tell Aunt Amalie that.

I finished my coffee and set down my cup. "This is only a short visit. I want to walk down to the beach before Elise calls me. I'll be back to see you again."

"I suppose you'll be coming to the affair at the Sea Oaks plant tomorrow morning?" Floria said.

"I haven't heard about it," I told her. "I'm flying home tomorrow by the late afternoon plane."

"There'll be plenty of time to catch that," Floria assured me. "We're all helping Giles with some sort of celebration at the new plant. It's to be opened up for full operation tomorrow, and there will be visitors from all over, and the family in attendance."

"I don't know——" I began, but Amalie nodded at me with reassurance.

"Of course you must go. If Elise is too busy playing hostess at the plant, you can come with us. We're all very proud of Sea Oaks brands, you know. We have a great pride in Giles's enterprise and success. Besides, it's an interesting place to see for itself."

"All right," I said. "I'll come, if Elise wants me to."

Aunt Amalie got up to go for her ride, and we all went

down the veranda steps into bright sunshine. I saw the iris bed at one side of the steps and paused. Circling the plants, tilted on edge, was a long row of cockle shells.

" 'And cockle shells all in a row,' " I said. "Floria, do you remember what a thing we made of shells when we were young? We found so many on the beaches. I remember the sand dollars, especially. I remember how you used to exact a tribute of sand dollars from us for your services as Merlin."

Floria laughed. "I did more than exact a tribute," she admitted. "For me those were magic shells. They were my one weapon against Elise. Those and being a few years older than the rest of you. Elise was queen, but with my magic I could almost make her believe that she was queen only because I permitted her to rule."

I remembered very well. We all collected the tawny sand dollars we found on the beach and paid them to Floria. When she wanted to be kind and encourage us, she would sometimes make us the open gift of a shell in return. But when she wanted to warn or punish us, a single sand dollar would be left among the possessions of the one to be warned, or in his path, or where he would be sure to touch it. I could still recall the shiver of dread that would go through me when one of those shells would appear in some unforeseen way. I could recall its chalky feel in my fingers and the way I believed implicitly in Floria's magical powers in those days.

"What a tyrant you were," I said. "Just because you were older and we were all a little afraid of you. King Arthur should have banished you from his court."

She smiled wryly. "He knew he couldn't. Besides, I'm not sure I wasn't possessed of certain powers when I was young. Something I've lost, unfortunately, in growing up."

Aunt Amalie was shaking her head over this interchange. She touched me lightly on the arm. "I'll see you at lunchtime, my dear. Elise has invited us over today, in your honor. I'm going for my ride now."

She went off around the house, and Floria and I walked through the white gate together and set out in the direction of Sea Oaks. When we reached the oleander thicket, Floria put a hand on my arm and held me quiet.

"Wait! Don't go out there till he's gone. I don't want to meet him now."

We stood still and watched as a man came down the steps of Sea Oaks and followed the drive, strolling idly beneath the live oaks.

"That's Hadley Rikers," Floria said. "I don't see how she can stand him. All that racing and hunting and shooting!"

"Stand him?" I said. "What do you mean?"

"Don't be an innocent," Floria told me. "You must know Elise's wonder-marriage is on the rocks. And it's her fault too. She's absolutely vile to Giles. Vinnie says they have separate rooms these days. And Elise's men keep coming to visit. Not that she ever risks a scandal. It's all done very quietly, with nothing Giles can pounce upon."

Her words were raw and blunt—which was the way Floria often spoke her mind. She was telling me what I had come here to find out, but because of Richard the truth struck through me mercilessly. I knew in my heart that this was the truth, but I couldn't admit the fact to Floria.

"That's hard to believe," I said. "After all, Elise has had everything she could want—"

Floria threw me a quick look. "You've forgotten what my dear sister is like. Anything is possible to believe when it comes to Elise. There—that man's gone down the drive. Come along."

She led the way and I followed her past Sea Oaks to the place where the well-worn path to the beach opened up. Once this path had been trod by the three children we had been. Now my son's feet would know it best.

Floria came a little way with me and then stopped. "Don't look so appalled. You must have been weaving fantasies about Hampton Island if you thought that marriage could last forever."

"But Giles—" I said, "how does he—?"

Floria shrugged. "Ask him. I've wondered myself. There's the boy, of course. Giles loves him devotedly, and for Richard the sun rises and sets in his father. Well—there's your beach. I'll go back now. See you at lunchtime." Abruptly she was off on her own way and I was left alone.

I turned toward the beach, suddenly running, dashing through the palmettos. I felt pursued, invaded, as if by nightmare. Floria's words had shaken my safe, sad, private little world.

The smell of the ocean is something one never forgets. I breathed it deeply as the wind came whipping into my face, tossing my hair. The tide was part-way out and the sound of surf rushing in over the low shore summoned me to follow it. I walked toward the sea wall.

There was no native rock on the island—no rock at all, except that which was brought in from outside. Originally this had meant rock carried as ballast in ships that sailed to Hampton Island, but now it came from nearer at hand. Outside rock had built the long sea wall that bisected this portion of the beach, running along it parallel with the water, protecting the banks from deeper erosion. It was not a proper wall in the sense of being compactly built, but was more like a stone row piled loosely together, with sand interlaced between the rocks. Down near the house there was a wooden walkway built over the piled-up stones, but I did not bother with it.

I remembered certain stepping-stones across the wall which I had made my own as a child, scorning the wooden steps, until these stones had come to be known as "Lacey's way." Once Floria, always delighting in her influence over my young imagination, had said, "It's lucky to have your own private way to the beach, Lacey,"—and forever after I clambered faithfully over the rocky wall.

I took the rocks now, fitting my feet into the natural steps I had discovered so long ago. There was no reason to risk bad luck at this late date, and I liked my way best. I climbed across to the beach and started over the sand.

Somewhat farther along, the old, abandoned lighthouse tower stood upon its spit of land, cutting into the beach. The circle of ground around its foot was still kept trim and neat, and the tower must have been given a coat of paint not long ago, because it stood white and dazzling in the morning sun. How we children had loved to climb to its top when some adult was willing to go with us, and once Giles had taken me up there on a moonlit night. Most of the time the door was kept locked, and its heights were taboo to us. I wondered if Richard found adventure in that climb, as I had done.

The sands of Hampton Island were neither white nor tawny, but a silvery gray. When I had crossed the loose dry sand to the wet band above the tide, I found it hard-packed and smooth beneath my feet. This was the scene of my dreams, but I would not think of that now. For this brief moment I had come home. For me this place would always be the heart of the island. The haunted heart of Hampton Island.

I sat down in a place where the rolling surf would not reach me and clasped my hands about my knees. Except for a few shells the beach was unlittered, free of debris. It seemed as though its very emptiness might empty my mind, lull me into ease for a few restful moments before I had to come to grips with ugly reality. It would be lovely to sit here in the early sunshine. For a little while I would not think of Floria's words, I told myself. I would not think of Giles being unhappy. Nor of Elise's waywardness. I would not think of the days when I had been a child. Most of all, I would not think of Richard. I would simply bask in the sun and let my mind run free.

But I found quickly enough that my thoughts must turn relentlessly to Hampton Island—to what it meant to me, and had meant for so much of my life. I had come here to shake off its spell, to free myself of the old, nostalgic magic it had laid upon me, and I was not succeeding. I knew the dangers of an island. It could offer a peculiar isolation which must be guarded against. Once felt, once lived through, that treacherous sense could be carried into one's outward life—always lying in wait with a false promise of safety. Safety for me lay elsewhere. I must be free of old dreams, old longings. If tragedy hovered in the wings at Sea Oaks, what could I do about it? Why had I come here? Must I always be greedy for a life I could not have?

I watched the waves rush endlessly in below me and followed the distant smoke of a ship on the far horizon. When

I turned my head toward the south I could see other purple islands floating in their own waters beyond this spit of land. They belonged to another world, not to this tiny, enclosed world of Hampton Island. It was up to me to be conscious of their reality, aware of the reality of all the outside world. It was what I experienced here that was unreal and must be banished.

I was lost in these uneasy thoughts when Giles walked down the path from the house and came over the wooden steps to the beach. He wore navy trunks with a white belt, and a towel was flung over one shoulder. His feet were bare and so was his dark head. I had not known it would be like this—the freezing inside me, the sickness of old longing.

He saw me at once. "Hello, Lacey. They told me you were here," he called, and came purposefully in my direction.

The words neither welcomed nor rejected me. The old coolness was between us again, as it had been the few times I'd seen him since I had run away that summer long ago, and he had not followed me. Perhaps neither of us would ever forget or forgive. And that was ridiculous. We no longer meant anything to each other. I had no business freezing, or feeling sick at the sight of him. I could afford to be more generous. I held out my hand.

"Giles!" I said. "It's been such a long time."

The coolness in him seemed to melt. He came toward me over the years and took my hand in his warm clasp. Then he lowered his tall frame to the sand beside me. He looked older, and a little worn, I thought, but his eyes were as deeply green as ever. He had gained no weight. His body was as lean and hard as I remembered. Try as I would not to stare, I drank in every detail of him like a woman who has been thirsty for a long time.

"What were you thinking of just now?" he asked me. "When I came over the steps your face was intent on some sort of dream. Not a happy one, I think."

I clasped my hands more firmly about my knees and gazed out toward the far line that marked the edge of the ocean.

"I was thinking about islands," I told him. "Thinking about the escape they seem to offer."

"Escape?" he said. "I'd have said a prison, rather."

"That, too. It's a false escape, of course. I was thinking about their dangers as well."

"Go on," he said.

I put my fancy into words. "I suppose I used to love the

feeling of shutting out the world, of drawing a line of water around myself and letting all my troubles stay outside the line. I used to do that when I came to Hampton. An island is like a castle with a moat around it. The world can't get at you—or so I used to think."

"Camelot?" he said, smiling. "Camelot floating in its own dream. Is that what you mean? But why do you say 'used to'? Don't you believe in the dream any more?"

I shook my head almost violently. "I don't believe in it at all. I suppose that's the reason I've come back—so I can put everything in its perspective and get rid of sentimental notions that belong to my childhood. I know there isn't any Camelot now."

He looked at me, and when I turned my head to meet his eyes I found a surprising tenderness in them—a tenderness that might be based on old affection for the child I had been. I would not accept it, would not meet it.

I stared out across the beach, where waves curled in and withdrew, leaving the sand a dark, wet silver. It was a calm morning. There were no real breakers today. Sandpipers ran along the wet sand, and now and then a gull soared in to light.

Giles went on, speaking almost as if to himself. "There's something to what you say about islands. Sometimes I wonder how different my life would have been if I had grown up in Malvern—or anywhere else. Sometimes I wish I'd never known the island at all."

This ground seemed dangerous with quagmire and I said nothing. Though we had taken a step toward each other, we were strangers, Giles and I. There was no comment I dared to make. Quite suddenly the urge to be away from him was upon me. The dangers were clear, and I wanted to get away. I had come here to learn how to be free, not to involve myself further. I had loved this man when he was a boy. He was my child's father. But I had no right now to either.

I glanced at the watch on my wrist and jumped up. "It's later than I thought. Elise will want me. I must . . ." I let the words trail off and ran up the beach. Ran heedlessly, so that I slipped on loose sand and went sprawling clumsily upon my hands and knees.

The fall made me angry with myself, and when Giles came quickly to help me up and set me on my feet, my cheeks were flushed over so ignominious a departure. He saw how I felt and laughed at me gently.

"You remind me of a certain coltish, bright-eyed little girl who used to bring me gifts of seashells and driftwood."

He pulled me to him, kissed me on the cheek in brotherly fashion, rumpled my hair teasingly—and I did not like the response that sprang up in me at his touch. Oh, no! I thought. Not again with Giles Severn. I must not feel this way about Giles.

He looked at my face and kissed me again, almost bemusedly, as though he had not expected to do this. Then he let me go and I fled back to the house along the path that led from the beach.

With my heart pounding, I went up the steps to the side veranda and into the big double parlor through a French door. The long, beautiful room was as I remembered it. The graceful Chippendale was the same. The black and gold chest with its chinoiserie ornament was there, and so were the Italian sofa and faded Persian rugs. Around the walls and over the mantel hung a number of good paintings, all chosen by Giles's grandfather, who had a taste for collecting art.

For a moment I thought the room was empty, and then a man rose from a wing-backed chair in the corner and came toward me. He was not as tall as Giles, though somewhat more stocky—handsome and virile, his brown hair swept by an early marking of gray at each temple, his mustache and beard neatly trimmed. His smile flashed at me in a room darkened against the later heat of the sun.

"You must be Lacey Ames," he said, and held out his hand. "I'm Hadley Rikers and I'm delighted to meet you."

I had no time to wonder why he should be delighted, because even as I gave him my hand, Elise came quickly into the room. Her small person seemed just a shade plump in beige slacks and creamy blouse, but becomingly so. She had never been a thin girl like me. Brushed smoothly, her fair, page-boy hair shone in the dim room, and her eyes were a deep violet-blue.

"Oh, there you are, Lacey. I see you've met Hadley. I've something of his to show you—I know you'll be interested."

She went to the piano and picked up what was obviously a manuscript box and carried it toward me. I suppressed a sigh as I took it from her. This, undoubtedly, was why I had been so urgently summoned to Sea Oaks for the weekend. I might have known.

"It's Hadley's book," Elise said. "His experiences as a racing driver. Absolutely fascinating. Will you read it while you're here, sweetie, and tell us what you think? You'll know exactly what should be done with it, I'm sure."

"I don't have much to say about publication," I warned her. "I can only recommend what I like, and I'm not sure this is my sort of book. I don't know anything about the subject."

"This is all Elise's idea, you know," Hadley Rikers said easily. "You needn't feel in the least obliged to do anything about it."

"Of course she's obliged," Elise said. "Lacey is my cousin, and she can't let me down. Can you, darling?"

Hadley Rikers smiled, and I promised to do what I could, carrying the manuscript with me when I went out of the room. In the mirror near the door I saw that Elise went close to him, murmuring something I could not hear. Probably to the effect that all would be well taken care of with his book in dear Lacey's hands.

Mildly curious, I took the box upstairs with me, but I did not go at once to my room. The door of Richard's room stood open and there seemed to be no one inside. I could not resist the opportunity to see what my son's room was like, and I went to the door and stepped through it.

This was a boy's room—not particularly tidy, but apparently enjoyed and well occupied. On a ledge near the window was spread a collection of sand dollars—some of them brown as they came from the beach, and some whitened by later bleaching. So he collected them, as I would have liked to do, except that in my time they had to be paid as tribute to Floria Hampton in her Merlin's cap.

A bookcase was packed with books and I recognized many of the titles as those I had sent him over the years. He had kept them all, and the worn jackets gave evidence of loving reading. I had to blink hard against the tears that came into my eyes. I knew so little about my son.

Over the mantelpiece was a painting, and I went to stand before it. The artist had done a water color of a sunny day and a sunny-haired boy in a boat on a creek. The scene touched me. It might have been something from the days of my own childhood visits to the island—yet this boy who lazed so pleasantly upon his oars was my own flesh. Once I had held him in my arms, as I could never hold him again. Because of me he had that boat, with the lapping waters of the creek beneath it. He had this room with its books and seashells. *I* had given him all this richness. I must not forget that or indulge myself. I must not suffer longings that would take all this away from him.

A step in the doorway made me turn guiltily. Elise was there, watching me.

"A sentimental visit?" she asked lightly. "I'm glad you're seeing the room when it looks better than usual. Believe me, Lacey, being the mother of a son is not an unmitigated blessing. Richard has a slightly wild streak in him that makes him do strange, unpredictable things. There've been occasions when every book in that case was tumbled frantically about, with the bed torn up as well, and the cushions out of the chairs and tossed about the room. All to get himself attention —to make himself the center of focus."

"Doesn't he get enough attention?" I asked quietly.

Elise laughed. "As much as is good for him. And those are only tantrums. At other times he's very sweet and wants to follow me around and smother me with affection."

I could see what she was doing. She was letting me know how thoroughly the boy was hers, and how completely she played the mother to him.

"I had a visit with him this morning when he brought me the snapshot you sent me." I said. "He seems a happy child."

"Happy? Of course he's happy. He loves the island, loves everything about his life here. Someday it will all be his. Someday Sea Oaks will be his. As it's really mine now, since Charles does little about it. Richard is being raised for that heritage."

Elise had always been possessive of the island. Floria cared nothing about it, so Aunt Amalie had always planned that it should be held for her younger daughter. That was what Judge Hampton had wanted too. Even as a young girl, Elise had played at being, not only Guinevere, but queen of Hampton Island as well. Now, apparently, Richard was being groomed as crown prince, which might account for that faintly imperious manner which I found distasteful in him.

Elise moved about the room, touching an ornament here, a fold of curtain there. "Sometimes I've wondered about you, Lacey. I've wondered how well you made your adjustment." Her violet eyes flashed me a curious look that might be malicious. "You're not really the mothering sort, are you?"

I caught my breath. "I don't know whether I am or not."

"Oh, I think you're not," she said. "To give him up so easily."

Easily? I thought, and turned toward the door. I did not want to be swept into remembering.

"I'll take the manuscript to my room and start reading it," I told her.

"At least you've kept your bargain well," she said.

There was anger deep inside me. She had no business talking of these things. She had no business stirring up old wounds. Perhaps she never knew the meaning of mercy.

"I'll keep my bargain as long as you keep yours," I said.

"Mine has been kept." She moved her hands to encompass the room. "He has everything. You can see that."

"Has he a mother?" I asked.

She laughed as though I delighted her, and there was cruelty in the sound. "Ask Richard. He dotes on me. He'd never ask for any other woman for mother. But don't let me hurry you off to your room, Lacey. Stay here for a while, if you like."

She slipped past me out the door, her lips still smiling spitefully. I turned back to the room, held there in my quivering rage, yet knowing that I must not give in to her baiting. It was like Elise to prod when she was in the mood. At another time she might have treated me with gentle consideration, and there was never any telling which to expect. Her shifts from one extreme to another had always tormented me, and I wondered what effect they had upon Richard. It was good that he had his grandmother's love, and her watchful eye upon him. His grandmother and his father could surely fill his life, even if his mother fell somewhat short in what she should be doing for him.

Richard found me there in his room, coming unexpectedly through the door and stopping to stare at me.

"Hello," I said, feeling awkward and caught out of bounds. "I wanted to see your room. I hope you don't mind."

"I don't mind." He came past me, holding something in his hands that he had wrapped in a handkerchief. Almost secretively he went to his bureau, opened a top drawer and tucked the small parcel in among his things. Then he closed the drawer and turned to face me.

"Is there something special you wanted to see?" he asked me, with a certain polite defiance in his voice. He did not really like my being here among his things, and there was something he had hidden from me quickly in his bureau drawer.

I was at a disadvantage, but I took a step toward the bookcase. "I was looking at your books. I see you've kept a number of those I've sent you over the years."

He relaxed a little. "I've kept them all, Cousin Lacey. I love to read and you've sent me some awfully good stories."

"I've enjoyed picking them out for you," I said lamely. This interchange was painful. I wanted to be comfortable and natural with him. I wanted to know him better, and have him see me as a person and like me. None of which could be quickly managed.

I turned once more toward the door. "Elise has asked me to read a manuscript written by Mr. Rikers, so I suppose I had better go and get started."

He went back to the tall bureau, opened the top drawer again and reached in his hand as if to make sure of the parcel he had hidden away. Then he turned to look at me.

"I'd like to have a job like yours—where I could read books all the time. Read them before they were even published."

"It's not always fun," I said. "A lot of them come from beginning writers and they're not very interesting. Besides, reading keeps you indoors a lot, and I remember when I used to come to Hampton Island the thing I liked best was to be outdoors."

"I have plenty of time for that," he said. "It's *my* island and I've explored nearly every bit of it."

There was the princely tone again, and I had to challenge it. "Your island? I thought it belonged to your Grandmother Amalie."

He shrugged carelessly. "Oh, it's hers for now. But someday it will belong to me. So I wouldn't have time for reading every day anyway, would I?"

"No," I said dryly. "I expect you'd be very busy."

We left it at that, and I went across the hall to my room, lest I wear out my welcome with Richard. Once there, with the door closed, I opened the manuscript box and took out a sheaf of paper. I might as well commence my bread-and-butter chore. I sat near a window and began to read, but it was hard to get started because the small, bright face of a boy kept coming between me and the words.

Not only the boy himself, but his relationship to those about him troubled me. My publishing firm had specialized in books on child guidance, and while I've had nothing official to do with their publication, I had read them fervently, and a little furtively. I knew something of what the best minds in the country had to say about the development of the young.

I had flattered myself that I was knowledgeable. I knew all the right terms and phrases—until I met my son! Now, confronted by the real boy, the books did me very little good. I could not apply those pat phrases to the child before me. This was something I had to play by ear and by instinct. My own good intentions, my own longings got in the way of an easy relationship with my son.

I felt the thick pages of manuscript beneath my hands and tried to give them my attention. I must not think of Richard now. Long schooling in concentration came to my aid, and in a little while I was able to attend to the words and their meaning.

Hadley Riker's style was vigorous, but a bit on the amateurish side. What I liked least was the way the character of the man came through in the writing. His ego was supreme. Perhaps that was a matter of necessity for a man in his line of work, where confidence was so vital. But whether he wrote about cars or women—the latter seemed to take up a good deal of his attention—he was completely sure of himself, of his own intelligence, his own charm, his own skill. I disliked him intensely, yet read on, unhappily fascinated. It would be especially dreadful if Elise were interested in this man instead of Giles.

I found my thoughts straying again. How did Giles feel about Elise? How much of the old attraction existed between them? If it was true that their marriage was not going well, how much suffering was involved for Giles? I did not want to see him desperately unhappy over Elise.

When my eyes began to tire, I put the manuscript aside and changed my clothes. It was nearly lunchtime when I was ready, and I went downstairs. In the hallway below, Paul Courtney stood before the glass case that held the pirate goblet. He heard me on the stairs and glanced up.

"Lacey! How good to see you—it's been years!" He came toward me with his hands outstretched, kissed my cheek and held me off to look at me.

He was tall, and still as slender as ever. None of Vinnie's feeding had ever fattened him, though what with being Giles's right hand at the plant, he visited Sea Oaks often. His hair was sandy and softly thick, and he wore it rather long behind the ears in a graceful style that became him. His features had a slight delicacy to them, and he was not at all the robust, overwhelming sort of person Floria could be. I had often thought that Paul Courtney would have suited another age

better than our own—perhaps an age of courtiers. At least
I was happy to see someone I could greet with a natural ease
that grew out of old acquaintance, and with warmth that
need not be denied.

"Congratulations, Paul," I said. "I've just learned this
morning that you and Floria are to be married."

"It's good news, isn't it?" he said quietly. "Why are you
back, Lacey?"

The question seemed an odd one. "I'm here for a weekend
visit," I told him. "Elise wanted me to have a look at a
manuscript by Hadley Rikers, and meet the author."

"I see." His eyes had a look of remembering. Paul had been
around that summer when I was seventeen and my world had
been tied up with Giles Severn. He must wonder if a return
to Hampton Island might be painful for me. Though he could
not know how painful.

He moved away from the subject of my unaccustomed visit,
and gestured toward the glass case he had been examining.
"Strange, isn't it, the disappearance of that old brooch, with
never a trace of it turning up over the years?"

The great jewel-encrusted goblet which, legend had it, had
once been the treasure of Stede Bonnet, stood in its place of
honor in the case, with the other smaller objects around it.
The story was told that the retired-British-army-officer-turned-
pirate who had plundered ships along the coasts of Carolina,
Virginia and Delaware, had made a rare foray south to the
Malvern River, and had hidden treasure ashore on Hampton
Island.

Paul pointed to the place in the case where a small sapphire brooch lay beside the pirate goblet.

"That's not the one which should occupy that place, you
know. The real Stede Bonnet brooch had a fantastic emerald
in it. Priceless because of age as well as size. It was found at
the same time and in the same place where the goblet was
found. Probably buried there by Stede Bonnet himself. It
disappeared years ago, and there was a story—" He broke
off and looked at me in some embarrassment. "I'm on
dangerous ground. I'd forgotten it was your mother—"

"That's all right," I assured him. "I remember something of
the story. Doesn't it run that Charles gave it to my mother
to show his undying love, and that she never gave it back?"

He nodded. "Something of the sort."

"She didn't have it," I said. "There was some mystery about
it, I think, but it was never found among her things after her

death. My father searched for it after Aunt Amalie wrote to him."

"I understand that there was quite an uproar here when it was first found missing," Paul said. "Charles had evidently put the small brooch in its place, and no one noticed for a long time that the Bonnet brooch was gone. He held out through all the commotion and never told anyone what he had done until years later. No one was blamed for the theft, so the guilt was never placed here on Hampton Island, and he could keep his secret without any damage being done to another person. He didn't tell the truth about it until after his father died. I gather that Charles was always afraid of his parental wrath."

Aunt Amalie and Floria came out of the long parlor just then, and found us studying the case. Floria had changed from her slacks to a flowered dress, and tied her hair back with a green ribbon, looking less informal than she had this morning, but still making a gaudy splash of color in the hall.

"We were talking about the emerald brooch," Paul said.

Floria tapped the glass. "That was a dreadful loss. I've always thought that Charles never took a properly responsible attitude toward what he had done. But then—Charles was in love, and apparently no one in love is ever responsible." Her words sounded faintly bitter, but she went on at once. "The chief thing about the old brooch that intrigues me is the legend that it has gained over the years. You remember, Lacey, that the woman who wears it at the Camelot ball assures herself of true love forever! And of course we all believe that fervently. I'd wear it myself if I could lay my hands on it. It's too bad, Lacey, that you don't know anything about what happened to that brooch."

Amalie shook her head at her daughter. "You mustn't blame Charles. Kitty never should have taken the brooch away with her, probably to misplace it, but once she had done so, what could Charles do?"

Vinnie came into the hall just then to ring the Chinese gong for lunch, and we let the subject go. Elise and her racing driver came in from out of doors. Richard ran down from upstairs, and Charles came out of the library and went at once to greet Amalie. Giles was the last person to come downstairs.

As we gathered in the dining room there was one small movement that caught my eye. Elise, coming through the doorway, brushed against Paul in passing, and paused to make

an apology. She touched his arm, looked into his eyes, and
then went on. It was the slightest of gestures, but I saw the
dark look on Paul's face, saw that Elise had in some way
disturbed him. She knew it too, for she smiled as she went
about seating us at the table. I threw a quick look at Floria
and saw the purposely blank expression she wore. She had
seen too, and was hiding what she felt. Elise's act had been
cruel, deliberate mischief, and I wondered if it meant that
Paul was still susceptible to Elise's old appeal.

As she seated us Elise was all the charming hostess. She
took her place at one end of the table, with Giles at the other.
I was seated at Giles's right hand, and as he pulled out my
chair I did not look at him. My memory of what had happened on the beach was still too vivid in my mind.

The beautiful old room, with its chandelier and intricately
carved plaster rosette, its shining, mellow furniture, its linen
and crystal and silver, reached out quite calmly to possess my
spirit. I breathed the fragrance of lilacs from the centerpiece,
and surrendered to beauty and graciousness. This was at least
something I had given to Richard. This was what I wanted
him to have.

Elise was an integral part of the picture. She sat at her
end of the table, beautifully at ease, cool in her white frock,
with its touches of ice blue at the throat and down the front.
Before it fell into its usual page-boy at the back, her hair had
been brushed in an upward sweep at each side of a central
part, giving the faint effect of pricked ears, reminding me of
a fox's mask. Her eyes seemed a little sleepy-looking, as
though she was pleased with her inner thoughts, pleased with
the disquiet she had roused in Paul.

Even as I was enjoying the room, a quick, ugly happening
wiped away all its bright charm. As I unfolded my napkin
something sprang from the folds and flew out upon the table.
I reached out automatically to pick up the sand dollar that
fell at my place. Quite suddenly I was a child again, freezing
in horror as I held the brittle thing in my fingers.

Elise gave a little cry. "Throw it over your left shoulder,
Lacey! Remember—that was what we always did to wipe out
Floria's spells."

I did not hesitate to make the gesture. I flung the brown
shell over my shoulder and heard it crack against the hearth-
stones of the fireplace.

Elise laughed softly at the sound. "Someone meant to

frighten you, Lacey dear. *Are* you frightened? Are you having prickles up and down your spine?"

"It was a childish trick to play," I said, and glanced quickly from face to face around the table.

Giles clearly found the incident distasteful, and he was frowning at Elise. Richard sat next to me on the other side, his eyes sparkling, his expression alert, as if he enjoyed the moment's excitement. Beyond him, Aunt Amalie looked mildly surprised, but less concerned than those of us who had played this unpleasant little game as children. Paul had gone quite pale, his lips pressed together in a tight line, his eyes on Floria. But Floria seemed undisturbed. Perhaps she was faintly amused that someone had chosen to use her old method of trying to frighten me. Charles Severn seemed uneasy, while Hadley Riker's bearded face looked merely bewildered. At Elise's left, Vinnie was helping her husband George at the table by serving the duchesse potatoes, and her expression was a complete blank—a little too blank, I thought, for innocence. I had the sudden feeling that Vinnie might know who had tucked that ominous little shell into the folds of my napkin, and that she would never tell what she knew, even though she might disapprove.

Elise shivered exaggeratedly. "Childish, of course," she agreed. "Someone is playing pranks. Later on, Richard, you and I will have a little talk."

Richard seemed unabashed. "I know what it means," he said. "When you were all young, Merlin—I mean Aunt Floria —used to send you warnings with sand dollars, didn't she? And the person who got the warning had to be very careful from then on, or something terrible would happen to him. So you'd better be awfully careful now, Cousin Lacey. You'd better be careful, so—"

"That's enough," Giles said sharply and firmly.

"We'll talk about this later," Elise repeated. "Though I must say this is the sort of trick I used to love to play when I was young. You never guessed, did you, Lacey, how many of those sand dollars you found among your things were put there by me, not Floria? It was rather fun—you frightened so easily."

The eerie sense of exhilaration was upon her again—a somehow wicked exhilaration that took pleasure in another's discomfort. I remembered my dream of flight, and the pervading sense of evil that had seemed to pursue me.

"If that's what you were doing, you should be ashamed to admit it," Floria said flatly to her sister.

Richard was watching his mother, bright-eyed and observant, and he gave me a sidelong look—a look of impudence and mischief. Yet it was far more likely that Elise had played this trick, though I could not guess what her action portended. Why should she want to frighten me now, when all the cards lay in her hands, and when it was she who had invited me here?

The incident appeared suddenly to bore her, and she changed the subject casually.

"How did you get along with Hadley's manuscript, Lacey, and what do you think of it?" she asked.

I answered noncommittally. "I find it interesting, but I really know nothing about the subject. I'll take the book back with me and put it in the hands of some editor more competent on this topic. I can't promise anything, though. You could have mailed it in cold with exactly the same results."

"But I wanted you to meet Hadley," Elise said. "When there's someone colorful behind a manuscript, I'm sure that must be a point of interest to the publisher."

Giles said, rather coolly, "I imagine any manuscript has to stand on its own feet," and that ended the matter, to my relief.

Vinnie's stuffed crab was delicious and we began to eat. I tried to forget the incident of the shell, but an uneasiness seemed to linger in the room.

Aunt Amalie began to talk about the doings which were to take place at the new Sea Oaks plant tomorrow, and soon there was general conversation about the plant and the people who would be coming in to see it the following morning. I could listen without taking part in the discussion. I could think my own thoughts.

Once or twice I caught Giles watching me in a questioning, rather troubled way. Once when my eyes met his he smiled at me reassuringly, as though he did not want me to worry about the incident of the shell. Once Aunt Amalie too smiled at me down the table and shook her head slightly, as if to say that I must disregard what had happened. I wondered if she had guessed who it was who had slipped the shell into my napkin, and if she had some reason to know that I need not worry. I would question her when I had the opportunity.

But there was no chance to do anything immediately because when we rose from the table, Richard caught me by the hand and reminded me of my promise to go to the beach with him. Giles heard him and broke in at once.

'That's a good idea. Will you let me come along? It's going to be a beautiful afternoon, and not too hot. Anyone else like to come? We can drive to one of the other beaches."

"If you're through with me, Giles," Paul said, "I'm going over to The Bitterns with Floria."

And Elise shook her head. "I've an errand in town. Hadley will take me over to Malvern." She spoke lightly, almost tantalizingly, as though she wanted to evoke some angry reaction from Giles. But if anything, he seemed indifferent.

Aunt Amalie said she and Charles had some details to talk over—so it was left for the three of us to drive to the beach. We went to our rooms to change our clothes, and Richard was waiting for me in the hall when I came out. I'd put on blue shorts with a white blouse, and tossed a light cardigan about my shoulders.

Out on the driveway Giles waited for us in the station wagon. Hadley was driving Elise into town in his red Ferrari. We followed the asphalt road past The Bitterns, and then turned along gravel that ran for a distance beside Turtle Creek, skirting the green marshes until the road reached the Atlantic shore of the island in the other direction from Sea Oaks.

I felt in a strangely suspended state. It was as if I accepted only this moment when Giles and Richard and I could be together. All the unhappy truths of the situation seemed to fall away, and leave only this core of temporary contentment. I was intensely aware of the man in the seat beside me, and of the boy in between.

Giles looked brown and fit in gray slacks and a gray shirt open at the throat. He had thrown off whatever burden had seemed to hang over him at the house. Richard wore slightly grubby shorts of his own choosing, and a shirt with a hole in one shoulder. He was comfortable and obviously did not feel that such things mattered. Elise, apparently, had let him dress as he pleased.

"I wish Mother could have come," he said when we were on our way, and threw his father a bright upward glance that told me a lot. Richard knew very well that there was trouble between his parents, and he was not above playing one against the other when the opportunity arose.

This I did not want for him. I hated to see a slight maliciousness creep into his behavior at times. Material advantages

did not compensate if he was to grow into that kind of
person. My mood of contentment and unreality shivered on
the verge of dissolving.

Giles said nothing, but I saw his hands tighten on the wheel,
and I wondered what lay behind his careful schooling of indifference to whatever Elise did.

It was a perfect day to drive about the island. The afternoon was sunny and warm, but not hot the way the weather would be a month or two later. Though Hampton never suffered from the heat to the extent that the mainland did, thanks to ocean breezes and water all around.

Richard sat between us, stretching tall so that he could look out in every direction, his light brown hair lifting gently in the wind, his tan a smooth golden glow. Away from Elise he seemed a different boy, less imperious, as though he felt no need to play the prince when he was with his father. I longed to slip an arm about him, but I dared not. There was something independent about the boy that I must respect. He was growing up.

I basked in my corner of the seat, grateful for the day I held in my hands, gradually forgetting to be on guard and watchful of my emotions.

"Do you know where we're going?" Giles asked.

It had to be one place. One perfect place, because this was that sort of afternoon. "Elephant Beach," I said.

Giles's laughter had a light sound, as though he too were momentarily carefree. "That's your beach, you know, Lacey. Ever since you named it years ago. Even Richard calls it that."

I remembered. I must have been no more than seven years old, and Giles ten. In the morning we had gone to a traveling circus over in Malvern. And in the afternoon I had fallen asleep on island sand. I'd had a frightening dream of elephants thundering through the waves and up the beach—sure to trample me. Giles had been there when I had come yelping

61

awake, and he had soothed me gently, while everyone else had laughed. No elephants had ever been seen on a Hampton Island beach, he assured me, but after that this particular stretch of gray sand had been called Elephant Beach, and it was one of my favorite havens on the island.

Swimming was good there, and when the car had been parked in a cedar grove where twisted trees, leaning grotesquely away from the ocean, gave us shade and protection, we took turns at changing to swim suits. Then we made our way past sea grapes and the inevitable rows of cabbage palms, and ran down to the sloping wet band that marked where the tide was coming in.

The water was pleasant and we swam vigorously for a while. Afterwards we came up the beach to lie on the sand and let the welcome sun pour over us. The island light was dazzling, and even the gray sands took on a more golden hue.

Richard was still at the sand-castle age and he went to work building a magnificent structure down near the water's edge. Giles lay on his back with an arm flung across his eyes, and I turned on my side so I could study him, memorize him against all the lonely months ahead of me in New York. His body was brown and smooth, his legs straight and powerful and long, his feet well shaped. All these things I remembered from the past. But it was his face in profile I studied longest —the nose strong and firm, the wide mouth with a faintly sad twist to the lips, betraying more than he meant to betray. I wanted to touch him—and did not. This was not what I had come to Hampton Island for. There was no exorcism for me here. I had been wrong in coming to the island—but for the moment I did not care. Giles was beside me, and I did not want to escape. I knew how much I loved him.

After a time I got up and strolled the wet sand where waves rolled in from the Atlantic, foaming about my feet as I searched for whatever I could find. The pickings were not very good—only a broken cowry, an unbleached sand dollar, an imperfect cockle shell. I gathered them up and took them across the sand to where Giles lay. He had turned over on his stomach and I knelt beside him.

"I've brought you gifts from the sea," I said.

He propped himself on one elbow and looked at me. I held out my hand with its meager offering, and he smiled at me, remembering as I had remembered. When he took the shells from me, he folded my hand into his.

"Do you know," he said, "I still have three or four of those ocean treasures you used to bring me. I came across them in a drawer in my room just the other day. They made me think about you, wonder about you."

"Of course!" I said lightly. "That's what they were supposed to do."

He sat up on the sand and crossed his legs. "I do wonder about you, Lacey. What is your life like in New York? Tell me."

"It's busy," I said, "but not very dramatic. I have a small apartment in the Village, and I ride a bus uptown to work every day. At the firm I have my own small office, and I live surrounded by piles of manuscript, with other people's words running through my head. It's interesting. I like it."

"Why no marriage?" he said.

I laughed uneasily. "You sound like Aunt Amalie. 'A suitable marriage is the proper thing for any girl.' There seems to be no other acceptable answer. But why can't a woman be happy in her own sort of life without all that dishwashing and bedmaking and child-raising?"

"I suppose some girls can be," he said. "But not you, Lacey. You've always been too warm and loving. I should think you'd want other human beings in your life. Someone to give yourself to."

Oh, but I do! I could have told him. *It's just that I can't have the one I want, so I'd better settle for the substitutes.*

"I go out often enough," I said. "There are two or three men I like rather well."

He shook his head at me, playing the stern uncle. "Liking several rather well isn't the same as liking one a whole lot. How old are you, Lacey?"

He should have remembered the three years between us. "I'm twenty-seven, and practically gray-haired, the way you're making me feel," I said.

A handful of sand slipped through his open fingers. "I'm sorry. It's none of my business, of course. It's just that I've always been fond of you, Lacey. Once there was a time—" He broke off and for a moment I think we both remembered Elise. Elise that vivid summer when I had been seventeen. He ended lamely. "I've wanted the best for you. I think you deserve it."

The best was Giles Severn, and I still knew it very well. I had to mock him to save face.

"Oh, I do—I do deserve the best!" I cried. "But it just hasn't come my way. And now you're talking to me as if you

were old and wise, and I was a child, and I don't think I
like it."

His smile returned my mockery. "That's for self-protection.
I find that I'm all too ready to see you as a woman, and it's
not altogether comfortable."

To occupy myself I picked up the sand dollar he had
dropped on the beach and broke it carefully in two across
the middle. When I tapped the broken parts on my palm, the
little "doves" fell out in my hand. I poked at the tiny winged
formations that every sand dollar contains. Giles was watching me, and I knew we were both thinking of the shell that
had been tucked into my napkin at lunch.

"It might have been Elise," he said. "She remembers how
I used to feel about you."

I tipped my hand and let the bits of shell lose themselves
in the sand. "That was a long time ago. And Elise herself
invited me here."

"Perhaps she shouldn't have," Giles said, still watching me.

Before I could find anything to say, Richard came running
toward us up the beach.

"Dad! Cousin Lacey! Come and see my castle. It's the best
one I've ever made."

He reached out and pulled his father to his feet, then offered a hand to me. I let him pull me up, and the three of us
went to admire his creation of turrets, battlements and court-
yards, with a circling moat to which he had carved a channel
leading in from the water. It was, indeed, the finest of sand
castles. And it was something else. It was a structure built by
Giles's son. A boy who needed his father. I might not care
about the woman Elise had become. I might turn a blind eye
upon a marriage that was not working out. I might evoke in
my mind old "rights" of my own. But Richard I could not
ignore. He was mine only in secret. He belonged to his
father in fact.

There was a sudden urgency in me—a hardly-to-be-endured
longing to say to him, "Giles, this is *our* son. He doesn't belong to Elise. He's yours—and mine."

I said nothing. The outcome of speaking would be disastrous—for Richard, as well as for Giles and me.

Instead, I gave myself to admiring the sand castle, and
after a time I remarked that the afternoon was getting along,
and perhaps we should drive back to Sea Oaks.

I was all too well aware of Giles's eyes, his searching look,
and I could not face him. The only safe thing to do was run

away again. I had a bargain to keep. I could not say to him, "This is *our* son."

We returned to the car hand in hand—the three of us, with Richard between. We pulled our clothes on over bathing suits that had dried in the sun, and I chattered about how I had enjoyed a lovely afternoon. Giles was silent, thoughtful. I wished I knew what he was thinking—and was afraid to know. He drove all the way around the island before he took us back to the house, and several times we stopped at some favorite place. There was a picnic grove of cedars above the Malvern River, where we had often gone as children with a basket of Vinnie's wonderful food. And there was a spot where one had a clear view of Dune Island to the north, with the causeway crossing Hampton marshes.

There we got out of the car and stood for a little while looking out across a great expanse of tall grass interlaced with water. Only birdcalls broke the vast silence, and I wished I might gather for myself something of the peace of this place to take away with me.

"It's always so—so lonesome," Richard said softly. "I like it here. There's nobody to pull me different ways at once."

His words gave me a painful insight. Elise, undoubtedly, pulled at him like that. Whatever the others tried to teach him, however they tried to help him, she would pull him askew for the satisfaction of her own vanity in binding him to her. I was beginning to think she turned him in new and wrong directions out of sheer maliciousness in order to even some score with Giles.

Giles did not reply to his son's words, but he put a hand on the boy's shoulder. Richard looked up at him and for a moment I saw the love that flashed between them. It was beautiful and touching, and tears stung my eyes. At least Elise had not been able to affect this bond between father and son —nor must I. I must go quietly back to New York and trust Giles to care soundly for our son.

All the way to Sea Oaks the urgent need to be off was upon me. I must return to New York as quickly as I could. There was still another day to live through here, and then I could escape. There was nothing I could do on the island. Nothing that would not make everything worse.

The rest of the afternoon I spent with Hadley Riker's manuscript. It was not always easy to concentrate, but I managed, and at least the typed words were a distraction to help me get through the time that must evolve before I could go.

When the last manuscript pages had been read, I found there was time for a walk before the seven o'clock dinner hour at Sea Oaks. I let myself out of the house without seeing anyone, and wandered in the direction of the old fort.

The original buildings had been placed at a strategic point commanding the river, and some of the crumbling foundations were left, marking where the fort stood. The construction was all tabby—that material made of burned shells and lime that was indigenous to this coastal region, and had been widely used by the early settlers.

The only building left partially intact was the one which had been a powder magazine. It boasted a square, flat roof, with broken steps leading up to it, and battlements all around. Beneath the roof two yawning black entryways led down into the earth beneath. I had thought them fascinatingly spooky when I was a child.

I climbed the steps, noting the rough shells in the familiar tabby construction, and walked out upon the battlemented roof. Across the river were the marshes, and on this side more marshes beyond the high ground of The Bitterns. The elusive odor was on the wind and I breathed it deeply. It was an odor that belonged to this coast.

On the far side of the river the sun was low in the sky, staining the air with a pale yellow and rose that would deepen as it set into the soft green of the horizon. I sat down on the battlements and was very still. There had been times in the past when I had run to this place for a few moments of utter quiet. Here the sound of the sea was hushed. Only the river lapped gently at stone banks beneath the battlements, and the marsh birds called to one another.

But this evening there was no peace for me anywhere. Inside me nothing was still. I was swept by longings I could not control, by pain I did not know how to overcome. The island offered me nostalgia and longing and more hurt. As I knew now, there was no surcease for me here.

A sound of voices broke in upon the outward quiet, startling me. I rose from the wall and walked across the roof. A man and a woman strolled beneath the sweet gums, a little way distant. They were Hadley Rikers and Elise Severn. I stood where I was, openly, but they were engrossed in each other and did not see me. As I watched them cross the clearing the sound of their voices drifted toward me, but I could not hear their words—and did not want to. Then, quite suddenly, they moved together. Elise was caught into the man's arms and his head came down to meet her lifted face. I stood frozen where I was, not wanting to watch, yet held there in spite of myself.

The embrace was long and fervent. It was Elise who broke suddenly away, pushing her hands against his chest, running a few steps away from him. He laughed softly and came after her at once, but this time she held him off, shaking her head, joining his laughter with her own, playing her tantalizing game. They went on together after a moment, walking toward Sea Oaks hand-in-hand.

I turned my back and looked out across marsh and river, tasting the purity of the air, sensing the stillness just before sunset. But I was sickened as though I had drunk some nauseating draught. In that moment I hated my cousin. How could she play at love with other men when she was married to Giles? She had everything I had ever wanted, yet she brushed it all carelessly aside for a man like Hadley Rikers.

Out beyond the river the marshes were darkening, losing their calm green radiance, their sense of peace. At night the marsh was a place of forbidding mystery. I ran toward the crumbling steps and down from the roof, hurrying toward Sea Oaks.

Halfway to the house I met Giles Severn. He came striding along the path at a furious pace, his assumed indifference gone, and I sensed that he must be trying to walk out his rage. He had met those two on the way, and there was anger in him, in his eyes, in the set of his mouth. When he saw me he came to a halt and tried to fling off the mood that drove him.

"Hello, Lacey. Out for a sunset walk?"

I nodded. "The old fort with its view of the river and the marshes used to calm me when I was upset. But the old spells don't work any more."

"Are you upset, Lacey? Why?"

I couldn't tell him, of course. "It's nothing. I shouldn't have come to the island. I had a foolish idea that if I saw it with adult eyes its spell would lessen and I'd be able to rid myself of old ties. But when I see the island again, they only bind me more strongly."

"Which of the old ties?" he asked carefully.

I spoke a little breathlessly. "Ties out of my childhood.

Times when I was happy. When my mother was alive and—"

"Why did you run away from me?" he asked.

I flung out my hands. "Do you think I couldn't see what was happening? You were in love with Elise and I wouldn't stand by and watch."

He shook his head. "Not good enough," he said. "No—you can't tell me that now. I understood clearly enough at the time. You were very young, and too impulsive and generous. Perhaps it was summer magic for us both. You got frightened, or perhaps a little bored, and you didn't know how to break things off. It was like that, wasn't it?"

There was nothing I could say. I could hardly blurt out the fact that I'd found I was going to have his baby, and I had been too proud and too young to know how to tell him. Too fearful of making a claim he might feel obliged to honor. Too convinced that *if* he loved me he would come after me.

I walked beside him in silence and after a moment he touched me lightly on the arm. "I'm sorry, Lacey. I was hurt and angry at the time, but I mustn't take that young anger out on you now. And there's Richard. Whatever happened in my marrying Elise, I could never regret Richard."

Somehow I was glad he had said that, even though he could not know the true meaning of his words. I would never regret Richard either.

We walked back to the house without saying anything more. His rage against Elise had died, but there was an unrest in both of us as we followed the path. My cousin was playing a dangerous game. How much did Giles care? How much would he endure of this sort of thing, whether he cared for her or not?

At the steps of the house we parted, and Giles went around toward the stables. I climbed slowly to the portico, and found Elise waiting for me near the door. She was alone.

"Did you enjoy your walk with Giles?" she asked, and I knew I was in for a tormenting.

I returned her look gravely. "It's always pleasant to walk with an old friend."

"Old friend?" Her delicate eyebrows raised a little. "What do you think of him now, Lacey? He was only a boy when you knew him. He's a man now. What do you think of him as a man?"

"I would think," I said steadily, "that he could be worth everything a woman might give to marriage with him."

Her laughter had a flippant sound that angered me. "So

you're still carrying a torch for him? I wondered about that. You were always such a loyal little thing. No wonder you came back."

"I came back at your invitation," I reminded her.

"I would have added mine, too, if I'd had a chance." Giles had returned to the house, and he spoke as he came up the steps. When he reached the top he held out his hand to me. "Going inside, Lacey?"

I didn't know how much he had heard, but I gave him my hand and we went into the house together. I glimpsed Elise's face as we passed her, and her expression was dark with venom.

"You're shaking," Giles said when we were out of her hearing. "You mustn't let her get under your skin, Lacey. She plays that game deliberately."

I wanted only to escape him. "I know Elise," I assured him, and ran away from him and up the stairs. A few shreds of pride were left to me, and I did not want him to see how true Elise's final words had been. I could not feel safe until the door of my room was shut behind me. Then I stood for a few moments with my hands covering my face. These last hours were going to be hard to get through.

At dinner that night Charles was away, having accepted an invitation from Amalie to The Bitterns. Paul had gone home to Malvern on the mainland. Only Elise and Giles, Hadley Rikers and I, and of course Richard were there. No pranks were played upon anyone, and the meal went smoothly enough on the surface, with Elise and Hadley carrying the burden of the conversation. Giles was the correct host, and that was all.

"I've finished reading the manuscript," I told Elise, and she insisted upon asking questions. I managed not to commit myself, on the grounds that I was no proper judge of the book, admitting only that it had held my interest. It was as if our interchange on the portico had never been.

Hadley listened with slightly amused interest, and I had the feeling that he had every confidence in his book's being published, and thought my hesitance rather silly.

When dinner was over I sat for a while in the long double parlor with the others, but as soon as I could I went up to get ready for bed. What I wanted most was to be asleep, to be hurrying the time that must pass before my leaving. Richard was beyond my reach, and Giles was deep in his own troubles.

Now I had only tomorrow and the affair at the Sea Oaks plant to get through before I could take my plane for home.

I went to bed as early as I could and listened fitfully to the sound of the ocean rolling onto the beach below the house. There was a strong wind tonight, and the waves rushed up the sand with an all-enveloping roar, then receded, only to rush in again—over and over, the everlasting, rhythmic voice of the sea.

I must have slept because the high sound of a human voice startled me, brought me wide awake, sitting up in bed. The sound came from below my window, and I recognized the voice as Elise's.

"Try and stop me!" she cried. "I'll do exactly as I please. I'll see exactly whom I please. There isn't anything you can do about it."

Lower tones answered her—a man's voice, Giles's. I did not hear the words.

"Oh, I know you'd like me gone!" Elise cried, her tone rising angrily. "Then you could be rid of me. You'd have everything for yourself—the island, Sea Oaks, Richard. But you shan't have them. The island belongs to me, and so does my son. He loves me first and best, and I mean to see that it goes on that way. I mean to see—"

Somehow he managed to hush her and get her farther away from the house. The sound of the sea took over and there was nothing else to hear.

I was wide awake now, and I did not think I would easily fall asleep again. If only I had something to read. After a little while I put on my robe and slippers and went quietly downstairs.

I half expected to find Charles home by this time, and reading in the library again, but he was not there. Instead, Giles sat alone by a window, with a glass in his hand. He sloshed the ice about in it and drank, then leaned his head back against his chair. His face was like a mask—something I had never seen before. Not angry now, not wild with rage, but with a stamp of hopelessness upon it. A stormy longing rose in me. I wanted to run to him, fling myself on my knees beside him and put my arms tight about him. I wanted to offer him solace, sympathy, understanding—love.

Of course I could offer him nothing. I had no right to do so. And I could imagine how surprised he would be at so emotional a gesture. So I stood there in the darkness of the hall a few moments longer. Long enough to witness his lonely, quiet drinking. Then I went back up to bed and lay tossing for most of the night. The picture at Sea Oaks had come clear, and it was the picture of the trap a woman had built about a man. A cruel trap, and perhaps a dangerous one. Because I did not think Giles would live in it forever, and when he made an eventual move to escape, a number of people might be hurt.

Whether I had the right or not, I wondered if I should help to effect that escape. What would the result be if I went to him and told him the truth—that Richard was my son, and not Elise's? There seemed little of a bargain to hold me now because of Elise's own behavior. Yet there was still the matter of my own conscience, and I knew I would do nothing of the kind. The time might come when I would fly in the face of my self-restraint, but that time was not yet. The consequences could be too grave. Grave for Richard himself. The shock of discovering that Elise was not his mother, when he apparently adored her, could be bitter and destructive—and the harm done would be permanent.

In the morning after breakfast, I phoned Aunt Amalie. "May I come and talk to you? Just to you alone?"

She told me to come right away. I let Elise know that I was going to The Bitterns, and set off on the walk between the two houses.

Floria was not about when I arrived, and Amalie met me at the door. We were all going over to the Sea Oaks plant later in the morning, and she was dressed in a simple gray-green linen frock that made her look trim and elegant, even at this time of day.

"Is something wrong?" she asked as she took me into the parlor of The Bitterns.

It was a room I had always liked. Aunt Amalie had a fondness for things Victorian, and the red velvet sofa, the occasional chairs with their oval backs, the faded India carpet, and the small pedestal tables, all gave the flavor of Victorian times.

I sat down on the dark red velvet of the sofa. "Everything is wrong at Sea Oaks," I said. "You must know that."

She moved about the room, not seating herself at once, idly touching books on the piano, a big conch shell on the whatnot shelf.

"What do you mean exactly?" she asked at last.

I began at an oblique angle. "Well, it's a trival meanness,

but who do you think put that sand dollar in my napkin
yesterday at lunch?"

She was equally oblique. "Who do *you* think put it there?"

"The only likely person seems to be Elise," I said. "And
that makes no sense."

Aunt Amalie seated herself in a small chair opposite me.
Light from a window touched the wide, high cheekbones of
her face, lighted her dark eyes, showed traces of red in her
hair. She looked younger than her fifty-odd years, and a little
sad.

"She's afraid of you," Aunt Amalie said.

"Elise? Of me? But that's ridiculous. She invited me here."

"I warned her not to. I didn't think you should be brought
back to the island and all it holds for you. But Elise takes
matters into her own hands when it suits her, and she would
see nothing except her wish to help Mr. Rikers."

I caught up the name and let the rest go. "What about this
Hadley Rikers?"

She was silent for a moment or two, her sadness reaching
out to touch me with the gentleness of an old affection for
her sister's child.

"You're thinking about Giles, aren't you?"

I heard her but I did not answer.

After a moment she went on. "I don't think Elise is serious
about Hadley Rikers. Or about anyone else, for that matter.
I think she craves admiration and excitement. I think she
must punish Giles for not loving her as much as she feels
it is her right to be loved."

"But what an unhappy way to live!"

Aunt Amalie nodded. "It would not be my way. But I've
waited a long while to marry Charles. I will value what I am
getting. Perhaps Elise married Giles too easily. Perhaps she
doesn't value him enough. Perhaps your coming here has
opened her eyes a little."

"I'm glad if it's done someone some good," I said dryly.

"My dear!" Aunt Amalie left her chair and came to sit beside me on the sofa. She took my hands and held them in her
own. "I know how hard it's been for you. I've seen the way
you look at Richard. I've seen the way you look at his father.
And you mustn't, you know. That road can only lead to
tragedy. For everyone. Elise knows, basically, what she wants.
She wants the island, Sea Oaks—Giles, even. She wants an
heir to those things she holds—Richard. She will never give

them up, and anyone who crosses her path in opposition will meet with merciless treatment."

"What does Giles want?" I asked, not meeting her eyes.

She patted my hands and then let them go with a slight asperity, as though she grew impatient with me.

"Giles wants the good of his son above all else. Perhaps that's what we all want, more than anything—what is right for the boy. I do, and I believe Elise does as well, in her way. She's very fond of him, you know."

"I've wondered about that." My tone was still dry.

Aunt Amalie sighed. "I suppose I've foreseen this moment from the time when you gave up your baby. With another woman the giving up might be complete, but not, I think with you, Lacey dear. You've never recovered from the loss. It's hurt me to watch you these two days. Because this is my fault, too. For your sake I sometimes wonder if I was wise in what I helped you plan. But then I look at Richard, and I know this was the only way."

Was it? I wondered. Had it really been? Or had I been too young and unhappy and frightened to do what was ultimately wise and right—and courageous? Sometimes one had to fight—how could I know now?

"Richard is happy," Aunt Amalie said gently. "He loves his father deeply. You've given him that above all else. And he adores Elise. You should see the way he follows her around at times—"

"Begging for her love?" I broke in.

"Richard doesn't beg for anything, as you'd know if you were here for a while. He's a very proud little boy. Don't torment yourself, Lacey dear. The affection Elise has to give him is different from what yours would be. Allow her the privilege of that difference. Perhaps it's not so all-consuming a love as yours would be, but Richard is not neglected in any way. There's no dearth of affection around him."

She was being fair, as perhaps I was not. There was a need for me to stop on occasion and examine my own motivation. Perhaps I was too ready to see Elise in an unfavorable light as Richard's mother. For all that I told myself I wanted Richard's well-being, wouldn't it give me a secret satisfaction to believe that no one could make him as good a mother as I? Aunt Amalie was helping me to see an unhappy truth more clearly than I wanted to.

"Perhaps you're right," I said. "When I watch Richard, sometimes I don't know what to think."

"You must allow him to be himself. He isn't always an easy child to be near. You'd find that if you were around him much. He can be sunny and radiant, and a joy to us all. And he can be a young demon filled with strange notions of revenge toward the very ones who love him most. You've only seen him on his best behavior."

I felt that I was still not reaching the heart of what was truly wrong at Sea Oaks. I was not touching on the trouble that lay between Elise and Giles. While I sought for the right words, Aunt Amalie returned to the matter of the sand dollar.

"You know Elise well enough to realize that she's given to whimsies. The sand dollar might be a way of warning you that you must say nothing, that you must not be tempted to speak out."

"Say nothing?"

"About Richard's birth, of course. Have you any conception of the upheaval there would be if you told the truth at this late date? Giles would hate you both. And I don't know what he would do as far as Elise goes."

"Whatever happened would be bad for Richard," I agreed. "I can see that."

She nodded at me briskly. "I'm glad you can. The cup is broken. It's too late to mend anything that way now."

"Just the same," I said, "I had to think of it seriously. Perhaps I still do. I wish terribly that I could do something to help."

"You can," Aunt Amalie said with a touch of her former asperity. "You can cut your ties with the island. With Sea Oaks. With all of us here. That's painful drastic treatment. I hope you have the strength for it. It's the only way I can see that will do any good."

I knew she was giving me her best advice, but I didn't know whether I could take it. "I'm not sure I can," I said. "I truly don't know if I can."

"We live with what we have to live with," Aunt Amalie said, and I knew suddenly that her own life lay spoken in those few words.

I slipped my arm about her. "I'm sorry. I shouldn't have come here to dump my troubles in your lap. I know I have to work this out myself. And I haven't taken the time to tell you how glad I am that everything is turning out well for you."

She embraced me warmly and then drew away. "In a little

while it will be time to start for Malvern. You'd better run
back to Sea Oaks and get ready."

"I will," I said. "And thank you, Aunt Amalie. I'm not sure
I can see things your way, but I'll try."

She came to the door with me, and I hurried across the
garden and out the white gate between the tall hedges. Beyond the gate Floria waited for me. She wore the same
flowered dress she had put on yesterday, and her legs were
bare, with thonged sandals on her feet. She greeted me with
no particular pleasure and fell into step beside me.

"I'll walk you back to Sea Oaks," she said. "What was all
that with my mother? What was so important that I had to
be banished from the house?"

"It was nothing much," I said evasively. "I wanted to have
a visit with her before I leave. There'll be no more time
today."

She glanced at me suspiciously, with her reddish brows
drawn down. "Paul says you're still in love with Giles," she
blurted out.

"Oh, come now!" I looked up at her as she strode along,
tall at my side. "Paul is taking something upon himself."

"He's more sensitive to such things than I am," Floria told
me. "And he hasn't forgotten about you and Giles when you
were young. All that had gone out of my mind."

"As it should," I said. "What on earth's the matter with
you, Floria? You can't put spells on me now."

"I'd have liked to that time when I thought you might
marry Giles," she said. "If I hadn't been too grown up I'd
have done some of my own sort of island voodoo."

I could only look at her in astonishment. "I didn't know
you had anything against me to that extent, Floria."

"Oh, I hadn't anything against *you*. It was just that I wanted
to see Giles marry Elise."

"Because you loved your sister so much?" I asked in some
astonishment.

"Because I hated her," Floria said.

There was such passion in her words that I glanced at her
again in surprise. Her thick eyebrows were drawn down in a
scowl, and her red hair was wildly massed on her shoulders
as she tossed her head.

"You shouldn't say things like that," I told her.

"I'll say what I please! And this afternoon when you get
aboard that plane out of Malvern, I hope you never come
back."

She wheeled on the path beside me and strode toward The Bitterns, leaving me shaken and not a little shocked. What on earth had gotten into Floria? What was disturbing her so much that she should pour this tumult of emotion into words directed at me?

There seemed no easy answer to that question as I hurried back to Sea Oaks. The others were nearly ready to leave, and I ran up to my room to change for the trip to Malvern.

While I was dressing I tried to plan. This would be my last opportunity to be with them all together. It would be my last opportunity for observation. My talk with Aunt Amalie had left me frustrated. I could see how she must feel—because of Elise. Yet she was trying to be fair to me too, and advise me for my own good. For the most part, I had failed in my reason for returning to the island. Now I was to be given another chance, and I must be ready for it.

When I went downstairs I found that Hadley Rikers had left the island. So at least he would not be present any longer, and Elise could not goad and torment Giles with her flirtation. The fact that Aunt Amalie felt she meant little by it did not improve the situation.

Floria and Charles were driving with Amalie over to Malvern, and the rest of us were going with Giles in the station wagon. Paul was already at the plant.

When we got into the car, I did a little quick maneuvering that placed me in the back seat with Richard. The boy was not altogether pleased, but Elise gave him a mischievous look as she took her place next to Giles, and he subsided rather glumly beside me. On the way I tried to get him to talk, but he was plainly bored with me this morning, and I realized that I was hampered by Elise's listening presence in the front seat. I could not be myself with the boy, and I suspected that he could not be himself with me. Elise would undoubtedly influence him against me.

We drove down the asphalt road and across bridge and causeway into the broad, palm-lined streets of Malvern. The Sea Oaks plant was a little way outside of town, and though we were early, people were already arriving, and Paul was in charge. I saw Aunt Amalie's gray car parked outside as we went in.

The freezing plant was already in operation, and Giles turned at once to his duties as host. Visitors were filing in, their lines controlled, with guides assigned to each group.

Elise and Richard and I went to join Floria, Aunt Amalie and Charles, as they moved about, watching what was going on, greeting those of the visitors whom they knew. The plant consisted of several high-ceilinged oblong rooms built of concrete, all opening into one another at angles. There were electric lights overhead everywhere, and high glass windows as well, along all the walls. I was aware at once of the clang and hammer of machinery, of the movement of conveyor belts, of women with white caps over their hair working at the cleaning of shrimp and other seafood, of men unloading the deliveries of shrimp and lobster, clams and scallops, bringing them by carton-loads into the plant. White and Negro men and women worked together throughout, and I knew this was Giles's successful policy.

Though there was a smell of fish, it was surprisingly mild, and not at all offensive. A great deal of water was used in the operation, and some of it inevitably spilled off on the brown tile floor, so that one had to move about with caution.

Richard came out of his bored mood and took it upon himself to act as my guide, perhaps because I made him a satisfactory audience. He showed me the women who were butterflying the shrimp with sharp knives and swiftly skillful hands. He showed me where the sauces were being mixed, where the finished dishes were being sent through the cooking units, and then put into trays for quick freezing. I saw where blocks of frozen foods were sent along a conveyor belt, to be sliced by machinery and quickly, neatly packaged, only to be stored instantly again in the great freezers.

The freezers themselves fascinated me, but Richard was reluctant to go near them.

"I don't like them, but you can go inside if you want," he said. "I'll see you later." He summoned a foreman to open a door for me.

The man raised one of the great doors and I watched it go sliding upward out of sight. Then someone called to him and he went off, leaving me to my devices.

There were lights inside the big room, and I stepped wonderingly into a world where frost vapors made a thin fog. At once the noisy clatter of the outer room faded, and I was in the deep, quiet cold of a northern night. Stacked in high, solid rows were racks of shelves on wheels, holding trays of food that were being frozen. I walked into the bone-chilling cold, meaning to stay only a few seconds, letting the big gray cavern draw me into its vast depths.

As I took a few steps along a wide main aisle, I heard a sound behind me that made me whirl about. I was in time to see the door sliding inexorably down into its locked position. Without warning, I had been shut into the freezer.

Someone had made a mistake, of course. Someone had carelessly closed the door, leaving me inside. I hurried to the great wood and metal expanse and banged on it with both hands, calling for someone to open it and let me out. Nothing happened. I remembered the loud roar of machinery beyond that must drown out any pounding or shouting of mine.

It had all happened so suddenly that I did not panic at once. I was more annoyed than anything else. But as the cold penetrated my flesh and set me shivering as nothing happened to the door, I grew frightened. The situation was ridiculous— and utterly menacing. Oh, where was Richard that he didn't see what had happened to me?

Frantically I began to search the door for buttons or knobs or bolts that might be manipulated from within to let me out. Surely there must be a way out of the freezers from inside. But if there was a way, I could not find it, and the cold was growing worse—a little numbing now.

Then, quite suddenly, the door moved beneath my hands. It slid upward with a clang and freed me to the warm outer world. I found myself staring into the faces of Paul Courtney and Giles Severn.

"S-s-someone closed the d-d-door," I said between chattering teeth.

Paul gestured. "There's an overhead chain you can pull to open it. See it there, hanging from the ceiling, right above where you were standing."

I could see the chain, but I hadn't known what it was for, and I might never have guessed. I clasped my arms about my shivering body and stared at them both, shocked and helpless.

Giles put an arm about me. "Come along," he said. "I'll get you into the warm sun."

As he led me toward the outer door, I saw Richard and tried to smile at him. "I wish you hadn't gone away," I said. "Someone shut me into the freezer by mistake."

He gave me a dark look, such as I had never seen on his face before. "I hate you!" he cried a little wildly. "Why did you come here when we don't want you here? I hate you!"

Giles reached out and grasped his son's collar, gave him a quick shake, but the boy squirmed out of his grasp and ran away across the wet tile floor.

"What was that all about?" Giles said. "Richard couldn't have shut you into the freezer. He couldn't reach the chain."

"He—he was all right just a few moments ago," I said. "He was being very nice to me."

"Never mind. It was lucky that one of the foremen told us where you must be, and we came to look for you." Giles opened a door and I stepped into the warm sunshine of late morning.

He led me around to the side where there was a long tulip bed and a stone bench. I sat down and lifted my face to the sun. The shivering had left me now, and the heat felt wonderful on my face and arms.

"I'm sorry I got in trouble," I said. "Go back to your guests, Giles. I'll sit here for a little while."

His eyes were concerned, his look grave. "I can't imagine what could have happened. Anyone who works at the plant would look inside as a matter of routine before he closed the door."

"It doesn't matter," I said. "I'll be all right now."

"I'll drive you in to catch your plane this afternoon," he told me. "Don't worry about anything till then."

He touched me lightly on the shoulder in a gesture of affection, and went back inside the plant. I sat very still in the sun, letting it seep into my pores and wipe out the last traces of that bone-chilling cold.

The truth was coming clear in my mind. It had not been an employee of the plant who had closed the door of the freezer. Another prank had been played on me, though a more serious one this time than that of the sand dollar. Someone was determined to frighten me. Not, I thought, to injure me dangerously—surely I would have been let out in time—but just to chill and alarm me. I could not know for sure that it was Elise who had done this, but I had a very good idea. Richard's behavior told me the truth. He might have seen what had happened, and allied himself on the side of whoever had closed the door.

It was a long half hour that I stayed in the sun. Then I got to my feet and walked back into the plant and sought out Aunt Amalie.

Chapter

Five

My plane was aloft. I watched the curving Malvern River far below, and looked beyond it for a brief glimpse of the roofs of Sea Oaks and The Bitterns, a vanishing view of Elephant Beach. Then there were only marshes for a time, and Hampton Island was left behind as we flew up the coastline. We flew over other islands that were equally fair, equally golden, but which meant nothing to me. My island was lost to me. I was flying into exile. I could never go back.

I turned from the window and rested my head against the back of the seat. Giles had kissed me good-bye and I still felt the sudden hard brush of his mouth across my own. For an instant I had responded to him with all the warmth I felt. Then I had pulled away and was out in the open, running toward my plane.

Now Hampton was lost in the haze behind me and even the odor of the marshes was already an elusive scent that I could not recall.

While we were still at the plant, I had told Aunt Amalie and Charles about being shut into the freezer. I had made no accusations, but I had let them know what a fright I'd had. I think Aunt Amalie understood perfectly what I was saying, that she knew very well what I believed. Once while I was telling her under the rattle and clash of machinery, I caught her looking across the huge room to where Elise stood talking to Paul, with Floria standing by, dark-faced and displeased about something.

"It's a good thing you're going home," she told me. "You

80

know how sorry I am to say this, Lacey, but for your own good I think you must not come back."

Charles, not altogether understanding, tried to soften her words, tried to tell me that I would always be welcome on Hampton Island. And of course I must come back for their wedding.

But I knew I would not.

It was especially hurtful to take with me a remembrance of the look and manner Richard had worn toward me right up to the moment when Giles had driven me away. At the plant the boy had not come near me again, but had stayed with his Aunt Floria, who was his good and usually sympathetic friend.

It was a relief to get back to New York and be caught up in the demands of my work again. Every day I was beset by the problems of the writers whose manuscripts I edited, rewarded with small triumphs. Every day I was distracted and reasonably content. But in the evening when I went home, it became more difficult to shut out the ghosts. I remembered the surly look on the face of my son when I said good-bye to him. I remembered Elise's light, silvery laugh when she had told me that I must come back often—knowing that I never would.

Particularly did my small apartment begin to be haunted by Giles. I kept imagining how he would look sitting in this chair or that. I could see him walk through the door, or stand beside a window. He was in my thoughts constantly and I seemed unable to banish him. I even began to give in to my fantasies in a whimsical way.

In my walks about the Village, with enticing little shops on every hand, I would buy "gifts" for Giles. Here a bowl from Greece of a graceful design and muted color that might appeal to him; there a handsome piece of English silver in the form of an inkwell. Or I would bring home a book he might care about reading, and try to read it with his eyes. Once I bought a painting for both of us.

The artist had depicted a stretch of sandy beach—it might have been Elephant Beach down to the last detail—and I discovered it with delight. But after I got it home and hung it over the mantel that topped my prized fireplace, I was sorry. I did not want to be reminded so constantly of sand and sea and island. The picture made my sense of exile all the more acute.

There were times when I even tried to be more generous to Elise, times when I questioned my own motives. Hadn't I always been too greedy for life—for what *I* wanted from life? I had not given Richard up emotionally as I should have done. I must try to do what Aunt Amalie suggested and allow Elise to be a mother in her own way. Then I would remember my cousin in Hadley Riker's arms, and I could not be kind to her.

Two months went by, and I had a desultory correspondence with the island. Aunt Amalie wrote to say that my visit had made her miss me all the more when I was gone, though she must reaffirm the wisdom of my decision to stay away. Richard wrote a scrawled note that barely thanked me for a book I sent him. And Elise answered my bread-and-butter note with her usual light chatter. My firm was still considering Hadley Riker's book, but though I did not think the final outcome would be favorable, Elise wrote as though publication were sure.

I was not happy, but I was not entirely unhappy, and I told myself that I was learning how to live my life as it had to be lived—without Giles Severn or Richard, without Hampton Island.

Then, late one summer afternoon, I came out of my office and found Giles waiting for me in the reception room. He had not given his name at the desk, but had simply made sure I was in that day, then sat down to wait for me.

I came through a door that opened into the reception room and saw him before he saw me. Saw him, and was shocked. He was thinner than he had been, and altogether grimmer-looking.

When he saw me his face lighted and for a moment he looked more like himself. He stood up and held out his hand.

"I've come to take you to dinner," he said. "I hope you're free."

I made an instant decision, which was surprising, considering the confused leaping of my heart and the unwarranted feeling of joy that flooded through me.

"Come to dinner at my place," I invited. "I've enough in the freezer for a simple meal, if you're not gourmet-minded."

He liked that. I said good night to the receptionist and we went out to the elevator bank together, stood among the evening throngs waiting to go down. I asked him about the island, about Richard and Floria, Charles and Aunt Amalie. Not about Elise. I could not so much as mention her name.

We found a rare, rush-hour taxi and rode down to the Village. On the way Giles told me he had come to New York to talk over a contract with a new customer for his Sea Oaks delicacies. So of course he had wanted to see me. Casually, naturally. Of course.

We walked up my two flights and I unlocked the door.

He belonged in my rooms at once. While I took lamb chops out of the freezer and lighted the broiler, he wandered about my living room, made himself a part of it. He picked up the Greek bowl I had bought, remembering his taste for subdued beauty, and admired it. He found the leather chair I had placed for his comfort, while hardly admitting to myself that it had been purchased with him in mind. Sometimes it had been necessary to fool myself, when the extravagance was great. He saw the painting over the mantel.

While I opened the gate-legged table and set out my best blue stoneware and bright fiesta napkins, he found the picture to his liking.

"Elephant Beach," he said without hesitation, and went to stand before it. "It's so true to life that I wonder if the artist came from Malvern."

I set down the silverware and approached the fireplace. "It's possible, I suppose. There's the very shape of the inlet, and there's that hummock of grass that creeps down the beach over the left-hand dune beyond the sea grapes. All it needs is one of Richard's sand castles to make it perfectly true to life."

He turned to look at me. "You've got the island in your blood, haven't you, Lacey?" he said. "You had to buy this picture."

I did not say, *I bought it because of you.*

"I'm afraid that's something I can't help," I told him. "I'm not content to have it that way. I'd rather not be pulled back to Hampton wherever I go. I'd rather not be haunted by the false notion that everything is safe for me there—and nowhere else."

"Is that how you still feel?"

I was too close to him. I knew him too well. I knew the very shape of his body under his clothing. I knew the laughter that could brim in his eyes, teasing me—though he was not teasing now. I knew the slow way a smile could begin at the corner of his mouth, and the way his laughter could burst out suddenly, engulfing me. This somber man I knew less well. He had not worn this mood when we were very young.

"Lacey," he said. The sound of his voice caressed, though he did not touch me. "Lacey, I had to come. I've tried to put you out of my mind and stay away from you. But I couldn't. I knew very well from the time you visited the island that you would pull me here. You felt it too, didn't you, that last time when we took Richard to the beach?"

I could smell the chops in the kitchen, but I stood quite still.

"Don't look so wide-eyed and frightened," he said. "I'm not going to rush you. The mistake that needs to be corrected was made years ago. But first I wanted you to know that I'm going to ask Elise for a divorce. I think you had a glimpse of how impossible our life together has become."

I couldn't dissemble. I did not want to. He must know by my eyes how I felt about him. He must have known very well that afternoon we'd spent together on the island. But this was not the time to go into his arms, though I knew he wanted me there. Too much must be thought about soberly. I was no longer a heedless child and there were too many things to be faced. I must remember Richard first.

I smiled at him a bit tremulously and fled back to the kitchen. He did not follow me, and I turned the chops under the broiler, checked the browning of the au gratin potatoes, stirred butter into the peas. And all the while I thought about Richard, who adored his father. Richard was the person I dared not forget.

When our supper was ready, I carried the dishes on a big wooden tray into the living room, and we sat down to the first intimate meal we had ever eaten together. Sounds came through the open windows from the brightly lighted Village night, yet it was cozy inside and there was a sense of being with each other that was satisfying to both of us.

Giles threw off his serious mood and was the old, teasing, faintly mocking self I remembered. His mockery laughed at himself first of all, and his teasing never hurt me. We sat long over our coffee and fruit.

"I'm glad to picture a place for you in my mind," he said. "You've made something warm and attractive here. It becomes you, even if it doesn't altogether suit you. It doesn't suit you because you need sunny space around you, and the sea wind tossing your hair." He nodded toward the picture. "It's strange that you should have the island so much a part of your heritage, when you've only visited spasmodically. Elise regards it as hers, of course. But it's not hers yet."

I pressed the knuckles of one hand against the palm of the other. "You're going too fast for me! I can't forget that you have a son. How will this affect him?"

"Elise is terribly bad for him," Giles said. "Her influence is all in the wrong direction. She wants to give him a sense of possession toward the island—the same sort of possessiveness she feels toward it. Though that might not be important if everything else were right. She encourages him in acts of rebellion that are not good for a child."

"What sort of acts?" I asked.

"He has begun to follow her example in the deceptive little tricks he plays, and in a readiness to lie. I've had to learn that truthfulness is not one of Elise's virtues. That's one of the main differences between the two of you, Lacey. You can be trusted clear through. You've kept the same clear-eyed honesty that you had as a little girl. Even when something might hurt you, you had to tell the truth about it. And that's a trait I value more than any other."

He reached across the table and covered my hand with his, but I could not respond. The touch of his fingers seemed to burn my flesh, and I sat very still, hardly breathing. That he should value honesty in me first of all was scarcely to be borne. Not when I had joined forces in so major a deception that it would rock his whole life to have it exposed, to say nothing of destroying me in his eyes.

After a moment he withdrew his hand, sensing a stillness in me he could not understand.

"Richard would be better off away from Elise," he went on. "I'm sure of that. You'd make him a far better, far more loving mother than Elise does. As for how he feels about me—I suppose I'm something of his pattern and his idol, right now. Though this may be a phase he's going through. At least we like and respect each other, as well as having a good deal of love in our relationship. The boy will have to stay with me, and I don't think Elise will really care, except that she will be losing her heir apparent to the island."

I forced myself to speak. "That's not how the courts figure these things. You'd have to have Elise's full cooperation or the boy would never be awarded to you."

"She'll give it," he said grimly. "I won't stand for anything less."

There was something in his tone that frightened me. "Oh, do be careful!" I cried. "Don't make her angry with you. Elise can be full of malice. She's unforgiving. She can—"

"Do you think I don't know?" He stood up and moved about the room, so that I could not see his face. I did not want to see it.

Not again that evening would there be a moment of tenderness when I might have gone into his arms—and I was thankful to have it so. The name of Giles's son had been spoken, and Richard stood between us, holding us apart. The destroying truth—that I still kept from Giles—held us apart. I tried to close off my pain and make his time with me one he would remember warmly and happily. That was all I could do.

For the rest of the evening we chose subjects that were safe. He talked with enthusiasm about his work at the plant, and of how satisfactorily his Sea Oaks brands were finding new customers and bringing work to more people around Malvern. The vegetables used were all proudly home-grown, and the men and women employed in the plant belonged to the town and the countryside. Giles had made a point of hiring both whites and Negroes, and both worked together in relative harmony with a good feeling of doing something for their own mutual benefit, and with mutual respect. Pride in a common product was something Giles took care to foster, and he had no disturbances or labor troubles. The Sea Oaks plant could use the old cliché about being one big family and have it sound true.

He spoke, too, about his father's coming marriage to Aunt Amalie. He bore Charles a very real affection, but he admitted they had never been understandingly close.

"He's been lonely since Mother died, and he and Elise don't get on too well. Not that he's ever in the least difficult to live with, but sometimes Elise is impatient with him, and too ready to regard the house as hers, when it still belongs to my father. I find myself wondering what he's thinking when he looks at her with that quiet air of his. Things will change for the better when Amalie comes to Sea Oaks. Though if there's a divorce, perhaps Elise will move into The Bitterns again. I could wish that she might leave the island, but her roots are dug emotionally deep, and I don't believe she ever will."

"Would you leave the island?" I asked.

His look of surprise answered me. Leaving Sea Oaks was no more a part of his pattern than leaving Hampton Island was a part of Elise's. Yet I could not imagine living in Giles's house, with Elise so short a distance away. I did not think there would be a divorce. I did not think it was possible.

Giles stayed later than he meant to, but I think I was good for him that evening. I could offer him a quiet, listening presence, and something of relief from the feeling of conflict that disturbed him when he was with Elise and in close contact with the unhappy truths of their marriage. For a little while I could furnish the companionship of someone who asked for nothing except his presence in my home.

My own anguish came later when he had gone. I busied myself doing the dishes, and straightened the living room, removing every evidence that I'd had a guest in my apartment that night. When there was nothing left to do, I went to bed at a late hour, and lay listening to sounds from the street, watching the flickering light of a neon sign upon my ceiling. I would not let myself weep, but I knew the tears were tight in my throat, burning behind my eyes.

Something had happened that promised me all I would ever want. But I dared not reach out to grasp it. Because I knew Elise. She would never let him go. She did not want him, but she would not release him to be happy elsewhere. She would not let Sea Oaks go. Especially not to me. I knew her so well. My cousin. My childhood friend and tormentor! If the truth about Richard ever came out, she would make the most of the deception I had played upon Giles. For it was my blame first—no one else's. Aunt Amalie had advised, and Elise had been willing, but unless I had given my consent, unless I had connived to the fullest in the plan that had evolved, it could not have been carried out. *I* had made it possible. I whom Giles considered honest and completely trustworthy.

When I fell at last into a restless sleep, my dreams were haunted by Elise's eyes watching me. I remembered them so well—blue-violet eyes that could charm and win, and betray utterly, if one believed in her too much. As a child, I had sometimes trusted. As a grown woman, I was wary. I knew now why I had dreamed of Elise pursuing me along a Hampton beach with a firebrand in her hands.

Sleep was hard to come by that night, and for many nights afterward. I did not see Giles for another month.

The second time he let me know ahead that he was coming. He phoned me from Malvern to ask if he could see me again. His voice was cool and noncommittal. It frightened me.

He came directly to my apartment this time, and I knew by his face that he had gone through a bad time. We were neither of us hungry. I fixed bowls of clam chowder and picked up a crusty loaf of French bread from the corner store. We drank

a rosé wine in my best glasses, and shut out the hot, noisy
street with the sound of the air conditioner.

While we ate, we talked of nothing important, but when
we were through and he had taken the big leather chair again,
he told me what had happened.

Elise had laughed at his request for a divorce. She liked
things the way they were and wanted no changes. Certainly
she would not give him up for another woman—if that was
what he intended. He had, of course, said nothing about me.
He told her that he was ready to give her the benefit of getting
the divorce, but if she would not, then, unpleasant though it
might be, he would take the necessary steps and file for
divorce himself.

This gave her reason for further amusement. She had been
careful—he would find legal cause hard to come by, she
pointed out. Besides, she knew very well that he would want
no scandal that would reflect upon Richard, or do the boy any
harm. If Giles went too far, he would then see what she could
do in turning the boy against him. Did he imagine for one
moment that she would not use her considerable influence
with Richard to make him wholly hers, and set him against
his father?

There had been an impasse. Elise was right. Richard must
not be injured. If Elise used her tricks to turn him against his
father, this would be to his ultimate harm. Elise was no
mother for him, but the only way she could be kept even
partially under control was for Giles to remain married to her.

I sat in my chair across the small room and heard him out.
When he came to a halt I went to him and knelt on the floor
beside him. I slipped my arms around him and pressed my
cheek against his chest. Holding him thus, the deep thudding
of his heart was part of the beating of my own. It was a quickening beat. I had only the comfort of my love to offer him,
and I would not hesitate. He needed and wanted me, and I
had wanted to belong to him again for a long while. Elise
could not have everything her way.

But it was Giles who stopped me gently and blocked any
travel down such a road.

"Not this time," he whispered, with his lips against my
cheek. "I took the chance of injuring you once before, and I
won't again. This time we're going to wait. There's too much
hanging in the balance to risk harm to you—or Richard. I
must try again to persuade Elise to give me a divorce, and in

the meantime I mustn't see you here. I must risk nothing that
will play into her hands."

He was wise, but I felt rebellious even as I bowed to his
wishes. Later that night when he had gone, I wept silently
into my pillow. This way perhaps neither of us would have
anything.

The months went by, through fall and into winter. Charles
and Aunt Amalie were married at Sea Oaks, but I did not go
to the wedding. I wrote to them both affectionately, knowing
they would understand why I could not be there for the
ceremony.

At rare intervals I saw Giles. When he was in New York
he would take me to lunch openly, since we were old friends.
He brought me no good news. Richard had been ill with a
virus that eluded the doctors, and all was not well with the
boy. Elise pursued her carefree life and held Giles off when it
came to a divorce. Nothing was happening on any front, and
I could see the marks of discouragement, of hopelessness
growing in Giles. I was glad for his work, which kept him
busy, as mine did me, but I could not forget that time when
I had come upon him drinking alone in the library. What was
happening could not be borne, yet by the time spring came
around again, there still seemed to be nothing I could do.
Then a letter came from Floria that changed everything.

We corresponded infrequently, and over the years her letters
had taken on a pattern that was now familiar. "Blowing off
steam," she called it. Perhaps she knew she had in me a
receptive listener when it came to all island affairs. This time
she was bitterly angry, and her wrath had to do with Richard,
of whom Floria was very fond.

Apparently the boy had been in a highly nervous state since
his illness, and he had been harder than ever to control. On
a recent occasion he had brought Vinnie's wrath down upon
his head. Usually, Vinnie was kindness itself to the boy, but
this time she lost her temper and scolded him as no one had
done for a long time.

"He's becoming too much the young prince," Floria wrote,
"and he took affront. A few days later he saw his chance and
he got Vinnie's fresh ironing from the kitchen table and took
it outdoors to drag it all in the mud. You never saw such a
mess! Yet Elise did nothing to reprimand him. If anything,
she was amused, and she took the attitude that Vinnie had no
business scolding him, but should have come to her. Giles
had better sense. He gave Richard the spanking of his life.

But it didn't end there. The next day Giles came into the library and found that piece of driftwood in the shape of a ship—something he's fond of and has had for years—smashed and splintered on his desk. Richard's doing, of course—to get even with his father. Elise was amused again and said openly that she couldn't blame the boy. Giles's hands were tied, though I know he had an unsatisfactory talk with Richard. He had to go away during the next few days, and things simmered down while he was gone. But I feel there's serious damage being done to the boy. Lacey, my sister is an evil woman. And Giles is helpless against these circumstances. It's alarming to see a strong man helpless. It's destroying him."

I sat long over Floria's letter. I read it several times, devastated by what it told me. Something must be done, and perhaps only I could do it. Perhaps the time had finally come to take Richard out of Elise's damaging hands. How, or if, it could be managed, I didn't know. But there was still Aunt Amalie to turn to. To some degree she might have an influence upon her younger daughter. Too, there was the possibility that if I could tell the truth about Richard, no matter what the cost to me in turning Giles against me, if I could prove that he was my son and not Elise's, then if there was a divorce the boy might at least be put into the hands of his real father.

I wrote to Aunt Amalie. I knew she did not think it wise for me to come to Hampton Island, I said, but I had to see her, talk to her. It was urgent for me to do so. She wrote back at once and her letter was a little surprising. Things were not well on the island, and it might be a good time for me to come—a good time for us to talk, she wrote me. She would like to see me, too. Why not take my vacation during the spring, if I could, and stay at Sea Oaks? She had consulted Elise, and my cousin was willing to have me come. Besides, this would be a good way to quiet any talk that might be going around.

The entire letter was enigmatic. Elise was "willing" to have me come. And there was talk to be quieted. Things were not "well" on the island.

The reference to talk told me it must be known that Giles had seen me in New York, that in spite of our circumspect and innocent meetings, there had been Malvern gossip which had reached Hampton Island. I still felt rebellious, and I did not want to care about secrecy. If it had not been for Elise,

I would have been willing to have it commonly known how Giles and I felt about each other. But Elise would turn such knowledge to her own use and Amalie's hint that there was gossip worried me more than a little.

Sometimes I thought of the sand dollar in my napkin, and of the incident at the freezing plant when that door had been closed upon me maliciously. But I must not worry about such tricks. They had done me no harm, and I was not a child to be terrified by hidden threats. If Elise wanted warfare, then let her bring it into the open. I would not let such happenings stop me.

I accepted Aunt Amalie's invitation and arranged for my vacation. When the time came I took a plane for Malvern. Since I feared his objection, I waited till the last minute to drop Giles a note and tell him my plans. He would know anyway, of course, since I would be staying at Sea Oaks, but I wanted him to hear it from me. I had no response from him, and I had a feeling that he would not approve of my coming.

This time it was Floria who met my late afternoon plane at the airport. Her red hair had been moderately tamed into a pony tail, and she wore brown, tapestry-printed slacks and a yellow blouse. She did not appear particularly glad to see me. When my bag had been stored in the back seat and we were on our way to the island, she blurted out what was on her mind.

"So you've been seeing Giles in New York?"

I kept my temper. "I would have lunch with anyone from Hampton who visited New York."

Floria kept her strong hands on the wheel and her eyes on the road ahead. "A friend of Paul's saw you together in a restaurant. It was the way you were looking at each other that gave you away. Mother was upset about it. Though I tried to tell her that you'd always had a crush on Giles, and this was probably nothing new or serious."

"Would it be so terrible if it was?" I asked her bluntly.

She threw me a quick look. "I suppose I'm thinking of Elise."

"—who cares very little for Giles," I said. "Why are you concerned about your sister? The last time we talked you told me that you hated her."

"Sometimes I do." She tossed her pony tail impatiently. "But we all want the status quo to continue. Elise's concern is for herself and her hold on what belongs to her. Mother's concern is for Charles and Richard. And mine is for me."

I didn't know what she meant, or how she could be affected by anything I chose to do.

"You sounded outraged by the incidents concerning Richard when you wrote to me," I said. "You didn't sound as though you liked the status quo at all. It's because of your letter I've come."

"I was upset. And I don't mean that things are ideal as they are. But it's none of your affair, and any changes might make things even worse."

It was my affair, but I could not tell her how much.

"What about you, Floria?" I asked. "Has the date for your marriage to Paul been set as yet?"

"We'll set it when we're ready," she said shortly, and I understood that this topic was taboo.

The island was in view now and I was silent for a time. Floria and I were irritating each other thoroughly, and I did not push her any further. I was concerned once more with my own thoughts, my own anticipation. In a little while I would see Giles again. I would see Richard.

We were across the bridge now, and onto island soil. The live oaks and the pines and sweet gums welcomed me. So did the sight of the tall white lighthouse.

"Are you staying at The Bitterns alone now?" I asked Floria.

"Yes. I'm not very gregarious. I don't mind being alone."

"How is everyone at Sea Oaks?"

"Richard's better, but he still hasn't gone back to school. He loves to run wild and Elise is indulging him. There's time enough for school in the fall, and he has been doing lessons at home."

"And your mother?"

"She has what she's always wanted," Floria said. "And Charles is happy to have someone to look after him again. Mother has fitted into Sea Oaks as though she always belonged there. Perhaps she really has."

"In that case, where would you be?" I asked lightly.

"I suppose I'd be somebody else. Perhaps that would be a good thing." Her words had a dryly bitter sound.

We turned off the asphalt and onto the shell drive. Moss-hung oaks framed the avenue, framed the way to the house. In the late afternoon sunlight it stood at the end of the way, white and shining—as beautiful as I always remembered it. But except for Aunt Amalie and her marriage to Charles, I knew it held unhappiness now. And my coming would not stir it to joy.

As we followed the drive, Floria spoke again. "You might as well know there's been an upheaval between Mother and Elise. Things were pretty bad a few days ago. Tread cautiously between them, will you?"

I wondered what this meant to me. How much might it put Aunt Amalie on my side? But I merely indicated to Floria that I would try to make no false moves.

When we reached the house Vinnie came running down the right wing of the steps, with Aunt Amalie descending more slowly behind her. I was greeted as warmly as I could have wished, though there was no Elise in sight to meet me with cousinly affection. My bag was heavy and I would not let Vinnie carry it in this time, but took it myself as Aunt Amalie led the way upstairs.

In my room, where windows had been opened and the curtains drawn back to let in the spring sunshine, Aunt Amalie put her arms about me and kissed me again, clung to me for a moment.

"Dearest Lacey. Even though I'm doubtful about your coming back, I'm glad your exile wasn't for good."

"I had to talk to you," I said.

She nodded at me and the soft wings of rusty-gray hair trembled at her temples. "We'll have a long talk soon, dear. But now you'll want to change your clothes and rest before dinner."

I held her at arm's length. "You're happy, aren't you? This is a wonderful time of life for you?"

"Now that I have Charles," she said gently. "Even though he doesn't approve of my daughter. But then—neither do I, always."

"It may be that I will have to tell Giles the truth about Richard," I said, blurting out what I had meant to lead up to carefully and slowly.

Aunt Amalie looked startled and a little shocked. "I think you must do what you have to do. But don't be precipitate, Lacey dear. Let's talk about this. At length."

"That's why I'm here," I agreed. "Floria says you know— about Giles and me."

She closed her eyes. Her lovely, composed face looked older than I remembered—and, for the moment, sadder.

"Yes," she said. "I know. Or at least I've suspected for some time."

"What does Elise think?" I asked. "About me, that is?"

"Who knows what Elise thinks? Or what she knows, for that matter?" Amalie moved toward the door. "Let's not discuss this any further now. I—I want to think about it all soberly before we have our talk."

She let herself out the door and closed it softly behind her, leaving me standing there in the middle of the floor, feeling that I had been foolishly impulsive, that I had accomplished nothing.

While I was getting out of my wrinkled things, Vinnie came tapping on my door, bringing me a cool lemonade, making an excuse for herself to come and talk to me. She did not go away at once, but stood shaking her handsome, graying head at me doubtfully.

"I don' know if you should be coming back here, Miss Lacey. Everything's all mixed up at Sea Oaks. I thought when Miss Amalie come here to stay things would be better. But they ain't. Miss Elise sure got the bit between her teeth these days."

I suspected there was little Vinnie did not know, and if I had been seen with Giles, she would know that too.

"How is Mr. Giles?" I asked her.

She gave me a quick look that confirmed her knowledge. "It's a good thing he got his work. This last year been hard on him, what with Richard being sick so much. That lil ol' boy's the apple of his daddy's eye, that's what he is." She reached out and patted my hand suddenly. "Don' you pay all this trouble no mind. Things work out someways. You just get you'self some rest, and eat a heap of good Sea Oaks food."

I squeezed her hand. "Thank you, Vinnie. If there's time before dinner, I'll go out for a little while."

She nodded at me. "There's time and that's a good idea. So you do that. And be nice to Miss Amalie, you heah? She's got a load to carry in this house."

"Because of Elise?" I said.

"Miss Elise don' give a thought for nobody. She just go her own way and laugh at other people. I don' think she hear too good when somebody criticize her."

I could believe that very well. Vinnie looked about the room with a proprietary air and then left me. I drank the lemonade, and put on a frock of watermelon pink. Then I went into the hall and toward the stairs. Richard's door stood open, but there seemed to be no one inside and I did not stop.

There was no one about in the downstairs hall and I went out the front door and down the steps to the driveway. The sky was showing signs of sunset, and the marshes would suit my mood. I wanted to be where I could breathe their scent and let my eyes follow their lonely reaches.

I took the short cut through the burying ground and went on past The Bitterns. I came to the place where higher ground ended, and wild, hardy sea myrtle marked the beginning of the marshes. It was possible to step onto a hummock of dry ground and feel myself a part of the marsh. The best way to be *in* the marshes was when you were out in a boat. But this would serve me for now.

All about were the wide stretches of marsh grass, the intervening patches of water—stained with rosy gold in the sunset—the quiet, the peace. And that tangy, elusive scent. When I had come here first as a child the marshes had touched my spirit indelibly. It was a strange magic because there was so little there to put your finger on. Just the wild, empty spaces, the occasional calls of water birds, the stillness.

Once I could have opened myself to this peace and let it heal me. Now I could not. All my feelings were too raw, too lacerated. Suppressing my love, trying to give it up, had been damaging. And now there was harm being done to my son. Floria's letter had made me sure there must be a change, and I was the only one who could bring it about. I must forget about everything except Richard's good. I must persuade Aunt Amalie to help me.

From the higher ground behind me a voice cut suddenly into the silence: "What are you looking at?"

I turned around, with water lapping at my feet, and saw Richard a few yards away, watching me.

It was a moment or two before I could speak.

"Hello, Richard," I said. "I'm glad to see you again."

He did not answer my greeting, but stood staring at me almost balefully, his eyes bright in the sunset glow, his hair touched with reddish gold. He was taller than when I had last seen him, and thinner as well. The old longing to touch, to fondle, was in me again, and I had to thrust the feeling away.

"Why don't you give it back?" Richard said.

I stared at him. "I don't know what you're talking about."

"The brooch," he said. "Why don't you give it back?"

"What brooch, Richard? What on earth do you mean?"

He came a few steps closer to me. "The Stede Bonnet pirate brooch that used to be one of the Hampton Island treasures. Mother was talking about it at dinner last night. She said she wouldn't put it past you to still have it and not want to give it up. Because your mother took it away with her."

"Oh, Richard!" I cried. "That was all so long ago. And there was no brooch found in her things. My father hunted for it and never found it. Of course I don't have it."

"If you were a thief, you wouldn't admit it, would you?" he said.

I climbed off my hummock of marsh grass and went back to higher ground where I could stand beside him with the sunset glow all around us. I was beginning to see the unhealthy change in the boy.

"Who said I was a thief?" I asked him.

The baleful look was still there, bright and steady. "My mother."

"And do you believe it's true? Can you really believe that of me?"

For the first time he looked a little uneasy. "I used to like you," he admitted. "But now I think I mustn't. I'm not sure about you any more."

He began to move away from me, and I put out a hand to coax him back. There was so much that needed to be said, yet I did not know how to talk to him, how to break down this fantastic belief he had about the brooch. If it was a belief. Perhaps it was just something he threw out to torment me with. Though why he wanted to torment me, I didn't know. Perhaps tormenting had become a pleasure to him, as it was to Elise.

"Wait," I said. "Don't go away, Richard."

He hesitated, waiting for what I might say.

"Please believe me—I don't have the pirate brooch. Or anything else that belongs to the Severns or Hamptons."

A certain impudence came into his eyes. He looked as though he wanted to say something more, but he did not. Instead he turned and ran away from me, back toward the burying ground and Sea Oaks. I stood looking after him in dismay, wondering what I could have said or done that might have made a difference between us.

Around me the marshes had turned gloomy and they no longer seemed peaceful in the fading light. Now my son was being turned deliberately against me. Elise was playing some game of her own to hold him at all costs. But before I could start toward the house and escape the darkening marshes, I saw Floria coming toward me from the direction of The Bitterns.

"Mooning over the marshes?" she said. "You always did like them, didn't you, Lacey? Though I could never see why. I've always hated their monotony. I've always wanted to escape them, and escape the island."

I began to walk beside her, back toward the house. "Won't Paul take you away from the island when you marry?"

She shook her head and the red pony tail danced. "Mother has put The Bitterns in my name. Paul likes that. He has island fever too, just the way Elise does. He's an outsider, but he has always wanted to live here. He wants to fix up The Bitterns, repair and refurbish it, the way Elise has done at Sea Oaks. And this pleases my mother. So what chance is there for me?" She broke off. "What was Richard talking to you about?"

"He accused me of having that old pirate brooch in my possession," I said. "The famous one with the emerald that was lost so long ago. Who could have given him that idea—Elise?"

"Of course. She hasn't been very friendly toward you lately, and she won't want Richard doting on you as his dear Cousin Lacey."

"But to tell him lies—" I said.

"That's something Elise does easily. You already know that. You knew her well enough when we were all young. She wasn't very truthful then." Floria stopped abruptly on the path beside me. "This is as far as I want to walk. I'll see you later at dinner. Since Mother has moved over there, I usually have lunch and dinner at Sea Oaks. Saves cooking for me alone."

She waved a hand at me and went off toward The Bitterns. I followed the short cut thoughtfully toward the house. Elise's shadow seemed to lie ominously across my path at every turn. But the matter of the brooch ought to be cleared up for Richard's sake, at least. Perhaps the best thing to do would be to talk to Charles about it. It was because of him the brooch had been lost originally.

When I reached the house there was still no one about, but when I looked into the library I found Charles there alone. He rose at once and came to greet me warmly.

"You look happy and contented," I said, and he nodded pleasantly.

"Why shouldn't I be? What brings you back to Sea Oaks, my dear? Not that we aren't delighted to have you. But it's not the happiest climate in the world just now. My daughter-in-law—" he hesitated and I saw the clouding of his eyes. "Never mind—we're glad you've come. But you look worried, Lacey dear. Has something happened?"

"Yes," I said. "Richard has just accused me—out of a clear sky—of having kept the famous Hampton Island pirate brooch after my mother died."

"What nonsense!" he said. "This is Elise's doing, naturally."

I had seldom seen Charles look angry, but he was plainly disturbed and indignant now. "Sit down, Lacey, do sit down," he said, and took a quick turn about the room before he returned to his own chair.

I seated myself and waited for him to join me. "I know the story of the brooch, more or less," I told him. "I know that you gave it to my mother when you were in love with her—"

"The extravagant act of a very young man," he put in wryly.

"I know she is supposed to have taken it away with her when she left, but I've wondered if that could be true. It seems unlikely when she didn't want to accept it in the first place."

"She tried to return it to me," Charles said, "but I wouldn't have that. So she took it away with her, as far as I know, and I never heard from her about it again."

I put my fingers over my eyes, trying to remember. "A letter from your mother came two days before my mother died. She was very ill, and I think at first it was hard for her to understand when my father read it to her. The letter inquired if she still had the brooch. I was there in the room and I remember that toward the end of the letter she began to get excited. I remember the way her hands fluttered and she tried to sit up. She cried out, 'No! No!' several times, and then fell back against the pillow and couldn't say any more. Afterwards she went into a coma. I sat beside her bed whenever they would let me, and I was alone with her when she died. She opened her eyes and said a few words quite clearly. She said, 'I wrote a letter . . . in the mailing place. Tell . . .' and then she was gone."

I broke off for a moment because the scene had returned to me too vividly. Then I went on.

"Later I repeated her words to my father, but he couldn't make anything of them. He thought she was wandering. So I forgot about them in all that happened afterwards. But I'm remembering them now. Do they mean anything to you?"

There was a light in Charles's eyes. " '. . . in the mailing place . . .' Yes, it's possible. We had a secret between us, Kitty and I. There was a place where we used to leave notes for each other. After she ran way from Malvern and the island—because she could not bear to come between her sister and me—I never went back to our mailing place again. Its memories were too painful, and there was no one left to leave notes for me there." I caught the sound of excitement in his voice.

"Then do you suppose—?" I began.

"It's possible. The evening's grown too dark now, but to-morrow morning, Lacey, you and I are going on a treasure hunt. It would be strange indeed—yet not, perhaps, unlikely, that the Stede Bonnet brooch has been resting safely in a special hiding place all these years. It's too bad you didn't repeat these words to me before this."

"They had no meaning. I was only a little girl when I heard them. And there was too much else to think about at the time. My father took over the writing of an answer to your mother, and he made no connection between the words Mother whispered to me when she was dying and that valuable brooch. Two days had elapsed, after all, since he had read her the letter. The subject of the brooch never came up again, until it was mentioned casually the last time I was here. And then just now, with Richard making his accusation."

"All the more reason to try to find the answer," he said.

I felt the same thing strongly. As I went up to my room, I knew that Elise must be confronted with the truth, and these new fantasies about the brooch must be brought to a halt. Richard was truly believing what his mother had said.

I'd left my suitcase open on the bed, but I had not yet unpacked my things. Now I began to busy myself, taking my clothes and toilet articles out and putting them away in closets and drawers. At one point an object wrapped in cleansing tissue came into my hand and I looked at it, puzzled. I did not remember wrapping anything in this way when I had packed my bag.

The thin stuff tore easily as I unwrapped it and stared at the object which lay upon my palm. It was the second brooch from the pirate case downstairs—the less valuable brooch which Charles had put into its place at a time of crisis, and which had been kept there ever since. It lay sparkling in my hand, alive with rhinestones and bits of sapphire and topaz—a pretty thing, but not precious, not valuable beyond redeeming as was the other brooch.

But why had someone tucked it away among my things? Why had someone hidden it where I would be sure to find it when I unpacked? It was a childish thing to do, and I thought of Richard at once. But an adult could imitate a child—which was what I felt had happened with the sand dollar. Was this a similar prank? Was it all beginning again?

In any case, I must now show Aunt Amalie what I had found, and let her place it in the proper place downstairs. If there were any conclusions to be drawn, suggestions to be made, I would let her make them.

I pulled open the door of my room, stepped into the hall-way—and met Giles coming up the stairs. There was no warm greeting for me in his eyes this time. I stood quite still, letting him come to me.

"I received your letter," he said. "There was no time to answer it. You gave me no time to tell you to stay away."

"Giles," I spoke softly, "I'm sorry, but I had to come. They've trapped you here. But I'm not trapped. Not yet. I'm still free to move about—and Aunt Amalie thought it best that I come."

"It's not wise to blow everything into the open at this point," he said. "Elise—"

"I think it's already in the open," I told him. "Floria says a friend of Paul's has seen us together in New York and drawn conclusions. Aunt Amalie wrote that it might help to stop any gossip if I came now. She wanted me to come."

"I imagine you gave her no choice." His look softened a little. "I remember how you used to be sometimes when you were small. Elise was willful and high-handed. But you could be more stubborn and persistent than anyone I knew. You had to take hold of life with both your hands. What do you think you can do here?"

"I don't know yet," I said frankly, and held out my hand with the brooch in it. "Look what someone hid in my suitcase while I was out of my room. What do you make of it?"

He recognized the brooch at once, but he did not touch it or take it from my hand. "More tricks," he said. "Who is it feels he must play them on you?"

"That's what I'd like to know. I'm going to show this to Aunt Amalie now, and see what she thinks about it."

He stepped aside to let me pass, and for just an instant I brushed close to him and saw him stiffen. For just an instant I knew we felt the same strong urgency to be in each other's arms. But that must not be under this roof. Not until many things were cleared up. I hurried to the room that had once belonged to Charles and Marian, and tapped upon the door. When I looked around again, Giles was gone.

Aunt Amalie called to me to come in and I went into the room. She had changed to a soft, blue-gray hostess gown for dinner—the sort of loose, flowing style that became her. She started to smile at me, and then saw my face.

"What is it, Lacey?"

I carried the brooch to her and repeated what I had told Giles.

She took the pin from my hand and turned it about in her

fingers. "I don't know what to say, or to think. Shall we call Richard and question him?"

I shook my head. "No—please. I met him outdoors just now, and he's angry enough with me, as it is. He accused me of keeping the other brooch myself. He told me that his mother thinks I'm a thief and that somehow I have the Bonnet brooch in my possession."

Aunt Amalie laid the shining bit of jewelry on her dressing table. "How very foolish! Leave it with me and I'll put it back where it belongs. Don't take Richard's words seriously. He has misinterpreted something that's been said, and I'll have to talk with him. It's true that there's a mystery about the brooch and its disappearance. It wasn't like Kitty to take it away and keep it forever. But Elise was only wondering out loud about it. I believe she said that it might be interesting to question you sometime—in case there was something about the brooch that you knew without knowing you knew it."

That had really been the case. But I did not put the thought into words. What I had told Charles was now his affair. If he wanted to tell his wife about the possibility of my mother's words meaning something, that was up to him. I would say nothing.

"I'm sorry this has disturbed you," Aunt Amalie said. "Perhaps it's best if I replace the brooch and we say no more about it."

She kissed my cheek, and I embraced her warmly, even though I wasn't sure whether her counseled action was the best course for me to follow. I would have liked to take the brooch with me to the dinner table and tell everyone what had happened—force some sort of confrontation. Perhaps my son needed a disciplining that his elders were not giving him. But I had to leave everything in Aunt Amalie's hands. He was not mine to discipline.

As I left the room, Charles came in the door, and he looked at me questioningly. I gave a slight shake of my head to let him know that I had said nothing to Amalie about our talk concerning the brooch. He caught the glitter of gems on his wife's dressing table and went to pick up the pin I had found in my suitcase.

"What is this doing out of the case?" he asked.

I started to speak, then flung out my hands to Aunt Amalie. "You tell him," I said, and fled from the room. I'd had enough of that brooch or any other for the moment. I'd had enough of pranks and tormenting from a boy who was my son.

When I went downstairs I found that I was bracing myself for a meeting with Elise. I had come here hoping to find some weakness, some chink in her armor that would help me in my purpose. But I had no idea what she knew or suspected. I had no idea how she would receive me.

When I went into the parlor I found Elise and Floria there, having drinks before dinner. Elise saw me at once and set her glass down carefully.

"Hello, Lacey," she said, and her violet-hued eyes were very bright. "Help yourself to something from the cart over there."

I had not known whether to expect resentment or disliking from her. Or perhaps the innocent blandness of ignorance. Instead, I saw that she was amused with me. The brightness in her eyes was that of mockery. Elise Severn had no fear of Lacey Ames. She was simply amused that I had come here to face her.

I poured myself a glass of sherry and sat down a little way off from the other two. Floria was watching us both with that dark, brooding look of hers that told me she approved of neither of us.

"It's nice that you're to spend your vacation with us, Lacey," Elise said lightly. "This means that you'll be here for the Camelot ball in about ten days. We'll have to find you a costume."

"Do I have to attend?" I asked, sipping my sherry and watching her uneasily.

"If you're here, of course you do," she told me. "We're not the same size exactly, but Vinnie can make some alterations, and you can wear one of my gowns from past years. No one will remember. Would you like to be a lady of the court?"

Our talk seemed unreal. As if I could care about the ball one way or another! But I had to go along with her line of conversation.

"I'd rather take my old role of the Lily Maid. If we can get her out of her tower, for once."

Elise shrugged. "Be what you like. Most of our main roles hold the same from year to year—with guests coming as anybody they please, except that there's supposed to be only one Arthur and one Guinevere. I have a white gown from two years ago that will do nicely. I was a little slimmer then, and we can lengthen the hem if necessary."

I could imagine nothing I wanted less than to join in the frivolity of Elise's ball, but there was nothing I could do but agree and hope that something would happen so that I could be far away from Sea Oaks by the time it was held.

The rest of the family began to gather for dinner from various parts of the house. Charles and Amalie came in, and so did Giles and Richard.

The boy seemed edgy and keyed up, and I wondered if it was because he expected me to say something about what he had hidden in my suitcase. I tried to get him to meet my eyes, but he would not. His shining green gaze slipped away from mine, and I could not pin him down.

In spite of the fact that Charles still owned Sea Oaks, Elise and Giles sat at each end of the table, with Charles and Amalie seated across from each other, on either side. I fancied this was Elise's doing. She had not released the reins as mistress of the house, even though her mother had married Giles's father.

We were filled with tension at the table that night. Amalie and Elise were carefully polite to each other, but there was pain in her eyes when Aunt Amalie looked at her daughter, and something close to insolence in Elise's return glance. Their falling out, whatever its cause, had not been healed. Giles was thoroughly uncomfortable. He did not want me there, and my presence put a constraint upon him. I think Elise was aware of this, and further amused by it. She would always be amused by anything which made others suffer.

Richard watched everyone, and particularly his mother. He seemed to be waiting with an almost unhealthy anticipation for something to happen. Something he held some secret about. Once when I looked at him suddenly, I found him studying me, though his eyes slipped away at once when I tried to catch his gaze and challenge it.

Floria seemed lost in her own private gloom, and joined very little in the talk. I noticed that Aunt Amalie seemed concerned about her, and that every once in a while she tried to throw some remark in her direction to draw her elder daughter into the conversation. But Floria simply glowered and refused the bait.

Only Charles, of all of us, seemed comfortable, and at ease. He answered Elise's banter cheerfully. He smiled at his wife, and tried to ease the tension between her and Elise. He engaged Richard in talk about the horses, and questioned Giles concerning some matter at the plant. When the meal was over he came around the table to speak to me as the others left the room.

"Tomorrow is Saturday," he reminded me. "So we may sleep late. But after breakfast you and I must slip away alone for our treasure hunt. I don't want to open up the subject with everyone until we've explored the possibilities. Then there won't be disappointment if it's only a false hope we're raising."

"I haven't even told Aunt Amalie," I assured him.

He hesitated as though he meant to say something else, and then let it go. The others had gone into the parlor, leaving us alone, and only Floria found us there and came in to say good night. When she had returned to The Bitterns, I asked Charles the question that had been puzzling me.

"Why doesn't Floria marry Paul? She's been in love with him most of her life."

"We all know that," he said. "Paul knows it too, and he's in earnest about wanting to marry her now. Perhaps she even represents safety to him."

"Then why—?"

Charles's pleasant look had vanished. "Because of Elise. All of our troubles seem to stem back to Elise. Floria isn't sure that Paul has recovered from his old feeling for her sister. It's no secret that he wanted to marry her at one time. That never worked out, but Floria isn't sure but that is still what he might want. It's a foolish, stubborn attitude on her part, but she's just the sort of woman to decide that she will have all or nothing. Foolish, very foolish."

Yes, I thought, thinking of Floria's mother. Aunt Amalie had not questioned the past. She had known the road to her own happiness and she had not minded that Charles had known other loves.

We returned to the parlor and I found Aunt Amalie waiting for me. She took me by the hand at once.

"Come along, Lacey. We've some visiting to do. Let's go into the library."

Giles looked up from the papers he was working over, and I saw the cool challenge in his eyes. A challenge directed at me. *Be careful,* he was saying, not wholly trusting me. But he could not know what lay between Amalie Severn and me.

Elise laughed lightly. "That will be nice, Mother. I know you'll enjoy a lovely long visit with Lacey."

I think she knew very well what we were going to talk about—and she did not care. Her position seemed frighteningly secure.

In the library I took a chair facing the long windows, where I could see the two pictures that hung on either side—

the picture of the shrimp fleet, and the one of marsh grass burning. They were familiar scenes and spoke to me of the island reassuringly.

Aunt Amalie sat in a favorite chair she had brought here from The Bitterns—a chair with a delicately carved frame, upholstered in pale gold damask. Her soft gray-blue gown fell in classic lines about her, and her rusty-gray head was held high. She was less beautiful than Elise, but she had a dignity and poise neither of her daughters could match. I always had the feeling that I could draw strength from her strength, and that was what I needed now.

"I've had a little time to think," she said. "And I know you don't want to wait any longer for this talk of ours. You've set your mind on marrying Giles—and I don't see how that can be."

"There's Richard," I said. "There's what Elise is doing to Richard. Floria wrote me about what happened with Vinnie's ironing that time, and then how he tried to get even with his father by smashing that bit of driftwood. All without even a reprimand from Elise. If anything, I gather she encouraged him."

"The boy's been high-strung since his illness," Aunt Amalie said. "Floria bears a grudge against her sister. Perhaps she made too much of what happened."

Her words disturbed me. She was too close to what had happened to see it objectively.

"His father disciplined Richard, you know," she went on. "You must have more confidence in Giles as a father."

"What can Giles do, with Elise undermining him on every side? It's an intolerable situation and one that has to be changed."

"By marriage to you? Oh, Lacey dear, don't you see that you can't go back on your bargain now? You gave these things up. You did what it was necessary to do when Richard was born. You've been brave about it all these years. You can't go back on that now."

I plucked at the arms of my chair. "I gave him up foolishly. I should have fought for him at all costs. But I was too young to know that then. I was too frightened of the consequences, and I thought I was doing what was best for him."

She spoke quickly, attempting reassurance. "I've watched over him, you know. Richard has never been neglected. Elise is devoted to him in her own way. I think she would never willingly give him up."

"Perhaps she would have to give him up to Giles if it could be proved that he is my son."

"That would be difficult, wouldn't it? All the hospital records, the doctor's records show—"

"I wasn't thinking of such records," I said.

She put a hand across her eyes and bent her head. For a long moment she was silent. "I see," she said at last. "I see what it is you want of me."

I left my chair and went to stand beside her, touching her shoulder with my hand. "I've loved you for a long time," I said. "You've been like a second mother to me after my mother died. I don't want to hurt you. I don't want to cause trouble between you and Elise—"

"There is already trouble between me and Elise," she said. But she returned the pressure of my hand and drew me close for a moment. "Now then, Lacey dear! You mustn't coax me like this. You tear me up more than you know."

I went back to my chair and waited for her to go on. There was a flush in her cheeks and her breath was coming quickly.

"I don't know whether I could ever do what you ask," she told me. "It would have to seem to me a clear-cut advantage to Richard, and right now I don't see that it would be. All the things that you agreed to when he was born still hold true. He leads a far better life here on the island than you could ever give him alone."

"I wouldn't be taking him alone," I said.

Her fingers clasped the carved arms of her chair, but she still spoke quietly. Her poise did not waver.

"We're back full circle again! I don't think Elise will ever give Giles a divorce."

"Then he will divorce her. He feels sure that he can get real proof of cause."

"At what cost to Richard?" she asked me.

"That's where you come in," I said. "That's what I've come to plead with you for. I suppose you know that Elise has threatened to turn him against his father. You're the only one who can prevent that from happening."

"She could do it," Aunt Amalie said. "The boy worships her. He has a good friendship with his father. But Elise knows how to charm him and keep him longing for her company and her approval."

"You could counteract whatever efforts she made to prejudice him," I pointed out. "You could prevent her success in

what she threatens to do. It isn't as though she loves him
deeply. I can't believe that, Aunt Amalie. You know as well
as I do that Elise has never loved anyone but herself."

Pain came into her eyes, but she did not let her gaze waver
from mine. "You ask too much of me. I don't know . . . I
don't know."

"You'll help me because you know it's right," I told her.
"And because, no matter how much you love Elise, you
know that what she wants is wrong."

Only then did she drop her gaze and cover her eyes with
her hand again. Emotion was breaking through her poise and
she was not a woman who liked to betray raw feelings to
anyone who watched her.

"There are still such enormous questions," she said at last.
"Elise has made Sea Oaks hers. But Giles would never give it
up. Where would she go?"

"She could return to The Bitterns," I said. "The island is
still hers. Though if it wasn't for Giles, I'd leave her Sea
Oaks and Hampton Island gladly."

"Floria will continue to live at The Bitterns when she
marries," Amalie said.

"But she needn't live there. You know how Floria feels
about the island. She could get Paul to live in Malvern, if
the circumstances were such that Elise must move into The
Bitterns."

"You've thought it all out, haven't you?" Aunt Amalie said
a little bitterly.

"Don't be angry with me. I've thought of little else. If it
hadn't been for Elise in the first place, Giles and I might
have married and none of this would have come about."

She put her hand down almost angrily. "Don't let yourself
off so easily, Lacey. You behaved like a little fool. If you'd
been wiser, perhaps you'd have held him. You flew off in a
jealous pique and left him to Elise. He was young, and you
hurt him badly. Elise was there to comfort him."

"I flew off because I didn't want to hold the threat of having a baby over his head. How could I take him under such
terms as that? I thought that if he loved me enough he'd come
after me. When he didn't——"

"More foolish pride," Aunt Amalie said. "But of course
that was where you were doubly foolish in the first place.
Getting yourself into such a predicament."

"I've paid for it since," I said.

I jumped up and took a quick, desperate turn about the room, pausing before a shelf of books to make myself read the titles. I had no answers I could give Aunt Amalie. I wasn't a young girl any more, but I had not forgotten how it had been with Giles and me. I would always remember how fiercely and splendidly the flame had come upon us. And how little we were schooled in self-discipline.

She watched me for a few moments and then spoke more gently. "Come back and sit down. I didn't mean to hurt you, Lacey. All that was done wrong lies in the past, and there's nothing there we can mend now. It's the present that matters."

"There's no one but you to help me," I said, and returned to my chair. "Giles doesn't understand why I had to see you. He doesn't know about Richard."

"And I hope you will never tell him," Aunt Amalie said.

I shook my head. "I would have to tell him before I married him. It's not a secret I could keep forever. Even if he could never forgive me, he has the right to know."

She was silent, her face grave and thoughtful. "At least you must not tell him yet. You must not tell him until after we've decided upon some course of action."

"Then you'll help me?" I cried.

"I haven't said that. I've made no promises, and I don't intend to. Not yet. Nothing must be plunged into hastily. You must stay here for the remainder of your vacation and see what we may be able to work out. Elise is unpredictable. Who knows—if you are here where she must see you every day, it may bring home to her the hopelessness of trying to hold Giles in her own way. And as I wrote you, it will stop people from gossiping. No one is likely to believe that Elise would invite her husband's mistress into her own house."

I spoke sharply. "There's nothing between Giles and me now. Not because I wouldn't be willing, but because he has some notion about protecting me. We've met only to dine out in public. After the first two times he saw me in New York, we haven't even been together in my apartment."

"I see," she said, and her expression softened. "Of course I believe you. It's just the sort of chivalric gesture our King Arthur would make. But while I believe you, I don't think Elise will. She's more apt to judge others by her own behavior. The frightful thing about it is that she doesn't care. If you wanted to have an affair with Giles it would probably be all right with her. Just so you didn't try to take away anything she regards as hers."

So this was why Elise could look at me in cool amusement —as though I were an insect she turned cruelly about on a pin.

Aunt Amalie stood up and held out her hands to me. "Shall we leave it at that for now, dear? You're to stay as long as you can. And in the meantime I will try to be honest with myself and see whether I have the courage to do even a little of what you ask of me."

I took her hands and kissed her cheek. She was my mother's sister, and I held her to me for a moment. "Thank you," I whispered.

She went ahead of me out the door, and climbed the stairs. I knew she did not want to face the others in the parlor just then. And neither did I. I could not meet Giles's questioning look tonight.

Shortly after breakfast the next morning Charles and I set out for our walk. We wandered, as if idly, toward the burying ground, and no one questioned us, or offered to come with us.

The morning was gray and the place seemed more gloomy than usual. The great live oaks dripped their veils of moss and the sweet gums stood tall, struggling with their clambering vines of fox grapes. Underfoot little brown seed balls lay scattered on the grass, pressing into the earth as we stepped upon them. Here and there the three or four tombs that were left in the place made shadowy patches of gloom.

"You'll remember this particular spot," Charles said. "You used to play here as a child."

He led the way toward the largest of the tombs. It was a structure made of tabby and brick, set half below ground and and half above. It was large enough to have held a number of caskets, and the roof was a shallow arch, meeting the ground on either side. The front end was open and steps led down into the shadowy interior. I had always found the place eerie as a child, and the same spell lay upon it now.

Charles went down the steps ahead of me, and I followed more hesitantly. Below ground the air was dank and smelled of musty dampness. The walls of the tomb rose around us and the roof arched blackly overhead. The rough tabby of the walls seemed scabrous and crumbling, revealing its layers of lime-embedded shells.

"There used to be a loose brick," Charles said, and began to feel along the foundation wall at one side. "It will not

111

have been moved for years and I may need a chisel to get it out. Let me see now."

His fingers touched and prodded, felt sensitively from one brick to the next. In the dim light that fell through the front of the tomb I saw something move under his hands.

"That's it!" Charles said. "It's loose, after all."

He worked at the brick until it came out, and set it down on the floor. Then he reached inside the space it had left. Apparently there was a hollow behind the spot where the brick had been, for he was able to reach in to some depth.

"There's something there," he whispered to me.

A moment later he had drawn out a small object like a box, wrapped in a scrap of gunny sacking. But before he could unwrap it, we heard voices out in the burying ground. The man's voice was loud enough to identify, though we could not hear the words. The woman's tones were softer, hushed to hardly a whisper.

Charles put a hand on my arm. "Be quiet," he said softly. "That's Paul Courtney. I don't know who the woman is. We'll be still until they go away. I don't want questions now."

It seemed more eerie than ever to be hiding in the tomb with Charles, waiting in secret so that we would not be discovered here. I tried to see his face in the faint light and was surprised to find it alive with eagerness, as though he played some game he remembered from long ago when he had hidden notes addressed to my mother in this place.

The voices moved away, and once more the gray morning hung dull and empty beyond the entrance to the tomb.

"They've gone," Charles said. "Come along, Lacey. We'll go out where there's a better light and have a look at what we've found. I don't think there's much doubt about what it is."

I followed him gladly from that dank, gloomy place, and we stood under the trees while Charles unwrapped the bit of sacking from about a small metal box which passing years had corroded. Charles's eyes were still alight with excitement, and he looked younger and more vital than I had ever seen him.

"So she left it for you, after all," I said.

He nodded eagerly, his finger on the catch of the box. It opened readily upon crumbling tissue inside. He pulled the paper out, but there was nothing else there, nothing hidden in its folds. The box was empty.

Charles held it out in one hand, turned it upside down and shook it, as if to wrest the treasure from it. Then he turned it over and closed the top.

"Nothing," he said. "The brooch has been taken from it. Taken goodness knows how long ago. Or by whom."

This was a stunning blow. I could only stare at the rusted metal container, which must certainly have held the brooch at one time. This was the place my mother must have put it when she left the island, though it seemed strange that Charles had never had any word from her as to where she had hidden it. She had spoken of a letter in those last words she had uttered to me, but if it was to Charles he had never received it.

"Back in those days when you used the mailing place, did anyone else know about it?" I asked.

He shook his head. "No one. I'm sure of that. Kitty and I both regarded the secret as privately ours. I knew her well enough to be sure she would never talk about it, any more than I would."

"Then someone must have found the place accidentally, just as you found it. Someone who took the brooch. It was very valuable, wasn't it?"

"Yes—priceless. But it's not only the value that matters. I suppose I've always had the pin on my conscience, and I've held it against your mother that she left me and kept the brooch. To recover it would wipe out something of that old guilt and resentment."

We had started to walk back along the path to Sea Oaks, Charles carrying the small box with him.

"I think there's just one thing to do," he said as we neared the house. "I'm going to tell the others about this, and see if there is anyone who possesses the slightest knowledge."

I did not think anyone was likely to admit to such knowledge, but he must do as he thought best.

When we reached the house and went inside, we found Amalie and Elise arranging flowers in the dining room, with Floria, once more in her tapestry pants, sprawled in a chair by a window, watching them.

Charles sounded a little grim as he paused in the doorway. "Will you all come into the living room for a few moments, please?"

Giles was already in the parlor, with Richard beside him as they pored over a book the boy was showing his father.

Charles went to the point at once. With all of us gathered around him, he showed the corroded little box with the empty tissue inside. He told of the words my mother had said before her death, and of the secret mailing place that he and Kitty had used to exchange their notes.

"Lacey and I looked behind the loose brick this morning," Charles said, "and this empty box was all we found. Do any of you have any knowledge of what may have happened to the brooch, if this was where it was hidden?"

"How silly of her to put it there!" Floria said. "She could have told someone so easily. She could have given it to someone else before she left, if Charles wouldn't take it back at that time."

"Her head was always filled with romantic notions," Aunt Amalie said. "This is the typical sort of thing Kitty would do. But she might have told us in later years, at least."

"There was a letter," I said. "I believe she wrote Charles a letter about it, but apparently he never received it."

Richard still sat at the desk with his book open before him, though he paid it no attention. His eyes were alight with interest at this revealing of a mystery. None of us noticed him.

Paul picked up the small box from the table where Charles had laid it, and began to turn it about absently in his hands, though he said nothing.

Charles watched him thoughtfully. "You were out in the burying ground just now, weren't you?" he questioned.

Paul dropped the box on Giles's desk as if it burned his fingers, and there was a moment's hesitation before he spoke.

"Yes—I came across from The Bitterns, where I stopped to look for Floria."

"I've been here in the house with Mother ever since breakfast," Floria said.

Elise had not spoken. She watched as Richard watched with a bright-eyed interest. Now she laughed softly.

"I know the next question," she said. "You were going to ask Paul if he was alone, weren't you, Charles?"

"We know he wasn't alone." Charles's tone was mild. "We could hear him talking to a woman." He paused, and then went on. "We heard nothing of what was said, and we couldn't hear the second voice clearly enough to identify it."

Paul's rather slender face had taken on a shade of color, but his eyes looked angry as he stared at Elise. Floria was looking at her too, and I sensed a smoldering rage. Giles turned away from the interchange and went back to Richard and his book.

"It doesn't matter." Charles seemed to recognize the suddenly explosive atmosphere in the room. "Whoever was near the grove this morning has no relevance to the brooch. It must have been taken from its hiding place long ago."

It was not in Elise to let well enough alone. "There's no point in making a secret of it," she said lightly. "I was talking to Paul out there this morning. Like him, I just happened to be passing through."

Aunt Amalie put a quieting hand on Floria's arm and drew our attention back to what might have happened in the past. "I remember the day before Kitty left. She was keyed up and rather desperate. I found her sitting out there by the marshes where she liked to dream, just as Lacey does. Perhaps I hated her a little that day. I think she was on the verge of telling me something, but perhaps my own manner changed her mind. It might have been about the hiding place for the brooch. At any rate, she didn't speak. Not even I knew that she meant to leave the next day."

"And now you're here." Floria had restrained herself and she did not look at either Paul or Elise, her tone surprisingly gentle. "You're here and married to Charles. And Kitty is gone forever."

Amalie's eyes brimmed with sudden tears, and Elise laughed again, unpleasantly. "How charmingly sentimental! I didn't know you had it in you, Floria."

Giles broke in on Elise's words. "The worst of it is that, as Father says, the pin has probably been gone for years, and there's no way to tell when it was taken."

Unexpectedly, Richard left his place at the desk and stood up. "Yes, there is," he said. "Because it was there yesterday."

An echo seemed to follow his words. Not one of us spoke for a moment, and we all turned to stare at him. He faced us uncomfortably, a flush rising in his face.

"You'd better explain that," his father said.

Richard put his hands behind him and set his feet slightly apart, so that there was an air of defiance in his attitude.

"I never meant to tell," he said. "Or anyway, not for years and years. I found the brooch a long time ago. I was looking for a good hiding place I could use, and that old tomb seemed right. So I started pulling at the bricks where I could reach them, and that one came out. The brooch was in the box,

and I left it there. That is, I left it there most of the time.
It was so beautiful that once in a while I brought it into the
house and kept it in my room. And I never told anybody."
The last words had a triumphant ring. Richard had clearly
enjoyed his tremendous secret.

I remembered such an occasion, I thought. When I'd last
visited the house and Richard had surprised me in his room,
he had carried something concealed in a handkerchief, and
put it carefully, secretly away in a drawer.

"Oh, Richard!" Aunt Amalie cried. "Why didn't you tell
us? You knew it was a family treasure and that it had been
missing for years."

He looked at her almost arrogantly. "It will belong to me
someday, won't it? It was mine to tell about, or not to tell
about."

"It was certainly nothing of the kind," his father said. "It
belongs to your grandfather Charles and your Grandmother
Amalie, and to no one else."

Stubbornly, Richard returned his father's look. Then he
ran to Elise, who slipped an arm about him. Watching him,
I could understand the power which the possession of the
brooch had given him. There must have been a certain solace
in knowing that he had a secret so marvelous it gave him
power over everyone. I could not condone what he had done,
but I could understand it. It was unfortunate that Elise should
now support him in his behavior.

"Don't scold him," she said to Giles. "If I had a secret like
that, I'd keep it too. If I had that brooch I'd never tell a
soul."

"The question," Aunt Amalie said, "is where it is now.
Are you certain, Richard dear, that it was in its box yesterday?"

"I put it there yesterday morning," Richard said. "I had it
out for a couple of hours, and then I put it safely away.
There's no mistake about that."

"Is it possible," Paul asked, "that one of the servants
followed Richard on some occasion, found out about the
brooch and took it?"

"I'd trust Vinnie or George with anything I own," Charles
said. "And the stable boys have been with us for years."

"I wonder—" Floria mused aloud, "which one of us wanted
that brooch enough to steal it from its hiding place and spirit
it away." Her eyes looked as bright as her sister's now, as
though the Merlin mood was upon her.

Charles shook his head, not smiling. "There seems to be no reason why any one of us would have the brooch. But I know what I shall do. I am going to return this box to its place behind the loose brick. I'll leave it there, and perhaps whoever has borrowed the brooch will put it back."

Elise laughed softly and moved away from the group. "Borrowed! What a lovely word. Imagine some member of the sacred Hamptons or the noble Severns playing a trick like this. It's quite delicious."

"I wouldn't put it past you," Floria said.

Aunt Amalie waved her hands. "That's enough. Charles is right. We will try it this way and see what happens. Then if the brooch is returned, there will be no questions asked, no accusations made."

"No questions or accusations," Giles said. "Only ugly suspicions of one another from now on."

"No, it mustn't be like that," Charles said. "We must make allowances for whatever the motive may have been." He looked about for Richard. "You may take the box and return it to its hiding place," he told the boy, giving him the container. "We will charge you to look there once a day and see if the brooch is inside. You make pick the hour you want to investigate, and let us know what it is. The rest of the time you are to stay away from the burying ground. No spying—understand?"

"I understand," Richard said.

There was still a tense excitement about him, but there was pride now, as well, and I was grateful to Charles for his gesture. The boy ran off with the box in his hands, and I knew Charles's instructions would be obeyed to the letter. Nevertheless, Giles looked thoroughly disturbed, and I understood that as well. Charles's way was gentle and carried forgiveness, rather than any sting of censure. Richard had gotten off too easily. He had learned nothing from what had happened. It was difficult to be a parent when you had some sense of responsibility to your son. Elise wanted only to bind him to her. She cared nothing about the cost to the child. I wondered what Richard thought. I wondered how he accepted the various attitudes around him. I did not know him well enough to judge.

Lunch was an oddly quiet meal that day. Perhaps what Giles had said about suspicion of one another was already taking root. And there was an uneasiness on another score

as well. Whether by accident or intent, Elise and Paul had
met in the burying ground this morning, and Floria's anger
still smoldered.

After the meal everyone dispersed about his own affairs.
Aunt Amalie took a nap in the early afternoon, so I could
not be with her, though I would have liked to talk over in
private this latest development. I did not really know what I
thought about what had happened. Perhaps I was a little afraid
to puzzle over it. No one on the island would take the brooch
because of its value. No one wanted it for money. Any one
of those who lived here would wish only to see it restored to
the glass case where it belonged. Its loss had been regretted
and resented through the years, with Charles having to live
with a good deal of the blame. Yet everyone loved Charles
and would want only to see him free of that blame after all
this time. In spite of these facts, someone had spirited the
brooch away and was keeping it maliciously for some secret
purpose.

I was in my room, standing idly by a window, when a firm
rap came at the door. I went to open it and found Giles
standing there. His eyes were green, like his son's, and they
had the same bright adventurous look in them that I had
seen in Richard's.

"Get into some outdoor clothes," he told me peremptorily.
"We're going for a boat ride."

There was nothing I would like better. I smiled at him and
closed the door. Then I rushed about my room, pulling slacks
and blouse from the closet, dressing as quickly as I could.
When I was ready in navy and white, I tied a blue-flowered
scarf about my hair, and hurried downstairs. Not for a moment did I permit myself to stop and think about what I was
doing. Giles had said, "Come," and I was coming as fast as
I possibly could. What consequences there might be, I was
not yet ready to face. Not until I stepped into the hall did I
suddenly realize that being alone with Giles was not the wisest
course of action I could take. He had spoken as though he
had reached the point where he was ready to throw caution to
the winds, no matter how he might play into Elise's hands.

He waited for me at the foot of the stairs, and I called
down to him, "Could we take Richard with us?"

"If you like," he said. "Only hurry along. The afternoon's
waiting for us."

I went to Richard's door and tapped on it. He opened it at
once, staring at me.

"Your father and I are going for a boat ride," I said. "We'd like to have you with us, if you want to come."

For an instant a response lighted his face, then he turned away and started to close the door. "I don't want to go if you're with him."

"Wait," I said, and put my hand out, my shock and hurt undoubtedly showing in my face. "Why do you feel this way about me, Richard?"

There was something of Elise in the expression he wore. "I still think that maybe you're the one who took that brooch. It's funny it should disappear the very day you came back to the island. Perhaps—"

"You can't believe that!" I broke in. "You're making up something foolish. You know that, don't you?"

He closed the door and left me staring at the wooden panel. I turned away and went slowly down the stairs.

Giles saw the look on my face. "What's the matter? The boy's always eager for any chance to get out in the boat."

"He has decided to dislike me," I said. "He doesn't want to go if I'm along."

"The skies won't fall because of that," Giles said. "Don't look so woebegone. He's a moody child and you can't count on what his reactions will be. He'll get over it."

We walked out the door together and down the steps. I still felt shaken by Richard's behavior.

"Ever since that time at the Sea Oaks plant when I got caught in one of the freezing rooms, he has turned against me," I said. "When I returned this time I thought he would have forgotten whatever struck him then. But he wants to taunt and torment me. I don't know what's happened to him, or what to think."

"Then let's not think about it for now," Giles said as we started along the path toward the beach and the boathouse. "I'll have a talk with him sometime soon and see if I can find out what's troubling him. He doesn't know you well, of course, but he has always spoken affectionately of his Cousin Lacey in New York. And he seemed to like you well enough that day we went to the beach."

"I think someone has been telling him lies about me," I said.

"That's possible." Giles's tone was dry. "We don't have far to look for the source, if that's true. But children change easily, and this mood may not be permanent at all. In any case, let's forget it for the time being. I want a free, happy afternoon with you. We deserve that, at least."

Giles's boat was fairly new and he told me about it as we got aboard. It was a nineteen-foot outboard, made of fiber glass, with a double hull—very seaworthy. He slipped behind the white wheel on the starboard side, and I took the seat opposite. The day had turned from gray to sunny, but a canvas stretched overhead to give us shade. The hull was painted a soft blue inside, echoing the sky.

Giles cast off and in a few moments we were planing around the point of land where Sea Oaks stood, following a calm sea toward The Bitterns and Malvern River. In a little while we were running past the tabby ruins of the old fort, past rocky embankments where fiddler crabs scuttled about. Then we were in the river proper, with wide stretches of marsh on either hand. Low in the water, all we could see was the green of marsh grass, with creeks and water indentations leading into the marsh at frequent intervals. At a distance, where the ground was higher, the sea myrtles began, and then the loblolly pines of the island.

I lazed in my seat, listening to the roar of the boat that kept us from talking. I watched the gray water flashing past, and now and then turned to see the foaming wake stretching out behind us, with muddy brown shadows churning in its midst. The soreness of my encounter with Richard was still upon me, but I was trying to put it out of my mind—to put everything hurtful out of my mind, and enjoy the fact that I was alone with Giles in this world of marsh and water.

We flashed past a sandbank where a white egret stood fishing, and followed a section of the river where shell banks fought off the erosion.

"Where are we going?" I shouted to Giles.

"Palmetto Island," he called back to me. "You remember the small, private island to the northwest of Hampton? The owners are away, and sometimes I look in on the place for them."

I was silent again, but not content. I could not, after all, put the thought of Richard from my mind. What was happening spelled disaster. My son could never grow up whole and well balanced in such an atmosphere. I remembered the time when he had said he was being pulled in different ways. How torn he must feel now, how bewildered and uncertain. His behavior in itself cried out for help. He needed to know where the boundaries lay. He needed to know where he must stop, and go no further. Instead, because of Elise, there was a lawlessness in the landscape about him, and instead of being taught to love, he was taught to hate. Yet no one had been able to stop Elise. Giles stood helpless against the force of her destructiveness, and Aunt Amalie was too loving and permissive in her approach. Not that she could not take a strong stand when she chose, but unless I could make her see what she did not want to see, she would do nothing. Oddly enough, only Floria, aside from Giles, had the perception to understand fully what Elise was doing. But there was too much hate of her sister in Floria for there to be wise guidance left over for Richard.

All that I'd witnessed left me sore and filled with a futile longing to help. But there was nothing to be done now. I tried to turn my attention to the scene around me.

Out in the channel an orange marker showed up brightly. We planed away from it in a wide arc to follow the opening to a creek. Hampton Island was behind us now, and for a little way there were high bluffs, with the forest growing close to their edge. Here rock had been used against the erosion that went on everywhere.

"Palmetto Island," Giles said. "We'll go around to the other side where the house is."

Where trees had fallen in this wilderness, the slashed gap was like a window into the forest. You could see deeply in among trees tangled with vines and choking with undergrowth, highlighted by streaming bars of sunlight. Giles slowed the boat as the banks of the creek narrowed and we followed a curving course around the island. The loud roaring of the motor lessened, and once Giles cut it back to a murmur so that we could watch a blue heron take off from a swampy hummock and fly above the mud-colored water of the creek. For an instant I felt a surge of deep happiness at the sight because I was witnessing it with Giles. He must have felt the same thing, for he reached across to touch my hand, and I held to him until the great bird was out of sight.

We were bound around the head of the island, and Giles told me there was a boathouse on the other side of the point of land on which the house was built. Through the trees, not far away, I could see the house now. It vanished as we drew closer to land.

"We'll stay on this side," he said. "There's a dock and we

can get up the bank without going clear around to the boat-house."

In a few moments the weathered brown dock came into view, thrusting into the creek. Giles drew the boat skillfully alongside and made it fast. Then he helped me out. With the motor silent, the world about us was very still. Those who lived on this island had a wilderness at their doorstep.

We climbed up a flight of wooden steps, and then made our way along a narrow path that led through scrubby palmetto, and loblolly pine. I could see the house on ahead of us—a low, one-story cabin, very spacious, with a roof that sloped to a wide overhang on either side of the front door. The timbers had a dark shine there among the sweet gums, and there were cabbage palms all around.

"I have a key," Giles said. "We'll take a look inside and see that everything's in order."

We went up the steps and found that the outer door stood slightly ajar. When Giles tried the screen door, he discovered that it was unlocked.

"That's odd," he said. "The Barretts usually lock up care-fully when they are away. Let's have a look around."

Inside, there was evidence of an occupant. Lunch dishes had not been cleared from a table, and an open book lay face down on a couch. Over the back of a chair hung a pale yellow kerchief that had a familiar look.

From the rear of the cabin beyond a partitioning wall, came the sound of running steps, then the creak of another door being opened and softly closed.

"There's someone here," I said.

Giles ran toward the door at the rear of the cabin, and I dashed to a window and looked out. Vanishing among the trees I saw a flash of intense green.

"That looks like Floria," I called to Giles.

He turned away from the door. "Then let her go. She probably has a boat around by the boathouse. Though what she's doing here, I don't know."

"Neither do I," said a voice from the door behind us.

We swung about together and found that we were facing Hadley Rikers. His neatly trimmed beard somehow gave him a cocksure look, and he smiled at us easily, confidently.

"Greetings," he said. "I didn't expect visitors. The Barretts said I'd have the island to myself."

Giles said nothing at all. The dark blood had risen in his

face, and I was almost afraid that he might make some move of violence.

"Hello, Lacey," Hadley said. "You'll be glad to know that I've come here for a few weeks' stay to work over that manuscript of mine. It appears that a good deal of revision is necessary before I make a resubmission."

"This should be a . . . a good place to work," I said feebly.

He nodded. "It is. I have the Barretts' boat for getting back to civilization, and my car is over in Malvern. I don't mind fending for myself. I'd planned to look in on Hampton Island before long."

It was difficult for Giles to be civil. He was staring around the cabin, a little white about the lips, and I edged backward toward the yellow kerchief that hung over a chair. I remembered it now. That last time I'd seen it, it was knotted about Elise's neck. While both men were regarding each other warily, I wadded the scarf up and stuffed it into a pocket of my slacks.

The moment of tension between the two men seemed to go on forever, but at last it was Hadley Rikers who turned away, the insolent smile fading from his mouth. Giles would not play his polite and outrageous game. He strode past him out the door and let the screen bang behind him. I hurried after him, and Hadley sprang to open the door for me, looking less poised and confident now.

Neither of us spoke, and I followed Giles back to the boat. Down on the strip of dock we were out of sight of the house, and he pulled me suddenly into his arms.

"Oh, Lacey, Lacey!" he whispered against my hair.

I put my arms about him and held him close. I lifted my face for his kiss and put my cheek against his. I knew the torment that he was feeling, knew the rage against Elise that tore at him mercilessly.

"Don't," I said at last. "Don't let it tear you up like that. If she's meeting him here, then they're playing into your hands. It should make everything easier for you."

"It could have been Elise running away through the trees," he said.

"No, I don't think so. I've never seen her wear that poisonous shade of green. That was Floria's color."

He helped me down into the boat, but before he untied the mooring rope, I spoke to him.

"Could we talk a little?" I said. "Once you start the motor

there'll be no chance. And I want to talk about Richard."

"Of course," he said. He slipped into the pilot's seat, and I took my place opposite.

"Floria wrote me about what happened a little while ago," I began. "I mean when Richard got angry with Vinnie—the malicious damage he did to her wash. And then how he tried to pay you back for spanking him by breaking that little drift-wood ship."

"Yes." Giles's eyes darkened. "We had a bad time for a while. I couldn't reach the boy. He seemed outside any punishment or counseling I could give him. It was unfortunate that I had to go away from the island just then. When I came back, he seemed changed toward me—like a different boy."

"He needs help," I said. "He needs help desperately. Even though I know him so little, I've seen the change."

Giles's hands tightened on the wheel. "What am I to do?"

"Persuade Aunt Amalie to aid you with Richard. I've been talking to her and I think she's wavering against Elise."

"Elise is defeating her too," Giles said. "They had a quarrel recently, though I don't know what it was about. There's always been a ruthless wildness in Elise, and it's growing worse. I don't think she'll listen to Amalie or anyone else."

"Richard loves his grandmother. And he respects her. If she can be persuaded to talk to him, oppose whatever Elise is doing, it may have some effect. She must come to your help."

Giles shook his head. "I don't know. His illness frightened her badly. She's been even more indulgent toward him since then. Charles is probably a better bet. At least to influence Amalie. I'll have a talk with him before long. Lacey darling, I appreciate your concern.

I wanted to cry out that Richard was my son as well as his. It seemed unbearable that I could not rightfully share these problems with him. But the time had not come for that rather terrible confession. It could only be made under happier—or more desperate—circumstances.

Giles unmoored the boat and started the motor. We roared off down the creek, and when we were out on the water, with the prow cutting the small waves a light wind was forming, I looked back and saw that Hadley Rikers stood in the door-way of the cabin, watching us go.

In my pocket I felt the bulge of the yellow silk kerchief that belonged to Elise. I was not quite sure why I had taken it. Perhaps because I was afraid of the violence I'd sensed in Giles there in the cabin, afraid of what he might do if he saw it. But there was another reason as well, and it was beginning to formulate itself in my mind. Perhaps the time had come for a confrontation between Elise and me. Perhaps I was the only one who could frighten her. Not for my sake, or even for Giles—but because of Richard.

When we got back to Sea Oaks we found Richard on his pony, Starlight, with Aunt Amalie putting him through his paces. She stood at the side of the practice ring that had been cut out of trees at a little distance from the house, and directed the young rider with crisp, no-nonsense orders. There was no indulgence, it seemed, when it came to something like being a good horseman.

Nearby Floria and Paul stood watching. Floria wore slacks and a cotton blouse of a particularly poisonous green. Giles and I joined them, and she threw us a quick searching look. Aunt Amalie greeted us with a smile and then returned her interest to Richard and his pony.

For me the scene was achingly familiar. When I was young, the one thing I had hated about Hampton Island was the riding. Everyone there rode well, except me. My mother had ridden when she was young, and she had considered it a disgrace that I was slightly afraid of horses. Amalie had always been the best horsewoman, with Elise running her a close second, even as a young girl. No one could quite match Aunt Amalie in a saddle. She looked marvelous on the back of her mount, and she was always in full command. Floria was expert too, but she rode recklessly to suit herself.

"Sit up straight," Aunt Amalie called to Richard. "And don't forget to keep your heels down and away from the pony." She turned to Giles impatiently. "The boy doesn't take to the simplest fundamentals. He seems to forget from one lesson to the next." Then she turned back to Richard. "Let's

126

see you trot around the ring now. And I want some good posting."

Richard rode grimly, as if he hated it. His grip was too tight on the reins, and his posting unrhythmic, uncertain. How well I remembered! Aunt Amalie's training had made a moderately good rider of me, but I'd never really enjoyed it, and now Richard, growing up in the midst of everyday riding, was taking after me.

He trotted all the way around the ring, and then tried a simple canter, looking as though he was terrified of falling off.

Paul had drawn Giles away from the ring and was talking to him about some matter at the plant. Aunt Amalie was concentrating solely upon the young rider and his pony. I stood alone with Floria.

"Why did you run away from us on Palmetto Island?" I asked.

She thrust her thumbs under her leather belt and turned slowly away from the ring to look at me. "So it was you who came into the Barretts' cabin? You and Giles, I suppose?"

I nodded. "He took me there in his boat. He wanted to look in on the house while the Barretts were away."

"I didn't know it was you," she said. "Though I think I'd have tried to get away anyway. Don't say anything about my being there, will you?"

"Not if you'd rather I didn't," I agreed. "Though I don't understand why."

"Elise would be furious," Floria said. "It's not that I mind making her angry. But I'd still prefer not having her know I was there."

"I suppose you're aware that Hadley Rikers is staying on Palmetto?" I said.

She was suddenly evasive. "That's none of my business, is it? Or yours, either."

"Perhaps not. But it seems to be very much Giles's business," I said.

She walked deliberately away from me and went to stand beside Paul and Giles. I didn't know what she was up to, or what had made her go to Palmetto in the first place, but evidently the subject was closed between us.

"Again!" Aunt Amalie instructed Richard. "Go around again, and try to remember everything this time. How we'll ever get you to jumping lessons, I don't know, if you don't manage the simplest part of riding."

Richard reined his pony in her direction and trotted directly over to the fence. His face wore the same dark look his father could wear.

"I don't want to jump," he said. "I don't ever want to enter horse shows and do all that sort of thing. If I could just bump around on Starlight in my own way, it would be all right. But there're so many rules, and so many right and wrong things. Why should I bother? I'm not ever going to ride when I grow up!"

"That is something you'll change your mind about," Aunt Amalie said. "Do you think your father would be content to have a disgraceful seat on a horse? Do you think—?"

Richard turned away from her rudely and spoke to me. "Can you ride?"

"After a fashion," I said. "And I learned the hard way, just as you're learning. I learned because Aunt Amalie was patient enough to teach me."

His grandmother went to Starlight and patted him before she put an arm about Richard in the saddle. "Don't be cross and rude, darling. Of course you must be a good horseman. You'd be ashamed to be the head of Hampton Island and not be able to ride properly. You know we do a lot of riding here. Now be a good boy and go back around the track again. Just once more, and if you do it well, I'll let you off for the day."

At Richard's urging, Starlight trotted back into the ring and they set off on another round.

"Why is he afraid?" I asked.

Aunt Amalie shrugged. "He's had a couple of falls, and I suppose they've frightened him. But he should be getting over it by this time. No harm was done on either occasion. He must learn to ride well."

"I'm glad to see he's being disciplined about something," I said dryly.

She raised her eyebrows at me. "You sound impatient, Lacey. But not with Richard."

"You've all coaxed him too much," I said, and walked away from her.

I was on the point of being angry, and I didn't want to be. At least I hoped we had seen enough of riding for the moment. But of course I really knew better. There was little else to do on Hampton Island, and riding had always been part of everyday life for both the Hamptons and the Severns. At Sea Oaks there was a small trophy room of cups and ribbons won over the years by Amalie, Elise, and Floria. Giles rode well, had always ridden, but he had never been interested in the showmanship that engaged the others.

I went back to the house and upstairs to my room. Vinnie was there, laying out a dress on the bed.

"Miss Elise sent you this," she said, smoothing out the folds of a long, flowing white gown. "It sure is a pretty dress. She say for you to try it on and see if the fit is right. If it's wrong I can fix the hem. I reckon it'll make you look pretty as anything for the ball."

I had forgotten the Camelot ball. I picked up the dress and held it before me, turning in front of the long mirror on the closet door. It was high-waisted, with a round, low neck, and long, tight sleeves. The skirt hung full, with a modified train at the back. It was a graceful style, and I could probably wear it.

"Thanks, Vinnie," I said. "I'll try it on in a little while."

I laid the dress down on the bed and she stood staring at it, as though there was something on her mind.

After a moment she asked the question that was troubling her. "You like your boat ride, Miss Lacey?"

It had always been that way with Vinnie. She knew what was going on.

"I loved it," I said. "It was wonderful to get out in the marshes and creeks. It was good to see nothing but birds and grass and water."

She reached out absently and straightened a fold of the dress. "Maybe I'm gonna say something I shouldn't ought to. But you never did scare me none, Miss Lacey, so I reckon I have to take a chance on makin' you mad."

I smiled at her. "This sounds terribly ominous."

"Maybe it is. But I'm gonna say it anyways. Miss Lacey, I think maybe you better not go off alone with Mr. Giles. I think it upsets too many people."

I knew who she meant by "too many people." Elise, who didn't want Giles herself, would nevertheless hold him jealously against all comers. Elise would not want him to be off on a boat ride with me.

"I don't think it will happen often," I told Vinnie.

"That's fine," she said. "In some ways it's too bad you had to go to Palmetto Island."

"You've been talking to Floria."

"Maybe yes, maybe no. That Mr. Rikers is back, ain't he?"

"He's going to work on his manuscript. Apparently the Barretts have loaned him their cabin for a while."

"Manuscript!" Vinnie snorted. "I coulda told by the look on your face when you talked about it last time you were here, that there weren't much to get excited about in that book of his. He don' come 'round here just for that."

"Do you think you ought to be talking this way, Vinnie?" I asked gently.

"I reckon I shouldn't," she agreed readily. "But I remember you as a lil' girl. And I remember Miss Elise too. I don' work for her, Miss Lacey. I work for Miss Amalie. And when I wan' to, I say what I please."

"Thank you, Vinnie," I said. A long time ago young Kitty had been loved by Vinnie, and now she was taking up a certain responsibility to Kitty's daughter.

She gave the white dress a last pat, smiled at me a bit sternly, and went out of the room. When she was gone I ran downstairs in search of Elise.

I found her in the small trophy room looking over her triumphs from the past.

"It doesn't seem that Richard will ever add to your blue ribbon collection," I said.

She looked around at me. "Did you enjoy your boat ride?"

"It was wonderful," I said. "I want to talk to you, Elise."

"That will be fine. It's time we had a talk, you and I. Let's go down to the beach where we can walk and talk without being interrupted."

I was willing. She wore sandals and a brief skirt that left her legs bare, and as she walked ahead of me out of the house she seemed enormously vital and as assured as ever. We went down to the beach together and I turned automatically toward the stepping-stones that led over the beach wall.

Elise laughed and came with me. "So you still take Lacey's way? The regular steps seem easier to me, but I remember Floria used to say this was lucky for you. I wonder if it still is."

I clambered over the rocks ahead of her, and found myself moving quickly, not wanting to be too close to her on the precarious stones. That was foolish, of course. I had nothing to fear from Elise in full sight of the house. Yet I moved warily, sensing the enmity in her, knowing that conflict lay ahead.

The day had turned cloudy, with the wind whipping in from the ocean, and gulls soaring the air currents, or gliding in to land on the beach as they sometimes did ahead of a storm.

We crossed loose sand and walked along that hard, wet band which rimmed the water's edge. Walked side by side as we had done so often as children. The gray waves washed in a foot or so away in a creaming curl that withdrew before it touched our feet.

I pulled the yellow kerchief from my pocket and held it out to her. "You left this on Palmetto Island."

She took it from me casually and knotted it around the neck of her white blouse. "How careless of me."

"We saw Hadley Rikers," I said. "He seems to have moved in quite comfortably."

"Yes. I helped him a bit in moving in." She was mocking me openly now. "After all, we do want something good to come of his book, don't we? And that's an ideal place to work."

"What does Giles think?" I asked.

"Oh—Giles! You sound like my mother. She wasn't pleased about Hadley's coming to the island either. We had something of a fight about it. But I shall do as I please. I always have."

So Aunt Amalie knew. So this was the cause of their quarrel.

"What you like may be damaging to Richard," I said. "Don't you consider that?"

For the first time she threw me a look of irritation. "I think you must allow me the right to know what's best for Richard. He's an intelligent, sensitive boy, and he can't be treated rudely."

"I know about what happened with Vinnie," I said. "And about the way he tried to get even with his father—with you taking his side. This doesn't sound—"

"Why should I scold him when he was behaving exactly the way I would in his place? You know, Lacey, you really aren't his mother any more. I think it's a mistake for you to come back here and stir yourself up. I should think you'd have better sense. Richard is in the best possible hands. Mine. I propose that he should stay there."

"Perhaps he shouldn't," I said. "If Giles divorces you, and it's shown that Richard is his son, but not yours, then the court may very well give him to Giles."

"There'll be no divorce," Elise said confidently. "Giles would never dare. I could make it all too unpleasant for him. And especially for you."

"I don't matter," I told her quickly. "Not when I weigh myself against what is happening to Richard."

She walked along in silence for a few moments and I thought I had brought her to a momentary halt. Perhaps I had even startled her. She must have been counting on the fact that Giles would protect me at all costs, and that I would expect to be protected.

"What do you want?" she asked at last.

"You could divorce Giles and let him take the boy. It would save the much more unpleasant way. And what difference would it make to you? You'd be able to marry Hadley Rikers, and—"

She whirled about on the sand beside me and that frightening wildness was upon her again. "I can have Hadley without marriage. And I'll never let Giles go—never!"

"Then he'll have to take steps to force your hand."

"So that you can have him, little cousin? Oh, no! He belongs to me and that's the way it's going to be, whether he likes it or not."

I saw something in her face then—saw the truth. She had no affection for him. She would not try to make him a good wife, but she meant to hold him somehow, no matter how hurtfully, and at whatever cost. She had never been able to give up anything once possessed. All the ruthlessness that was part of her nature reached out toward him with a relentless grasp. The only way Giles could win would be if he were as ruthless as she—and I was not sure he would ever reach that point. There was always Richard to be considered. That was where she could defeat Giles, because if it was to her interest she would not trouble to think of the boy.

"Well—you've had your talk," she said. "And it's been a waste of time, hasn't it? Except that now you know a little better how I feel. You lost Giles a long time ago, my foolish little cousin, and there's nothing left for you to do but accept the fact—as you should have done years earlier."

"I don't accept anything that is harmful to my son," I told her.

She gave me a quick look in which there was a certain disbelieving surprise. "I suppose that's true, isn't it? You really are trying to think of Richard first. Even though mistakenly. Richard is fine, and he loves me dearly. He loves me as he loves no one else—not even his father."

"A child's love changes easily," I said. "If his circumstances were changed, he would quickly—"

Elise broke in on my words. "I know a lovely thing I could do!" She reached out to touch me lightly on the arm, to draw her fingers along my skin from wrist to elbow in a way that made my flesh crawl. "I could tell Richard the truth about who he is. I could tell him that he's not my son, but yours. I could tell him the trick his father has played upon him, with your help."

"You'd never do that!" I cried. "You'd never risk—"

"Oh, yes, I would. Think about it, darling. Use that clever little mind of yours. Look at the ramifications. If you press me too closely, if you force my hand—that is exactly what I will do."

She turned from me and ran up the beach toward the wooden steps that led toward the house. I walked along the sand slowly in her wake, my mind coming fully alive to the dreadful possibilities of the thing she threatened.

It would be the cruelest of acts to Richard to tell him that the mother he adored was not his real mother at all. To tell him that his real mother was a woman he did not even like. And I knew that Elise would tell him in a way that would hurt him most, that would make him think the truth was too terrible to be borne. She was right about his being a sensitive, intelligent boy. To see his father in this new light, to give up every right to the woman he believed to be his mother, would be to set loose destructive forces in his nature that might never be mended. The damage would grow worse as he grew older. In today's world bastardy might not matter as much as it had in the past—except to the bastard. With the years, Richard's knowledge that he was illegitimate and not the true heir of the island through Elise, would become more and more painful to realize. He might well learn to hate his father, and he would easily hate me. That he might hate Elise as well was a risk she was clearly willing to take. Basically, to Elise, Richard was a tool to be used. As her son, as her heir to the island, she would hold him to her. But if there was a greater gain to be made by telling him the truth, she would snatch at that gain ruthlessly. It might even be that he would not hate her because of the way she would handle the telling. She might so win his sympathy that she would come out of this as the one person who could still hold his love. She could play the role of the misused to perfection, I was sure, and she might very well bind Richard to her.

If she chose that course, there was nothing I could do.

Nothing Giles could do. The damage to the boy would be deadly and disastrous.

I crossed the sand toward the rocky barrier and followed the stepping-stones. I felt shaken, desperate—and completely helpless.

For Sunday noon Elise had planned a picnic. There were not enough horses to go around, but those who had mounts were to follow the trail to the ruins of Bellevue, the old slave hospital which had served the island more than a hundred years ago. The others would go by car. Paul Courtney kept a horse at The Bitterns, so he and Floria went with Elise and Amalie. Giles rode, and so did Richard on his pony, but Charles no longer kept a horse, so he took his car, and I went with him.

I had no heart for the cameraderie of a picnic, but I knew I must go. I was the watcher now. I was the frightened observer on the sidelines. My nerves, my emotions, had been tightened to high tension, but there seemed nothing helpful I could do to lessen the strain of these new fears.

The riders were to go on ahead, and Charles and I watched them mount. Floria had dressed herself in the Western clothes she affected for riding—a fringed jacket and tight yellow riding pants that flared at the ankles. Paul, a quiet contrast in gray riding clothes, did not seem to mind Floria's giddy love for color.

Elise and Amalie both looked marvelous on horseback in their different ways. Aunt Amalie wore beige-colored jodhpurs, short boots and a proper riding coat of a darker beige than her trousers, while Elise was informal in jeans and a short-sleeved blouse and sweater. The two of them sat their horses well, straight in the saddle—a handsome pair. I watched Elise and ached with despair. She was so thoroughly in command. She always had been. Without conscience, or rules she needed to abide by, she could go her own dangerous way.

I think Giles had no heart for a picnic that day, any more than I had, but he was keeping up an appearance, and at least he and Richard rode together comfortably as father and son. So far Elise had said nothing to the boy, and I tried to tell myself that she never would. She had wanted to torment and frighten me, but it was unlikely that she would do anything so drastic unless she regarded the situation as desperate. Which meant that I must keep it from becoming desperate—at whatever cost to Giles and me.

Charles and I watched the riders on their way, and then got into his car. Giles's father had seemed somewhat subdued for the last day or two, and I knew that he was disappointed because his plan for recovering the pirate brooch had not worked. The metal box rested in its hiding place, and every day at the appointed time Richard went to look inside the big tomb. But so far the box remained empty and no move had been made to return the brooch.

The car followed a dirt road that wound off through the island toward Bellevue, and was a longer way around than the course the horses would take. We drove slowly because in places the road was overgrown with vegetation, and once or twice there were dead saplings that had fallen across our path and had to be dragged to the side of the road. Charles complained over the way much of the island was returning to the wilds—which was the way Elise liked it. I gathered there had been some controversy between them over what Elise called his "manicuring efforts." Nevertheless, we reached the old ruins well ahead of the others.

I had not seen this place since I was a child, and I got out of the car with a sense of nostalgia flooding through me. Long ago, on happier days, we had come here for picnics. I could remember a time when I had adored both Elise and Giles, and when it was a joy to go on any outing that included them. Now I dreaded the afternoon in Elise's company, and found it difficult to know how to behave in her presence. It was necessary to dissemble so that no one would suspect that a crisis had been reached between us, but that was hard to do when I despised her so thoroughly. She would know how I felt, and she would laugh secretly and enjoy all the more the power she held over me.

Charles said, "I'll stay in the car until the others arrive. No use making myself uncomfortable until I have to. But you can get out and explore, if you like, Lacey. I know this place must have memories for you."

I took him at his word and slipped out of the car. He had parked a little way off from the ruin, and I walked around its high, crumbling walls and was quickly out of sight.

Bellevue had a proud, humanitarian history. If anything in slavery could be called humanitarian. It had been a proper hospital for the Hampton Island people in its day, with a visiting doctor who made the rounds regularly. Three of its outer walls were partially standing. They no longer reached two stories high, as they had once done, but they marked the boundaries of the lower floor of the building. Within these three walls window shapes stood open to the weather, and in the center wall an immense fireplace gave evidence of a once warm hearth, its chimney pushing steeply into the sky. At the upper level a second fireplace was still visible.

The front wall that had housed the main door had crumbled to something no more than waist high, with the door space left open where it had originally been. Inside, tabby foundations marked where dividing walls had once stood, separating the structure into two large downstairs rooms. Once there had been two more such rooms upstairs, forming wards for the patients. I stepped through the broken doorway and found that the spell of the old place was upon me, just as it had been when I was a child.

Grass and vegetation had been reasonably trimmed here, and it was possible to walk about the two rooms and think of the days that had been. Dorothy Hampton, mistress of The Bitterns at that time, had been a kind and selfless woman. History had it that she had hated the slavery her husband enforced and that she had built the hospital to care for the people who worked for him in raising Sea Island cotton.

But for me, I remembered more recent days—the time when I was a little girl. I walked beside one wall and found a chunk of fallen tabby masonry that made a seat. Watching out for snakes, I sat down on its top, resting in the shade of a tall pine tree that had grown inside the ruins of the hospital. I tried to conjure up in my mind the memory of a former picnic here, when I had been happy with my secret love for Giles, asking nothing more than that he look at me kindly now and then, and accept with pleasure the small gifts I brought him.

But I could not think of these things for long because Elise's face interposed itself as I had seen her yesterday, walking beside me along the beach. A face alive with a recklessness of purpose which threatened everything that mattered to me in

life—threatened the destruction of those I loved. What was
I to do? What move was I to make?

Aunt Amalie was no good to me now. She had already
pitted herself against Elise when it came to Hadley Rikers,
and she had apparently lost. She would be frantic now, if she
knew of her daughter's threat against Richard, yet she would
be as helpless as Giles or I to control Elise in whatever she
chose to do.

I heard the riders when they arrived—heard the neighing
of the horses, and the stomping of hoofs, the voices calling to
Charles. I heard Richard's tones, high with pleased excitement,
but I did not go out to meet them. Somehow I had to steady
myself first, brace myself for each new encounter with Elise.

As I sat there, something flashed past the opening to the
ruined building—perhaps someone on horseback. I caught no
more than a streak of movement from the corner of my eye,
and I paid no attention, lost in my unhappy thoughts. I rested
my arms upon my knees and my head upon my arms—and
was thus mercilessly exposed to what happened next.

There was a sound over my head, but I looked upward too
late for my own safety. The falling block of tabby struck me
on the side of the head—and then I saw nothing at all.

How long I lay unconscious before Giles found me, I don't
know. It seemed that his voice came to me from a great distance and that I heard him calling my name before I felt his
arms raising me, pulling me back to consciousness.

The others were all around me. I lay on a stretch of grass
well away from the ruins, where he had carried me, and
someone was bathing my face with cool water. I opened my
eyes and looked up at Aunt Amalie. At once I tried to struggle
to a sitting position, but she pressed me back with a firm hand.

"Stay still, Lacey dear. Everything's all right. You've had
a bad blow, but you'll be fine now. Giles thinks a chunk of
loose masonry struck you."

I turned my head slightly and saw Giles looking down at
me in anxiety, saw Richard beside him, his expression unexpectedly sympathetic. My son had kindness in him, I
thought dreamily. He would not want to see anyone hurt. I
pushed Aunt Amalie's hands away more determinedly and
sat up.

"Something fell from the wall," I said. "It struck me on
the head." I looked from one to another as they watched me.

Floria stood near the broken doorway, holding her horse
by the bridle, with Paul beside her. Beyond them, Elise was

still mounted, watching with interest, but little sympathy. Charles had apparently decided to ride, and he was on Paul's horse. He too watched me from the saddle, more anxious than Elise.

"I know that wall is cracked along the top," Charles said. "I've meant to get a man down here to cement it in place, or else break away the loosened portions."

Giles stepped inside the ruins and picked up a good-sized piece of tabby—the one that must have struck me. If I had not looked up when I did, the impact might have been full on the back of my head, instead of striking me a glancing blow.

"I wonder why it came loose just then?" Giles said.

There was no answer to that and I looked fearfully at the broken walls. There was no wind. I had not touched the tabby. There would seem to have been nothing to jar the piece loose at that particular moment.

Charles got a bit creakily out of the saddle and came over to me. "Can you walk, Lacey? Can you get as far as the car? I'm going to drive you into Malvern to see Dr. Lane. We can't let a blow like that pass without an examination."

I tried to say that I was feeling better, that it wasn't necessary, but Giles added his own plea.

"Do go with him, Lacey. Father is right."

I still felt a little numb. I was confused and worried and doubtful. It was better to get away from the others and go with Charles. There was a swelling lump near my temple, and my head ached a little.

Charles helped me to the car and I got into the front seat. We were nearly silent on the drive across the island and causeway. Now and then he asked how I was feeling and I murmured that I was all right.

I was not all right. My thoughts were increasingly in a turmoil, swinging back and forth from one pole to the other. I was remembering that moment when something had flashed past the opening to the ruins—something I had not seen clearly. Had it been someone on horseback going around the outer wall? Someone who could easily have reached that loose chunk of tabby from the height of a saddle? But that was fanciful. This was surely a thought that grew out of my fears, and the knowledge of past pranks. If this had been intended, however, it was no prank. It would then be a serious attempt to injure me. Still—loosened stones could fall from a wall for no reason except their own disintegration, and this might have been only that. I mustn't alarm myself needlessly. Yet all the while my thoughts continued without restraint, following the pendulum swing.

In spite of the painful bruise on my head, I felt a sense of disbelief. It seemed impossible to think that someone hated me so much that my life had been threatened. Elise might torment me in other ways—but would she go this far? I didn't know. I only knew that I must find the courage and wisdom to solve the insoluble. This time I could not run away. I must stay and see it through, whatever happened. There must still be something I could do besides giving up entirely—giving up my love, and giving up Richard to Elise's merciless hands.

At the doctor's office the results were reassuring. An X ray was taken as a matter of precaution, and we were back at Sea Oaks long before the riders returned from their picnic.

The lump on my head subsided in the next few days, but my anxieties did not lessen. Everyone was kind to me. Perhaps a little too kind—and I was distrustful.

The days ran on toward the evening of the Camelot ball, and preparations were well under way. All the chandeliers were washed, and every crystal brought to its shining perfection. The smell of lemon polish pervaded everything, and extra help came over from the mainland to assist the regular servants in the readying of the house.

There had been no further untoward incidents of any kind. Elise treated me as she always had, except for a certain slyness and watchfulness that reminded me of our walk on the beach. For the most part, her attention was given to getting ready for the ball. The occasion had always been enormously important to her, and she gave it her full consideration.

I was not sleeping particularly well at this time, and one night a few days before the ball I was awakened by some sound from the corridor. My small clock told me it was nearly two in the morning. These days I found myself nervous about anything unexplained, and I slipped out of bed, threw a robe about me, and softly opened my door.

Richard stood at the head of the stairs, fully dressed in blue jeans, sweater and sneakers, one hand on the banister, as if he was about to descend. The sound of my door made him turn his head. He frowned in displeasure, raised a finger to his lips, warning me to be silent, and started down the stairs.

I followed him quietly to the hall below. Only the usual night light burned at the foot of the stairs. The other doors showed dark, and there was no one in the library. Now that we were out of hearing of the upper hall, he turned to me angrily.

"Go back to bed," he said. "Leave me alone."

I looked at him for a moment and something strange happened to me. It was as if I were a little girl again, remembering my own escapades on this very island. For the first time I could meet him on his own ground.

"Why should I go back to bed? It's a wonderful night, with the moon nearly full. Take me with you."

My words surprised him and he blinked at me uncertainly. "You'll tell," he said. "And then my father will beat me."

I laughed at him softly. "Your father doesn't beat you. You're making that up. He spanked you not long ago, but that was hardly a beating. And you had it coming to you."

He regarded me curiously. "You're different tonight."

"It's the moon," I said. "It makes me adventurous. Where are you going?"

"Up the lighthouse tower," he told me, and waited for inevitable adult protests and objections.

I smiled, still remembering. "I wonder if the key is still kept on the brass hook?"

I went past him to a place beside the front door and stretched an arm above my head. The same hook, supposedly set well out of the reach of young fingers, still held the key. It had always been easy to stand on a chair and get it down when there was urgent need, such as now. There had always been rules about the lighthouse tower. No one was supposed to climb it alone. Children must always be with adults. I lifted the key from its hook and handed it to him.

"Once when I was your age your father took me to the very top on a night like this. Will you take me with you now?"

"Because I'm not supposed to go alone?" he asked.

"Because I'd like to go with you," I said. "Because I remember the tower."

He waved a hand at me. "You can't go like that—in a robe and slippers."

"Of course not. It will only take me a moment to change. Wait for me."

He looked uneasy. "I don't think I want to. I don't think—"

"Wait anyway," I told him. "There's something I want to show you up there. Something your father once showed me. Don't make any noise. Don't waken the others."

I ran up the stairs, pausing halfway to look down at him. He stood near the door, still uneasy, uncertain. I put a conspirator's finger to my lips. Unexpectedly he smiled, looking like his father, and I turned from him with a pang to run up to my room.

Never had I dressed so quickly. This was touch and go, as I very well knew. For these few minutes he had accepted me. He was curious and puzzled, but at any moment he might reject the whole idea of my coming, and be off on his own.

When I'd put on slacks and a sweater, and drawn stout walking shoes on my feet, I ran down the stairs. He was nowhere to be seen. I opened the front door and found him sitting on the top steps of the portico. I crossed the bricks to join him.

"You've still got the key?" I asked.

He patted the right pocket of his jeans. "Sure. I've got it."

We went down the steps in silence, and headed toward the beach. The moon was nearly full, and very bright in a clear, windy sky. A breeze from the water made me glad for a sweater. On the path to the beach we went single file through low palmetto and came out upon the free, wide sand. Ahead of us, far along the beach, the lighthouse stood tall and white, gleaming in the moonlight.

"I know your way across the wall," Richard said. "I like it too. I hardly ever take the wooden steps."

He led and I followed. My son's feet found the stones my own knew so well, and in a few moments we were at the water's edge where we could follow the band of damp, hard-packed sand.

"Race you!" Richard cried.

We flew along the beach running together at first. But he was faster than I, and in a few moments he had outdistanced me. I came to a stop with my heart pounding, and waved to him in defeat. Kindly, he waited for me to catch up. The lighthouse was near now, the grassy bank on which it stood rising above the bare sands of the beach. The tall white tower blazed with reflected light under the moon, and its head, where once a lifesaving lamp had burned, reached into the dark, deeply blue sky. The smell of the ocean on the night wind was wonderful.

"You're not very good at running," Richard said.

"I did better when I was your age," I told him. "But I can't keep up with you now."

He was pleased by the small victory and his uneasiness with me was fading. For once, the anxieties that beset me so self-consciously when I was with him were gone. Tonight he and I were equals.

We climbed the grassy sandbank to the foot of the lighthouse, and went up three cement steps. Richard took the key from his pocket. It was an old key, and quite large. He handled it with assurance and it went easily into the lock. The door creaked open upon utter blackness.

"Are you afraid of the dark?" he said.

"I think I am—a little," I admitted. "The time I went up with your father he turned on the lights."

"Did they see them from the house and come running out to scold you?" he wanted to know.

I shook my head. "No one woke up at all that night."

"Sometimes they wake up," he said. "But they're never in time to catch me before I get to the top. My mother doesn't care, but Grandmother Amalie and my father worry about me. Aunt Floria thinks it's okay. She understands about adventures. She did the same thing when she was young, she says."

"Elise"—I could not say "your mother" to him—"never liked the lighthouse. She only climbed the stairs once that I remember, and she got dizzy at the top."

"I know," he said tolerantly. "She told me about that."

We went through the yawning darkness of the door. Richard fumbled for the switchboard and found a lever. Dim lights came on all the way up. I could stand in the center of the stone floor and look all that dizzy way to the crown of the tower.

"If they see the lights tonight," Richard said, "it won't matter. Because you're along. I meant to come by myself—" There was doubt in his voice again and he hesitated.

"Thank you for bringing me with you," I said quickly. "I don't think I'd ever have the nerve to come alone."

He gave me a fleeting smile that was somehow touching, and started ahead of me up the circling iron steps. I took hold of the metal railing and climbed after him, around and around on the wedged steps, until I was out of breath and had to stop for a moment. He waited for me three steps ahead.

"You're not a very good climber either," he told me. "My father can go all the way up without stopping to rest, and so can I."

I smiled at him apologetically. "You're in practice. I'm sorry to hold you back."

"That's all right. The moon will be out for a long while yet, and there's lots of time. Isn't it peculiar how there's lots of time in the middle of the night, when somehow there's no time at all during the day?"

"Do you often come outside and wander around at night?" I asked.

He shrugged. "When I feel like it. Mostly I sleep too hard, and I forget to get up."

Which was just as well, I presumed from my adult point of view. We climbed again, up to the place where the great light was housed—a light that no longer served. Here a door opened upon the narrow catwalk that ran about the tower. Richard stepped through it ahead of me.

"Are you afraid?" he asked again.

I had always been a little uneasy in this high place, but I had never admitted the fact to Giles, and I would not admit it to his son.

"Of course not," I said, and stepped onto the circling wooden walk, holding the railing with both hands.

The night made a marvelous radiance around us. Far below, the island seemed composed of great banks of soft, dark trees that moved tremulously beneath the windy sky. Here and there the white band of a winding road was visible, and I knew one of those roads led to the ruins of Bellevue, where I had been struck by a chunk of tabby only a few days before. My head no longer hurt, and the lump was gone, with only a faint bruise remaining to show what had happened. But standing there under the moonlit sky, with the shadowy island spreading away at my feet—and a dark patch of shadow off there somewhere that was Bellevue—it no longer seemed unbelievable that I had been struck down by intent. I knew the conviction was in me to stay. For all her bravado, Elise was afraid of me now. And Elise, afraid, was dangerous.

We moved on around the circling walk to where we could see the stretch of beach, no longer dull gray, but glistening like metal, with the moon forming a wide path upon the ocean. Behind the beach the white columns of Sea Oaks could be glimpsed among its live oaks, and still farther away the sloping silver roof of The Bitterns. No lights burned anywhere. The houses slept, and the night was still.

"What were you going to show me?" Richard asked.

There was something his father had made me see that long-ago night when we had climbed this tower together.

"Look out at the island," I said. "There's a place on the tower from which you can see nearly all of it at once, with the lights of Malvern in the distance over the causeway. Here —this is the spot. At night it looks as if the island were floating on the ocean and the river. It has almost the shape of a ship at sea, with the prow pointing into the Atlantic. The lighthouse is the bridge of the ship, and any minute now we may take off across the ocean."

My son did not disappoint me. He was gifted with imagination and he rested his arms along the rail and savored the picture I had given him. Where once I had stood beside his father in this place, with all my senses open to the beauty of the scene, now I stood with our son and felt for the moment tranquillity between us.

"It really is like that," Richard said softly, as if he did not want to break the spell of the night.

I dared to reach out and touch his hand. "Moon magic," I said.

He did not pull away, but looked up at me with something like affection. "I'm glad my father showed you this when you were my age, Cousin Lacey. So you could show it to me now. I wonder why he never did?"

"Sometimes we lose the magic when we grow up. Sometimes we forget."

"I never will," he said. "Someday when all the island belongs to me, I'll bring my son up here in the middle of the night, and I'll show him the ship sailing out to sea in the moonlight. Maybe by that time I'll have taken the name of Hampton, the way my mother wants me to do. So my son will be a Hampton too, and it will be our ship, with me the captain."

I drew my hand from his and shivered in the wind that whipped about the lighthouse, all tranquillity gone. He caught me at once.

"You're cold," he said. "Ladies always get cold when everything's most interesting."

"I'm not all that cold," I denied valiantly. "I'm doing fine."

But I was not. The ship was gone, and the moon magic with it. Richard Severn was no Hampton, and he would suffer if he knew the truth as Elise would tell it to him.

He was still studying the outline of the island. "It's the same shape as that piece of driftwood that used to sit on my father's desk," he mused soberly.

"I know," I agreed. "I found that bit of wood on the beach a long time ago when I was a little girl. I gave it to your father and he kept it all those years."

The boy beside me was silent.

"The trouble with smashing something is that it can never be put back together again," I said. "Once when I was small I broke a cup that belonged to my mother, because I was angry with her. She was fond of it, and afterwards I suffered because I couldn't bring it back to her. I got over being angry, but I never got over having smashed the cup."

"It *is* like that." Richard looked up at me in wonder, as if it surprised him to realize that someone else had experienced anger and reprisal and pain as he had done.

He moved on around the tower, and I followed him. When we paused again to look up at the moon sailing its dark blue ocean of sky, he asked me a question, almost wistfully.

"Why doesn't my mother like you?"

I was unprepared and I lost him then because I answered evasively.

"I don't know," I said, and was sharply aware of the false note in my voice, aware that his sensitive ears had heard and responded to it.

He turned his face away from the moonlight, and dark shadow lay across it. "My mother would hate it if she knew I was up here with you."

"Elise is my cousin," I said. "We shouldn't hate each other."

"But you do," he accused. "Perhaps it's because you hated her first that she has to hate you back?"

"Let's not talk about it," I pleaded. "We were happy together up here, Richard. We were friends. Let it stay that way."

Even his voice had a dark note in it as he reacted to the sense of a change in me—a change I could not control. "It can't stay that way. I don't know what got into me. I don't know why I let you come up here with me. I must have been crazy. You're not really my friend. You're an enemy." His guilt no longer had to do with injury to his father, but with what he regarded as betrayal of Elise.

I tried to answer him reasonably. "Even if Elise and I have our differences, that doesn't mean that you and I can't be friends. I've loved you from the time you were a baby, and I don't want to give up loving you now."

"Well, I don't love you," he said. "I don't want to be with you at all. I'm going down from the tower. You've spoiled everything for me tonight."

There was nothing I could say to him with this change upon him—and upon me. He had gone thoroughly back to

Elise and out of my reach, even as I became a concerned and worrying mother. I stepped ahead of him through the tower door and started down the wedged steps circling round and round the empty center space beyond the rail. Richard came after me and I was aware of a certain stealthiness in the way he moved, of a softness in his tread as his sneakers found one iron step after the other behind me.

I took the steps as fast as I could, moving with my back stiffly erect, not looking around at him. I did not like that feeling of stealthiness on his part, or the fact that he believed himself Elise's son, with his first loyalty to her.

When we were halfway down I felt a sudden slight pressure in the small of my back and knew that he pressed a hand against me. It was all I could do not to jerk away from his touch and put my back against the rail. But I did not, though my fingers gripped the railing more tightly than ever. After a moment he laughed, and the sound echoed eerily through the tower, though the touch at my back was gone.

"I could have pushed you," he said. "I could have pushed you and you might have rolled all the way down the steps. Or even gone under the rail and fallen clear to the bottom."

Only then did I move closer to the wall and turn to look up at him. His small face was very white in the dim lighting.

"But you didn't push me," I said.

"No, I didn't—I didn't!" he cried, and ran past me down the steep stairway.

I followed more slowly, watching his slight figure circle below me and disappear at the foot of the stairs. When I reached the bottom the lower room was empty. I found the proper lever and plunged the lighthouse into darkness. Then I opened the door and stepped into shadowy moonlight.

I would have expected Richard to run away home, leaving me to make my way back alone. But once more he had waited for me. He did not speak as I came out of the tower. When he saw me, he started down the bank ahead, and hurried along the beach. Not once as I hastened after him did he look back to see if I was coming. I did not try to speak to him, or call his name. I simply hurried, as he did, across the moonlit sands toward Sea Oaks.

We saw at once that lights were on in the house, upstairs and down. Giles, wearing slacks and a jacket, came out the door just as we started up the steps to the portico.

Richard faced his father defiantly. "I had somebody with me. I didn't go alone."

Giles stepped aside and let us go past him into the house.
Beyond in the lighted hallway, Aunt Amalie stood with
Charles, both in night clothes and robes, while halfway up the
stairs behind them, Elise sat on a step, wrapped in a filmy
pink gown. She yawned deliberately as we came through the
door.

"You gave us a fright," Aunt Amalie said. "We saw the
lights and thought Richard had gone up the tower alone, as
he's not supposed to do."

Charles supported her words. "You might have tapped on
our door, Lacey, and let us know about your adventure."

"I'm sorry," I said. "I didn't think of doing that." Nor
would I have. I had been thinking only of my son.

Richard ran past us up the stairs to Elise. He flung himself
into her arms and she held him sleepily.

"I didn't mean for Cousin Lacey to go with me!" he cried.
"She wanted to come along, and there wasn't any way to
stop her. I didn't want her with me!"

"That's all right, dear," Elise said, looking at me slyly over
his head. "I know you're my boy."

He clung to her until his father spoke from the foot of the
stairs. "Let's all get back to bed."

Charles agreed. "It's after three by this time."

We started up the stairs. Elise released Richard, and rose
from her step. Like the others, I went to my room, but when
I was inside I stood with my ear to the door listening. When
all was quiet I waited ten minutes longer, and then opened
the door just a crack.

Giles was coming out of Richard's room, and I waited until
he had gone down the hall to his own room. The upper hall
was a shadowy place, but Giles had left Richard's door open,
and a band of moonlight came through the crack. I crossed
the hall quietly and looked in. If the boy had been tucked in
by his father, he was no longer there. In his pajamas he stood
before a window, staring wistfully out in the direction of the
lighthouse tower.

"I came to say good night," I whispered. "I came to thank
you for taking me with you up the tower."

He turned from the window abruptly, and then switched on
a light so he could see me. His face worked unhappily, and
for one concerned moment I was afraid he might burst into
tears. But he managed to control his emotion.

"Good night," he said and went to fling himself into bed.
I stepped into the room and turned off the light.

He spoke in a muffled tone from under the bedclothes. "I wouldn't have pushed you," he said.

I went to the bed and touched the sheet near his cheek. "I know that. I know that very well."

No sound came from beneath the covers and I went quietly out of the room.

The next two days passed in a rush of preparation for the ball. There was a quickening of tempo that seemed to catch Elise and Aunt Amalie into it. Richard was keyed up with anticipation, and even Charles, being so much a part of the island, seemed to enjoy the flurry. Only Giles and I were set apart. Apart from participating in the preparations, and apart from each other. At least Giles had his work and could get away from the house.

On the day before the ball a storm blew out of the north and rain beat down upon the island. During the morning I left Elise and Amalie to their busy preparations, put on my rain things, and went outside. I'd had enough of Sea Oaks for the time being. I considered asking Richard to come with me, then thought better of it. He had been uneasily distant toward me since the night we had climbed the lighthouse tower. It was as though he wanted to please Elise by snubbing me, yet could not be altogether set against me as he had been before our middle-of-the-night adventure. It seemed best not to disturb his tenuous uncertainty.

Once away from the house, I struck out across the burying ground toward The Bitterns, walking fast through a light drizzle. I had nearly reached the house when the rain came down hard again, and I ran for the white gate in the hedge.

I could hear the music before I ran up the steps. Inside, Floria was playing the piano. The sound brought back old memories. Elise used to say that Floria played up our island storms—that when she played her hurricane music, the wind always blew. But I think it was the other way around. When it

150

stormed, Floria liked to pit her music against the tumult outdoors. There was something about bad weather that brought
out in her a desire to play music that matched any storm in
its intensity. What she was playing now sounded like Mous-
sorgsky, and it suited the day.

The front door stood open. I did not attempt to ring above
the sounds, outside and in, but flung off my wet things and
left them in the hall. Then I went into Aunt Amalie's Victorian parlor.

The piano was near the front windows, and Floria sat at
the keyboard facing me. Somehow there was a look of storm
on her face as well, as her fingers flew across the keys. She
looked up and saw me, but she gave no sign, continuing to
play, so wrapped in her music that she could not surface to
greet me. Her red hair was loose upon her shoulders and she
wore her favorite tapestry pants with a deeply yellow blouse.

I went to the velvet sofa and sat down, not caring whether
she paid any attention to me or not. Her music suited my
mood too, and I closed my eyes and listened to its violence.
Outside there was a rumble of thunder above the rumble of
bass notes, and the sound satisfied some need in me, released
something of my own suppressed desire for storm and fury
that would rip away all the evasiveness of deceit.

When the great chords finally came to an end and sound
died away, a quivering silence hung in the room, with only
the slash of wind and rain against the panes to contrast with
the stillness inside. Floria put the piano lid down with a
strangely contrasting gentleness, and looked at me across
the room.

"I feel that way, too," I said. "It was good to hear."

"It's better to play it out than to bottle it up," she said. And
then, with her usual abrupt change of topics: "How much
longer are you going to stay here and torment yourself?"

"Why should you want me gone?" I countered.

She swiveled about on the piano stool. "No one likes to
look at what's happening to you. You're being punished on
every hand, and unless you're masochistic, I can't see what
good it's doing you."

"I came closer to making friends with Richard the other
night," I said. "When we climbed the tower together he accepted me for a little while."

"Why should you care so much about Richard?"

"He's Giles's son."

"And if there's a divorce he'll be your responsibility—is that it?"

"I suppose so."

"But there won't be a divorce. Haven't you convinced yourself of that as yet? Haven't you seen how cleverly Elise will oppose that at every turn? Oh, Lacey, give up and go away."

"I can't," I said. "It isn't finished. Your mother may help me yet."

"Against Elise? Never. You're tearing Mother up too, and I wish you wouldn't. She has her Charles now—even though to my mind he's no great catch—and she was beginning to be happy before you came. Let her be. She can't persuade Elise to divorce Giles."

"No one can do that!" said a laughing voice from the doorway, and I swung about in dismay to see Elise standing there. We had not heard her come up the steps because of the rain sounds, but she had come through the doorway in time to hear Floria's words.

She wore a dripping rain cape, bulging over something she carried beneath it, and Floria flew to unsnap the cape at her neck and carry it to the hall to hang it up.

"You needn't slop all over the parlor," Floria said.

Elise paid no attention. "I've brought your Merlin costume —all but the hat. You have that over here, haven't you? Let me see you try it all on. Here's the beard I bought for you in Malvern. I'm tired of that substitute Spanish moss you always wear." Elise ran on as though the snatches of conversation she had overheard did not matter to her at all.

Floria came back into the room and picked up the black cape with its appliqué decorations of white crescents and stars. "Why should I try it on? It's the same old thing. You wanted to come over and see what Lacey was up to, didn't you?"

"As if it matters what Lacey is up to," Elise said. "Here— what I really want is to see you in the beard. Put on the hat first."

Grumbling, Floria flung the cape about her shoulders and hooked it at the throat. From a chair in the corner of the room she picked up a tall black cone of a hat, pasted with more crescents and stars, and put it on. Then she took the gray strands Elise held out and stepped before a mirror, pressing the adhesive onto her chin. When she turned around I saw Merlin again, as I had not since childhood. Floria sucked in her cheeks mockingly, to make them look hollow, just as she'd done as a girl, and her eyes seemed dark and sunken under the narrow black brim of the hat. The gray beard gave her the look of an elderly wizard, and only her unruly red hair spoiled the picture.

"You'll have to stuff your hair under the hat," Elise said. "Merlin may have worn his hair long, but yours is the wrong color. I'll count on you to be properly spooky for our guests."

Floria unhooked the cape, snatched off the beard and hat, and flung them aside on top of the piano. "That's a fanciful version of Merlin, anyway. We never grow up on Hampton Island, do we? You'd think we'd have more serious matters to attend to this year than one more Camelot ball."

"But I love our balls!" Elise cried. "And everyone looks forward to them. I'm glad we're getting this storm out of the way ahead of time. The radio promises good weather tomorrow. Well, I won't keep you two from your fascinating talk about me and Giles."

She swung toward the hallway, and then paused for a look over her shoulder at me. "Do you remember our walk on the beach? Don't forget what I said to you, Lacey. Don't forget what I promised."

She picked up her wet cape and threw it about her. In a moment she had run down the steps and was gone into the rain. "What was that all about?" Floria said.

I shook my head. "I can't tell you. I don't want to tell you."

"Could it have something to do with Richard's being your son and not Elise's?" Floria said.

I could only stare at her, shocked.

She laughed disagreeably. "You needn't look so surprised. You don't think a secret like that could be kept forever, do you?"

Who had told her? I could not imagine Elise doing so, and certainly Aunt Amalie was far too discreet to trust such a secret with her elder daughter. But there was no one else who knew. Certainly not Giles.

Floria grinned at me and tossed her red hair. "You've forgotten Vinnie. She's been carrying this on her conscience for years. She knew what I never knew—that Elise couldn't have a child. So Vinnie got the truth out of my darling sister back in the beginning. Now Vinnie's worry about Richard has got the best of her and she had to talk to someone. She knew it couldn't be Elise, and she wouldn't bring it up with Mother. So the other day she unburdened herself to me. What a good job you've done of fooling everyone, Lacey—including Giles. And what a mess you'll weave if you try to do anything about

it at this late date. That's why I say you'd better go away
and not stir up any more trouble. Richard can't mean anything to you now."

"What's being done to him means a great deal to me," I
said.

Floria stood beside the piano, plucking at a pasted crescent
on her Merlin hat. There was little sympathy or sentiment in
her for me, but that was Floria's way. She had grown up a
little hard, and not at all given to weeping for others.

"Giles will explode in all directions when he finds out,"
she said.

"It may be that he will never find out," I told her miserably.

She gave me a long, cool stare. "Seemingly, it's not to Elise's
advantage to tell him. But you can never tell about Elise.
There are times when she would rather damage someone else
than save herself."

"I know that," I said, thinking of our walk on the beach.
In any event I did not want to stay here and talk this over
with Floria. I needed to talk to someone who could help me,
but Floria was not that person. I needed someone who could
be more objective, and who felt a little kindness toward me.
Aunt Amalie's affection for me was diluted by her fondness
for Elise—in many ways she was as confused as I as to what
could be done in the present situation.

"I'm going back to Sea Oaks," I said, and went into the
hall.

Floria came with me, her look somber and disapproving.
"Stay for the ball, and then leave," she warned me. "It's the
only way."

"While I'm still alive?" I said mockingly. "Before someone
succeeds in what they tried to do at Bellevue?"

There was a long moment of silence, and then Floria spoke
quietly. "Don't underestimate my sister."

I caught her up at once. "So you guessed what happened
there?"

She regarded me with an odd blankness in her look. "A
chunk of tabby fell off a wall and knocked you out."

There was no use expecting real corroboration from her.
I got into my rain things. Outside, the downpour had lessened.

"Floria," I pleaded, "don't talk about what Vinnie told you.
Don't let it go on from you to anyone else."

"I'm not likely to." Her eyes were suddenly bright with
venom. "What a scandal it would make if it all came out! Not
that I'd care a great deal. But it will be safer if you just go

away. Except for Mother, not one of us wants you here. Not even Giles. You must be nothing but an embarrassment to him."

"Just so you don't talk," I said, and went out the door.

The trees were dripping heavily. I pulled my rain bonnet over my head and walked along quickly.

At Sea Oaks Elise and Aunt Amalie were directing the rearrangement of furniture in the double parlor. I left them to it and went across the hall to the library. Charles was there, and I dropped into a chair near his. He smiled at me and laid his book face down on his knees.

"Don't stop reading," I said. "I just want to be somewhere quiet." Floria's music had washed the tempest out of me. I felt disturbed and uneasy, but no longer stormy.

Charles said nothing, though he did not pick up his book again. As I sat there, I began to think about him. Was he the person I might confide in? He always seemed a little removed from what was happening around him. Might I count on his objectivity? Could he see what those of us who were too close to the center of the storm could not see? Or would any perception on Charles's part be too ineffectual, too uninvolved to help me? His mother had been living when I used to visit the island, and I remembered her as a rather dynamic and commanding figure, far less gentle than her son. She had managed him utterly, though she had never managed Giles's grandfather. In turn, Charles's wife, Marian, had taken his mother's place, and perhaps this was the sort of woman he needed. Aunt Amalie was like neither his mother nor his first wife, but she was not helplessly yielding either. Completely feminine, and very much in love with Charles, she would never rule him with a high hand. Yet he would listen to her counsel, I thought, and depend on her in many ways. My mother would have made him a very different sort of wife. She would have been the dependent one, and I wondered if that would have suited Charles, or if it might have changed him.

When our silence grew too long, he spoke to me. "I wish we could see you happier, Lacey. I wish events had turned out differently for you. And for Giles."

There was nothing I could say without blurting out the truth.

"I never wanted to see him married to Elise," Charles went on. "But then—I would not have wanted to see him married to you, either."

I gave him a quick look, startled and uncertain of what he meant.

He smiled ruefully. "Oh, that's all in the past, my dear. There have been times when I felt rather bitter about you, though I hope I always concealed the fact."

"Bitter? About me?"

"Why not?" He closed his book and laid it aside. "Your mother should have stayed here and married me. You should have been my daughter—not the child of another man."

I could only listen in surprised silence.

"I'll admit now that there was a good deal of jealousy and resentment in me toward you for a long while. Of course none of this was your fault, and I could not let such instinctive feelings rule me. I went out of my way to make friends with you, as I remember. I grew used to swallowing my hurt."

"You had Marian," I said.

He smiled at me benignly. "Yes, and now I have Amalie. I've been a fortunate man. But I think it can be known just between the two of us that in spite of the fact that I came to resent her mightily, I never got over loving your mother. Perhaps even now I'm not wholly recovered from old resentments and old loves. Perhaps one never recovers."

No, I thought, I could tell him nothing. Charles was not so uninvolved as I had believed. All these years he had watched me growing up, watched me falling in love with his son, and behind that quiet, benign manner, these disquieting thoughts were going on. I wondered suddenly if Aunt Amalie knew him as well as she thought she did, and I hoped he would not hurt her.

He seemed unaware that his words had disturbed me. "Memories of your mother have been with me a great deal lately," he went on. "That's because your resemblance to her when she was young is so great. She was a pretty thing, with so much life throbbing in her that it was exhilarating to be near her. You're quieter, and your unhappiness subdues you, but there is the same passionate love for life in you as well. I can sense it sometimes when you don't even know that it's showing. You want so much that it's a little frightening to watch you at times. One wonders where the breaking point is and what will happen when you reach it."

"Do you think, as Floria does, that I should go away? Give up?"

"You must eventually, mustn't you?"

I got up restlessly. There was no point in talking to him any longer. He was right about one thing. I wanted too much. I wanted greedily what I could not have. If I was honest with myself, what I was seeking now was some imaginary counselor who would show me the way to find what I wanted. I did not want someone who would tell me to go away. I no longer trusted Charles. What he had said about holding my mother's actions against me left me shaken.

"Yes," I said, "I must eventually leave. But I'm not ready to make that move yet."

"Do you ever feel frightened?" he asked surprisingly.

"Frightened? Of whom?" I was wary now. I dared not admit how frightened I had been lately.

He looked as though he had said too much, and knew it. Yet now he had to say a little more. "Elise can be ruthless. Unscrupulous. Being sure that Giles cares about you, she will stop at very little to break up whatever exists between you."

I knew all this. It was all embodied in Elise's plan concerning Richard.

Charles left his chair and crossed the room to where I stood beside a window. He took my two hands into his own and held them gently.

"I am concerned for you," he said.

He was also concerned for his son, and he had said he would not like to see me marry Giles.

I took my hands as gently away. "Thank you," I said. I left the library and hurried upstairs to my room.

I no longer felt that I must have a counselor who would urge me along some road I already wanted to take. Talking to Charles had at least made me face my own feelings more directly. It was true that I must talk to someone about what Elise threatened to do, but there was only one person to whom I could turn. Only one person whom I could wholly trust. Yet the moment had not yet come when I could go to Giles and tell him the truth.

The hours that carried us toward the time of the ball passed swiftly. The following evening was fair and a full moon lighted the sky. A breeze rustled gently through the palm trees, but the rain was over and there was no great wind blowing across the island tonight. I stood at my window, dressed to go downstairs, and looked out at the night.

In one sense I would be sorry to see the ball over. Preparations for it had so occupied Elise that she had forgotten about me, ignored me. Once the affair was over, she could give me her full attention again. Yet at the same time an uneasiness pervaded me. The last two or three times I had come upon Elise about the house, she had seemed possessed by that high excitement which seemed to border on some sort of explosion. As if a pressure were building up inside her—something that would be forced to vent itself in action that was likely to be destructive. I was aware that the others had taken to watching her warily, and I knew that Aunt Amalie had tried several times to calm her, to bring down the building pressure. Floria glowered at her sister watchfully, Paul kept out of her way, and Giles was guarded when he spoke to her. Charles seemed to watch her from a distance that kept him unengaged, but aware, and only Richard put himself constantly in her path, demanding attention, as though her very excitement drew him like a magnet. She treated him with little patience, her focus elsewhere.

By this time of the evening, everyone but me was downstairs, and the guests had begun to arrive, driving across the causeway, over from the mainland. It was after nine o'clock, and I could hear the sound of music.

I left the window and went to stand briefly before the long mirror on my closet door. Vinnie had worked skillfully to fit Elise's white gown to my figure, and now it flattered me subtly, contrasting with my dark hair. The neckline was square, the sleeves long and tight, ending in points at my wrists. I wore a jeweled girdle about my waist and a jeweled circlet in my hair. When I moved, the long lines of the gown flowed about me gracefully.

But the woman who looked at me out of the mirror seemed a stranger, and I took no great satisfaction in her appearance. The evening ahead of me seemed an ordeal to be endured, to be somehow lived through and submitted to. There would be many people at Sea Oaks tonight whom I had known in the past, but there would also be strangers. I could not help but be aware of how they would look at me, wondering about Elise, wondering about Giles. I had no desire to face the eyes of Elise's guests, or meet their unspoken questions, but the minutes were speeding by and I must go down.

When I stepped into the upper hall, the sound of the band grew louder, and I knew that the dancing had begun. As was the custom, King Arthur would have led Queen Guinevere out upon the floor to open the ball, and other couples would have followed. I could imagine Giles's reluctance to dance with Elise, and I could imagine how boldly and triumphantly she would circle the floor in his arms, perhaps taunting him under her breath, daring him to object to whatever unpleasant surprises she might have planned for this occasion.

I found Richard in his pajamas sitting at the head of the stairs, and paused beside him to watch the colorful, patterned motion of the throng below. Tonight the great hall had the look of another time. It had been hung with banners of scarlet and gold, while crossed lances stood on either side of the front door, the small triangular pennants fastened to their tips ready to flutter on the breeze as mounted knights carried them upright toward the place of the lists.

I looked down at Richard and saw that a book lay open upon his knees. It was the copy of *Idylls of the King* that I had sent him long ago.

At the sound of my step, he glanced up at me. "You look beautiful, Cousin Lacey," he said without guile.

If my son thought I was beautiful, the dress was worthwhile. I turned gravely before him, lifting my arms so that he could admire the sleeves.

"I remember that dress when Mother wore it a few years ago," he said. "It looks different on you, but very nice."

I was glad that it looked different on me. I went down one step and sat beside him, my long white skirt spread across the carpeted runners. From between the balusters we could look down upon the heads of the glittering crowd below. The music had paused, and a rush of sound came up to us—the chatter of voices, the laughter of women, the more resonant tones of the men. A blending of perfumes rose on the air, and the eye was caught by the bright movement of color and rich cloth. The ball was as lavish, as splendid, as always.

Richard tapped the book on his knees knowingly. "The real King Arthur—if there ever was a real King Arthur—lived back in 500 A.D. People wouldn't have dressed like that then. But Mother says medieval costumes are more fun, and I guess everyone comes pretty much as he likes. Look—there's King Arthur!"

There was a ring of pride in his voice, and I looked beneath the banister to see Giles in the golden-brown robes of the king, with a scarlet cape about his shoulders. He wore the costume with the graceful dignity that befitted a king, and on his head was the jeweled crown of his rank. He stood out nobly in the crowd, as though royalty came naturally to him.

"He looks like a king," said Richard softly.

I nodded. "He's been practicing that role ever since we were children. He plays it well."

"On Hampton Island he *is* king," Richard assured me, dismissing the thought that any play-acting was involved. "Just as my mother is queen. Have you seen her, Cousin Lacey? She's the most beautiful of all of them down there. Look—do you see her coming toward us?"

My eyes found her quickly. She wore a round-cut bodice that met the blue velvet band at the high waist, and then flowed into a parti-colored skirt. Half of her gown was azure blue, with gold fleurs-de-lis appliquéd upon it, the other half gold, with azure decorations. As Guinevere, she wore the feminine version of Arthur's crown, and her page-boy hair had been braided into two false golden plaits that fell over her shoulders.

She had seen us, and she was indeed coming toward us. But before she reached the foot of the stairs, Giles too looked up and saw me sitting beside his son in the upper hall. He had not noticed Elise, and he ran up the stairs ahead of her. I saw her hesitate below, her hand on the newel post.

Giles smiled at me and there was warm admiration in his eyes. "You look like the Lily Maid tonight," he said. "The dancing is going to start again soon. Will you give me the next dance, Elaine?"

I shook my head at him unhappily—not because Elise stood at the foot of the stairs listening, but because I did not want to go into his arms and be aware of the eyes watching us, the whispers starting.

"I'd rather not dance," I said. "Please don't ask me."

"If King Arthur commands you, you have to dance," Richard said.

"My son is right." Giles held out his hand to me. "Come on, Lacey."

I looked past Giles and saw the challenge in Elise's eyes as they met mine, saw the tightening of her hand on the banister. Suddenly my mood changed. I felt that this moment at least could be mine, and I would not let Elise stop me from dancing with Giles. Charles was right—I wanted so much, and I had so little. I gave Giles my hand and let him pull me to my feet.

At once Elise came up the stairs. She gave us hardly a look, but bent toward Richard, her eyes dancing with a wicked light.

"I have a secret to tell you tomorrow," she said. "Tomorrow afternoon, when we are all rested up from the ball, you and

I will go off together and I will tell you something that will surprise you very much."

Richard smiled at her lovingly. "You won't forget? You promise?" He knew her changeability so well.

"I promise," Elise said, and ran past him and along the hall toward her room.

The band had been placed at the far end of the wide downstairs hallway that opened from the front door. As it began to play the charming, sentimental tunes of two or three decades ago, brightly dressed lords and ladies, knights and maidens, separated into couples.

Giles would have led me downstairs at once, but I hesitated beside Richard. What could I say to counteract his mother's words? What could I do to stop them from being spoken? My defiance had died and I was truly frightened now. A dance with Giles was not worth this revengeful action on Elise's part. Yet my hand lay in his and there was no turning back. What Elise planned could not be stopped by my not dancing. I gave Richard a wavering smile and went downstairs with his father.

We were caught up quickly by the music, and we danced well together. Strange that we had never danced with each other before. I moved smoothly in his arms and held my head high. Around us I was aware of the looks and the smiles— ostensibly greetings to Giles, greetings to me—but with the chance of hidden meaning beneath every look, as I knew very well. I could take no pleasure in my nearness to Giles, though I was intolerably conscious of his touch, of the closeness of his body to mine.

Before the dance was half over, I saw that Elise had come downstairs again. She moved around the outskirts of the hall, shaking her head prettily at men who asked her to dance, moving as though she looked for someone. Hadley Rikers? I wondered. Had she invited him over from Palmetto Island? It would seem likely enough.

We were near the library door and the room looked empty. I had seen Charles earlier, moving about with Amalie on his arm, and apparently no one else had gone into the library. Giles and I were unobserved for the moment.

"Come in here with me," I whispered. "I must talk to you."

We slipped from among the dancers and stepped into the stillness of books and the quiet of inviting reading lamps. Across the room a breeze stirred the long draperies at open French doors, but we were alone in the shadowy library.

Giles's look was concerned. "What is it, Lacey? Something has frightened you? What has Elise done now?"

"It's what she means to do," I said. "I must talk to you, Giles."

From beyond the door came the lilting music of an old song from a Fred Astaire picture. Dancers circled past, and once the light of a chandelier flung a long shadow into the room—the shadow of someone who had stopped for a moment to look into the library. Before I could turn, the shadow was gone, but this was no place for a talk of such gravity as I must have with Giles.

"Not here," I said, as he would have motioned me toward a chair. "Let's part when we go out of this room, and meet again in an hour down on the beach. It will be empty tonight, and I can talk to you there. This can't wait until tomorrow, Giles—it must be tonight."

He responded to the urgency in me. "Of course, Lacey. But don't look so terrified, darling. Whatever it is, you can count on me."

Could I? I wondered. Could I, when he knew the truth?

Outside one of the French doors there was the sound of a board creaking—the sound of a footfall, as though someone moved away. Giles heard it too. In a moment he was across the room and through the door, and I was beside him. The night was still except for the sound of music and voices drifting through open windows. Moonlight filtered through the great, raised arms of the live oaks, but no one moved beneath them. The side stretch of veranda ran toward the columns at the front of the house, empty and shadow-embossed in the moonlight. A little way along, the door of the trophy room stood open upon darkness within. If there had been anyone on the veranda, it would have been possible to step quickly through the empty room and rejoin the throng of dancers in the downstairs hall.

"Never mind," I said. "On the beach we can see for miles if anyone is approaching."

"I'll meet you in an hour," Giles said. He walked along the veranda toward the front of the house, and I slipped back through the library and out among the dancers.

Now I moved like Elise around the outskirts of the hall, smiling briefly at acquaintances, not wanting to be caught by anyone and forced to speech. When I reached the nearest door to the parlor, I looked inside. Aunt Amalie and Charles were moving among those who were not dancing. Charles

wore a long, dark blue tunic, with red sleeves and red hose—
the same costume he had worn to most of these Camelot balls,
while Aunt Amalie was a grand lady in a flowing purple
gown, with a white hennin on her head, its purple veil cas-
cading down her back. The style became her and gave her
the regal look fitting to the queen mother she was.

She saw me in the doorway and came toward me among
her guests. "You look lovely, Lacey. Why aren't you dancing?
Let me find you a partner."

I put my hand on her arm. "No—please. I'd rather sit on
the stairs with Richard."

She did not argue with me. "Have you seen Elise?" There
was the light of worry in her eyes.

"A moment ago she was there among the dancers," I said.

Aunt Amalie bent toward me. "Hadley Rikers has come. I
warned her not to invite him, but of course she has paid no
attention. There'll be talk now. More talk than ever."

A figure in black cape and tall conical hat appeared in the
doorway beside me.

"There's already talk," Floria told her mother. "Lacey, I'd
expect you to have better sense than to make yourself con-
spicuous by dancing with Giles."

"I won't again," I promised her. "It was only part of a
dance."

She fumbled at the beard on her chin and pulled it off
crossly. "I've had enough of Merlin." She took off her hat and
cape and flung them down on a chair. Beneath her black
costume she wore a gown of saffron yellow that flowed into
a short train, and her red hair was piled high upon her head.

"Where is Paul?" Aunt Amalie asked.

Floria gestured and we looked out to see him among the
dancers. He held Elise in his arms and his head was bent
toward her as if he was engrossed in talking to her. His
costume of silver and blue became him, and he looked every
bit the courtier.

"Of course he must dance with her," Aunt Amalie said.
"Just as you had to dance with Giles, Lacey. Don't behave
like a child, Floria. You'll never hold him with jealousy."

"She doesn't want him," said Floria bitterly. "She never
has. She only wants to torment me and hurt Paul. How could
I dance with him in that awful beard and cape? That's why
she wants me as Merlin. But I've had enough of it now. I'll be
myself, and she can whistle as she pleases for Merlin."

Aunt Amalie went back to Charles, and Floria looked after her unhappily.

"Now I've upset Mother. And she has enough to worry about. But I'm always doing the wrong thing as far as she's concerned. You think you have all the trouble there is, Lacey. But you haven't—not by any means. Elise is capable of tricks you'd never dream of."

I let that go. I knew what tricks Elise was capable of.

"Your yellow gown becomes you," I said. "I could never see why you wanted to play Merlin anyway."

"I don't any more," Floria admitted, and went out of the room, leaving her cape and tall hat on the chair.

When she had gone, I made my way toward the stairs. There was so much I had to think about, so much I needed to plan. At the newel post I caught up the long draped skirt of my gown and went slowly up to where Richard still sat watching the dancers, his forehead resting against a baluster, his slightly sleepy gaze following the color and movement on the floor below. He did not look around as I came to sit beside him.

"I danced a little while with your father," I said.

He nodded. "I know. I saw you. You looked nice together. You danced better than some of the people down there."

The music stopped and there was a rustle of movement as the dancers stepped apart. I could see Elise in her gold and azure fleurs-de-lis moving out of Paul's arms. He led her across the room, where she stopped to speak to someone, while he vanished into the crowd. I heard the rustle of Floria's skirts on the step behind me, saw the saffron hem of her gown as she started past me from the upper hall. Her face looked white and strained, and her eyes were fixed intently upon some spot across the room below.

But before she could run down the stairs in search of Paul, Elise slipped from among the throng and came toward us.

"Come down to me, Richard," she called, paying no attention to either Floria or me.

Richard sprang up, his sleepiness gone, and ran barefoot down the carpeted stairs.

"Will you look for Mr. Rikers for me, darling?" she said. "Find him and tell him to meet me in the trophy room. Tell him right away, please."

"I'll find him," Richard promised, clearly delighted to be asked to go on an errand for her.

Only then did Elise glance slyly up at her sister and me.

She gave us a slightly mocking smile and turned away from the stairs.

Floria muttered angrily under her breath. "Sending Richard on an errand like that!" Then she saw Paul across the hallway and ran down to meet him.

I left my place at the head of the stairs and returned to my room, where I sat in a chair and leaned my head in my hands. I had less than an hour to wait before I must go out on the beach. And I was not ready. I was afraid. For all that I had known Giles most of my life, I was uncertain about him. I did not know whether he would ever forgive me for what I had done, whether he could accept this long deception and still care about me, ever trust me again. Though these things did not come first any more. What mattered was the vicious harm Elise meant to do Richard. I could see only too clearly how she would embroider her story, and how she would make Richard believe that she suffered with him. That she loved him as a true mother, just as he loved her as a son —yet they could no longer belong to each other because of what other, wicked people had done to them. Oh, she would do it well, playing upon Richard's sensitivities, lacerating his feelings as if she wielded a surgeon's knife. When she was through with him, he would be hers forever, and he would hate the rest of us fervently.

What could be done to stop her? Could Giles counteract what she intended? Perhaps if he told the boy himself it would make a difference. Perhaps if he cemented the closeness of the relationship he had with his son, he could prevent the damage Elise intended to do.

So my thoughts wove and interwove the fabric of this desperate drama. And the minutes ticked away to the accompaniment of distant music and laughter, and all the gay sounds of a ball.

At last I felt I could wait no longer. I would go down to the beach and walk the sands alone until Giles came to meet me. It was unlikely that anyone would see us there. From the downstairs windows palm trees and shrubbery hid the beach from view. From upstairs it might be seen, but who would have time to look tonight?

I let myself out of my room. Richard had not returned to his post on the stairs. Perhaps sleepiness had overcome him and he was in bed by this time. I looked into his room, but the bed lay empty in the moonlight and I felt an uneasiness. Where had he gone when he had finished his errand for Elise?

Double doors across his room stood open and I went to them and stepped out upon a small balcony. At once the sense of *island* was upon me again. Ocean and river lay all around, holding the tiny ship of land in its liquid clasp, severing it from all else. Those who danced to the music downstairs were alien visitors who did not belong. This empty vista was truly Hampton Island, alone and aloof from all intruders. Yet tonight it did not spell safety for me. Tonight the island held in its compass not solace, but evil. The evil that grew from the mind of one woman.

From my high balcony the entire sweep of the beach was visible. The palm trees were so placed that I could look between them and see the lighthouse tower rising tall and white into the moonlit blue of the sky. I could see the stretch of silver sand edging a dazzle where moonbeams shivered upon the water. The white froth of waves curled inward endlessly, and far down along the sands a dark figure walked with its back to the moon.

Giles was there already. I need not wait any longer. I could go to him at once. But I stood for a moment more at the balcony rail because another movement caught my eye. Near the sea wall something stirred. Someone in a long gown, washed of color by the moon, but plainly the dress of a woman. As I watched, she ran toward the stones where I always crossed the wall, and started over them.

I waited to see no more. That was surely Elise! Elise hurrying to intercept my rendezvous with Giles. I must go after her. I did not know why, but something told me urgently that Giles and Elise must not be left alone there upon the sands. There was danger loose upon the night.

I ran out of Richard's room and fled down the stairs. No one noticed me as I let myself out the door, and I ran toward the path that led to the beach, my light slippers sliding on the sandy earth, slowing me down. Overhead the moon went under a cloud, and palmetto fronds snatched at the skirt of my long gown. The rushing sound of the surf was a roaring in my ears—a sound louder than the music that drifted after me from the house.

I burst from the path and ran headlong toward the sea wall.

❁

Elise was no longer in sight, and that seemed strange. On toward the lighthouse, Giles walked, his back still to the moon and the house.

I could not cross the sand easily in my slippers, and I opened the buckled straps to kick the shoes aside, ran on in my stocking feet. The first stones of the wall were cold and rough as I stepped upon them, but I hardly felt the harshness in my urgency. I climbed swiftly among the rocks and clambered over.

The moon came out brightly overhead and showed what lay before me. I flung out my arms to balance myself, to stop my headlong flight—because there in my path, golden braids streaming over the rocks, lay a figure in a medieval gown. Directly at my feet Elise lay face down and very still, her arms flung out as wildly as my own, as if in an effort to save herself from a terrible fall. A little way off in the sand lay the small jeweled crown she had worn as Guinevere.

I let my arms drop to my sides and went to my knees on jagged rock. I crawled toward her and felt the movement of rock beneath my hand. One of the stepping-stones was dangerously loose—it must have thrown her when she put her weight upon it. I reached out my hand and touched the still figure before me.

"Elise!" I cried. "Elise!"

She did not stir at the sound of my voice. Far down the beach Giles heard my cry and turned back. I stood up and called to him frantically. He began to run along damp sand, hampered by his robes, and his shadow ran with him up the beach in my direction. I was aware of the sea breeze on my face, of the brightness of the stars overhead, of the pale gleam of Elise's hair, the brocaded sheen of the gown which covered her body. All my senses were alive to the night and to the terror it had brought to fulfillment.

Others had heard my cries because before Giles reached me, Floria and Paul were there, standing among the rocks, staring down at what lay sprawled on the far side of the wall. Paul moved first. He knelt beside her, turned her over gently. The gash across her forehead was black in the moonlight, her face lifeless.

Paul looked at Giles as he came up the sand toward us. "Help me with her," he said.

Giles flung off his scarlet cape, then bent and picked Elise up in his arms. Stepping carefully, he made his way over the wall and went ahead of us toward the house. I ran after him, and Floria and Paul closed in behind me. No one spoke. We reached the house in that desperate silence, and Giles went across the side veranda to the open doors of the library. The music from the hall assailed our ears, the tune entreating, "Dance with me!" We followed Giles into the room, watching as he laid Elise upon the long couch. Paul went at once to the telephone, calling Malvern for Dr. Lane.

"I'll get Mother," Floria said, and slipped out of the room, incongruously vivid in her saffron yellow dress.

A moment later she was back, with Aunt Amalie at her side. The older woman went directly to her daughter and knelt beside her. The draped veil of her hennin got in the way and she snatched off the headdress with a quick gesture.

"She's gone," Giles said quietly. "There's nothing we can do for her now."

Floria made a choking sound. Aunt Amalie gestured to her at once. "Stop it! Get me a basin of water quickly."

While Floria fled from the room for a second time, Giles put his hands beneath Aunt Amalie's elbows and raised her to her feet.

"It's no use, dear," he said. "It's too late."

Amalie met his look, standing there regally in her flowing purple gown. But her face was white, her lips trembling.

He held her so she would not stumble. "The fall must have killed her at once. She was climbing across the rocks in the sea wall, down on the beach."

Amalie drew herself from his support and knelt in anguish

beside her daughter. "No!" she cried. "No—I won't believe it. I can't believe it."

Paul put down the telephone and I saw his hand shake. "Dr. Lane is coming as quickly as he can," he told us.

Floria came in, with Vinnie behind her carrying a basin of warm water, and a pile of clean cloths. Aunt Amalie held out her hands for the basin, dipped a piece of soft cloth into it, and bent to bathe the dreadful gash on Elise's forehead. It was plain that she had closed off her attention to everything else. She would not listen to any voice that told her Elise was dead. But when the blood had been washed away, the lovely face was white and lifeless as before.

I found myself looking about the room dazedly, noting the brilliant colors—Giles in his golden-brown robes, Floria in her saffron, Paul wearing blue and silver, and Aunt Amalie in her regal purple. It was as if I watched some dreadful carnival at which Death had moved among us, unrecognized till now.

I thought of Richard, wondering where he was, and who was to break this dreadful news to him. An inner voice whispered that Giles was free now, and that Elise could never try to harm Richard again, but horror silenced the voice. The cost was too high. I would not have wished for this. Once, long ago, the woman who lay upon the couch had been my playmate and my idol. Once Giles had loved her.

Outside the library door the music wailed ". . . these foolish things . . ." and dancers circled the big hallway.

Aunt Amalie rose upon her knees. "Make them stop playing that music! Someone, please, send them all away!"

"I'll do it," Floria said.

She ran out of the room as though she was glad to escape, and in moments we heard the music break off, heard the flurry of shocked voices that burst into the sudden hush.

Within in the library we were very still. Vinnie had stood by while Aunt Amalie bathed Elise's face. Now she set the basin of water aside and took the cloth from Amalie's hands.

"Come, Miss Amalie," she said. "Come rest you'self in a chair. There's nothing to do till Doctor comes."

Aunt Amalie let Vinnie draw her to her feet, help her across the room to Charles's easy chair. There she lay back with her eyes closed. For the first time I wondered where Charles was. No one had thought to summon him. Aunt Amalie had not asked for him.

I went to the door and looked out into the hall. The first hubbub had ceased, as guests filed quietly toward the door.

Already the hush of death lay upon Sea Oaks, and the gay dress of the dancers looked shockingly out of place. Near the front door I saw Charles, with Floria beside him. The two of them were acting as hosts, bidding the guests good-bye, doing what the rest of us could not do. I looked down at my own white gown that had belonged to Elise, and for the first time I realized that I was in my stocking feet. I had left my slippers on the beach. It did not matter.

When I turned back to the room, Paul was bending over Aunt Amalie, speaking to her softly. Giles stood at one of the open French doors, looking out at the night. Now that the music had ceased, the sound of the ocean filled the house again, the waves rolling endlessly up the beach toward the straggling rock line of the sea wall. There was nothing I could say to Giles. Strangely, Elise's death had set us apart as though some barrier had been raised between us. I did not know yet how serious that barrier might be.

When the last guest had gone, Charles and Floria came to join us. Charles went at once to his wife, the full red sleeves of his dark blue tunic falling gracefully as he bent toward her. She opened her eyes and looked at him as though she did not know who he was until he kissed her cheek.

Then she found her voice. "Does anyone know anything more about how it happened? Did anyone see her fall?"

Giles turned from the veranda door. "I don't believe anyone saw her, but she must have slipped on a stone in the wall. Perhaps her dress tripped her."

Aunt Amalie moaned softly. "Why was she near the wall? She never went down to the beach that way!"

"Perhaps I can answer that," a voice said from the library door.

We all looked around in shocked surprise to see Hadley Rikers standing there. He was dressed entirely in green—the dashing dress of a hunter—and the red-feathered cap he wore was set at a jaunty slant that seemed to match the very tilt of his dark beard. It was as though Robin Hood had stepped suddenly among us, defiant and more than a little challenging.

He paid no attention to our blank shock, but went directly to the couch where Elise lay. For a long moment he stood gazing down at her white face, at the rumpled gold and azure of the fleurs-de-lis on her gown. Then he spoke without looking at any of us.

"When Lacey and Giles were talking in this room earlier, she stood outside a door to the veranda. She heard Lacey ask

Giles to meet her in an hour down on the beach. She meant to play a trick on him in the moonlight and make him think it was Lacey coming toward him over the wall. She meant to take him by surprise and see how he would react. Whatever happened, she meant to spoil the meeting between them."

We heard him in silence. No one moved. He stepped back from the couch and faced Giles, his look challenging.

"I advised her not to play games," he said. "I didn't think you would welcome them."

There was a certain arrogance in the words, as if he flung down the gauntlet and dared Giles to pick it up.

Giles said nothing, made no move, and I found myself speaking into the quiet of the room. I was not sure what Hadley meant, but his challenge could not be left hanging without an answer.

"When I went down to the beach, Giles was a long way off near the lighthouse. He couldn't have been anywhere near the wall when Elise started across. I saw them both from the balcony upstairs, and he was nowhere near her then. I came downstairs at once and followed the path to the beach. When I came out into the open, Giles was still walking toward the lighthouse and Elise wasn't in sight. I didn't see that she had fallen until I climbed over the rocks of the sea wall."

Aunt Amalie made the same soft moaning sound she had made before.

"I think there was a loose rock," I went on. "When I got down on my hands and knees to reach her I felt it tilt under my hand. If she stepped on it, it would have thrown her."

"You're not telling the truth, Lacey," Floria said abruptly. "I've waited to see what sort of story you'd offer, but I needn't wait any longer. Mother, Lacey pushed Elise down on those rocks. We saw her, Paul and I. She must have pushed her from behind before Elise ever knew what she was about. My sister didn't stand a chance—she fell directly forward on the rocks, and the fall killed her."

"No!" Aunt Amalie said. "No!"

I choked over my dismay at Floria's words, but before I could find an answer for her, Paul put a hand on her arm.

"It wasn't exactly like that. I was there, too. I saw what Floria saw."

"Oh, it's not that I blame Lacey!" Floria cried, paying no attention. "I'd have been tempted if I'd been in her place. If Elise had been trying to do to me what she was doing to

Lacey, I think I'd have felt the same way. I'd have taken any chance that came my way."

Giles spoke sharply. "What really happened, Paul?"

Floria twisted her arm from beneath Paul's hands. "You're afraid to tell them the truth! You're trying to save Lacey!"

"Lacey doesn't need saving," Paul said quietly. "When we came out of the path onto the open beach, Lacey was standing on top of a big rock with her arms outflung as if she balanced there. A moment later she called to Giles, and he turned and came running toward her. We never saw Elise at all until we reached Lacey and looked down among the rocks of the wall."

"Lacey's arms were flung out because she had just pushed my sister," Floria said. "Not that it matters. Not that I will tell anyone else. Elise has only received what was coming to her."

There was hysteria in Floria's voice, and Paul put an arm about her, holding her still when she would have struggled.

Aunt Amalie covered her face with her hands and Charles leaned over her, murmuring.

I looked from one to another around the room. Paul was quieting Floria. Vinnie watched Aunt Amalie solicitously. Charles gave me a quick, pitying glance, and turned his attention back to his wife. Aunt Amalie would not look at me at all, while in Floria's eyes there was only accusation, and and certain angry triumph. Giles came swiftly toward me across the room.

"Lacey wouldn't hurt anyone," he told the others. "We all know that. What happened was an accident—nothing more. It's nonsense to believe anything else."

"Of course you'd stand by her!" Floria said shrilly. "Now you can be together. Now everything will be fine for the two of you!"

I had to disengage myself from Giles's arm. He meant to help me, but I could not accept that help now.

"What Floria thinks she saw, didn't happen," I assured them all. "Elise must have been lying there for ten minutes before I found her. She must have fallen shortly after I saw her from the upstairs balcony and started down to the beach. When I came across that part of the wall, she was already lying upon the rocks."

The room was quiet again. No one answered me or contradicted my words. Aunt Amalie rose slowly from her chair, moving like a very old woman. She returned to the couch where Elise lay and reached for the brown wool throw that lay folded at her daughter's feet. With hands that were as controlled as she could manage, she drew it up over Elise, covering her face. It was brave acceptance at last. But in accepting, she had aged.

Floria seemed to deflate like an empty balloon. She turned to Paul and began to sob softly in his arms. Aunt Amalie turned away from the couch, her shoulders back, her voice steady.

"Who is to tell Richard?" she asked.

"I'll tell him," Giles said. "But let him sleep for tonight. There will be time enough in the morning."

"Thank you," Aunt Amalie said. "I don't know how I could bear to—"

I broke in on her words. "Has he gone back to bed? When I came downstairs a while ago he wasn't in his room. Elise sent him on an errand, but I don't know what he did after that."

Vinnie moved quickly toward the door. "I'll go see," she told us, and hurried out of the library.

For the first time I noticed that Hadley Rikers was no longer among us. While we were absorbed in what Floria was saying, he must have slipped away. He was hardly missed. He did not belong.

"Come and sit down," Charles said to Aunt Amalie, and she walked to the big leather armchair and let her husband help her gently into it. She had no sooner seated herself, than Vinnie was back, her dark eyes wide with alarm.

"He's not in his bed! I called for him upstairs, but he don' answer me."

Giles moved quickly. "Go back and look in every room upstairs, will you, Vinnie? Paul and I will take the downstairs rooms. We must find him quickly."

Floria came to herself and pushed Paul away from her. "Yes—hurry! Perhaps he heard what we were telling the guests."

I felt suddenly weak with alarm. If Richard had learned in some shocking way that Elise was dead, he might be capable of wild and frightening action.

Charles went to one of the French doors and stepped out upon the veranda, calling Richard's name. There was no answer. There was no answer from anywhere within the house. In a short time Giles and Paul and Vinnie were back in the room.

"We'll have to search for him outside," Giles said. "We can't let him run about in the dark if he's frightened or uncertain. I'll call the stable boys and George—they know the island better than the other servants."

"There's the lighthouse," I said. "He might go there."

"It's possible," Giles agreed. "I'll look there myself. Paul, will you take the drive to the road, and circle back by way of The Bitterns?"

"I'll search the fort area," Charles said. "I've got a good flashlight."

"And I'll look through the burying ground and the tombs," Floria offered. "But I'll get out of this dress first. I'll put on something of Elise's. I don't want to take the time to go home."

Aunt Amalie made a slight movement, but she did not object. "I'll stay here and wait for the doctor," she said dully.

"Will you stay out in front, Lacey?" Giles turned to me. "Then if he comes back, or if anyone finds him, you can ring the bell on the side veranda."

In a moment they had all scattered—Vinnie to rouse her husband and the stable boys, the others to begin their searching. I left Aunt Amalie to her sad vigil, and went into the hall. Lights still burned brilliantly in two great chandeliers, but the wide hall was vacant—empty of revelers. Scarlet banners hung above emptiness. The band had dispersed along with the guests, and the empty chairs where the musicians had sat looked singularly deserted. A music stand lay overturned—mute evidence of sudden disaster. With the rugs gone and the hall empty, the space had an echoing, hollow sound to it. In all that bright bareness no one could hide.

I went into the long double parlor, feeling like a ghost in my white dress—Elise's white dress—as though only I inhabited this empty, deserted world. In this room, with the chairs drawn back against the walls, where men and women in medieval costumes had stood about smoking and drinking, there was more of an air of wreckage than in the hall, where they had danced. Ash trays were full, and glasses stood on small tables. The extra servants had been sent away, to leave everything till morning. Floor lamps still burned, and for some reason I went about turning them off, one by one.

I hardly knew what I did. I was thinking of Richard, perhaps shocked and frightened and grieving—somewhere out in the moonlit darkness, with no one to comfort him, no one to reassure him, to tell him that though Elise was gone he would still be loved and sheltered. I wondered why he had not come to his father. I wondered why he had not come to us in the library, where Elise lay. Why had he chosen the path of flight instead?

Slowly I walked back into the wide entry hall that bisected the house, my thoughts troubled and busy. How differently the night had turned out from what I had expected and planned. If all had gone as I had intended, I would have crossed the wall myself, and Elise would not have been down on the beach at all. I would have run along the sands to meet Giles and I would have faced the truth, as it had to be faced, there beside the rolling surf. By this time Giles would have known that I was Richard's mother, and Elise was not. How he would have reacted, what he would have said about the long deception Elise and Aunt Amalie and I had played upon him, I could not know. Instead, Elise had fallen upon the rocks and lay dead upon the couch in the library. And Giles still did not know the truth.

I had reached the front door in my slow walk down the hall and I stepped between crossed lances and out upon the portico. The bricks were rough and cold beneath my stocking feet. The lamp that hung above the small second-floor balcony burned brightly and set the shadows of tall columns fanning away from the house. Beyond the columns, the two rows of live oak trees marched along the driveway, their high rounded tops gilded by the moonlight, their lower branches black with heavy shadow. Between them, making a white aisle under the moon, the shell drive wound its way toward the distant road. Above the sound of the surf I could hear voices breaking the night's stillness as searchers called for Richard. Wherever he was, he could hear them calling him. He would know they were searching for him. Yet it might be like him to hear them and make no response. If he chose to, he could hide for a long time on the island.

My thoughts ran on as if they could not pull themselves from the rut they had chosen to follow. If only Elise had stayed away from the sea wall, if only she had not attempted to play one of her cruel tricks on Giles, then she would be alive now. She would be moving among her guests in her gown of azure and gold, moving in her own confident, living beauty.

A cold whisper rushed suddenly through my mind. A voice I had not listened to until now: "And where would you be, Lacey? Would it be you lying dead upon that couch in the library? Would it be you whose foot found that dangerously tilting rock that was one of your stepping-stones across the wall?"

All about me night insects chirred their individual sounds. Their utterances seemed to buzz loudly in my ears, dizzying me. I moved close to a soaring white column and put my hand upon it to steady myself. The last time I had gone over the wall had not been long ago, surely—and there had been no loose stepping-stone then. So what could have jarred it free from the socket in which it had rested all these years since I had been a child?

The sound of an approaching car on the drive caught my attention, and I was glad to thrust the sudden terror from my thoughts. This would be Dr. Lane coming, and someone must be ready to meet him. I went to the edge of the portico and waited while he stopped his car and got out of it, came running up the steps toward me. He had been the island doctor for a long time.

"Hello, Lacey," he said. "Where is she?"

"In the library," I told him. "Aunt Amalie is with her. Will you go right in, please. Richard is missing and everyone is out searching for him."

He thanked me and hurried into the house. I walked the width of the portico, finding it difficult to stand still, difficult to wait and do nothing, when it was my son who was lost somewhere out there in the moonlit island. Near where I stood a live oak reached heavy, gnarled branches across the balustrade, dripping strands of moss toward the bricks of the floor. I idly pulled a strand loose and twisted the brittle gray stuff in my fingers.

I did not think this was merely a prank Richard had chosen to play on his elders to get himself attention. He had been content enough this evening, and happy to be privileged to watch from his post on the stairs. No—desperation had driven him into hiding tonight, and I could not bear the thought of his lonely grief, his terror of the unknown, the hopelessness, perhaps, that drove him to hide from comforting hands. Elise had sent him upon an errand to Hadley Rikers. He could well have been downstairs moving among the guests when Floria came out to stop the music and send everyone home. In their consternation, who would have noticed a small boy who chose to slip away by himself and hide from adult eyes?

I reached along the dark branch for another strand of moss, and the branch moved beneath my hand. It swayed gently, although at the moment there was no wind. Startled, I reached into a place where thick clumps of foliage met, and parted the leaves. Far along the branch, huddled into a dark hollow against the trunk of the tree, was a spot of something light. I held the branch steady in my hands.

"It's time to come out now, Richard," I said as calmly as I could manage.

He did not speak, but he began to crawl toward me along the branch, coming out of the depth of his hiding place. When I held out my hand, he took it in his and let me draw him to the flat top of the balustrade. Once he stood on the rail I forgot all caution. I put my arms tightly about him and held him close.

"Darling!" I said. "You've given us all a fright. They're out looking for you now. Your father and your Aunt Floria, and—"

"I know," he said. He did not struggle against my embrace, but settled into my arms like a small boy who suddenly wanted to be comforted. Though the night was warm, I could feel his shivering through the thin stuff of his pajamas, and I placed a hand on his cold bare feet.

"It's best if we get you back to bed," I told him. "Tomorrow we can talk about all this."

He clung to me. "I don't want to go in there. I don't want to see *her.*"

I held him tightly. "You needn't, darling. Your father will come back to the house as soon as I ring the bell to let him know you're found. He'll take care of everything."

Behind us, the door to the house opened and Aunt Amalie came through, walking slowly, with the doctor at her side.

"Why is *he* here?" Richard asked me.

"Because Elise—" I began, and then broke off because I could not put the rest into words.

"Is she ill?" Richard asked.

I looked at him blankly. His question told me he did not know what had happened. Something had driven him to hide from us, but it was not because of his mother's death. What had he meant when he said he did not want to see *her?*

Aunt Amalie saw us and came running across the bricks, her arms outstretched to her grandson. "Richard! Richard, dearest, where have you been?"

She reached up and drew him away from me. He jumped down from the balustrade and let her hold him to her. Over his head her eyes met mine coolly. I knew why she drew him away from me. Floria's words stood between us. Aunt Amalie no longer trusted me. I wanted to cry out to her that she must believe me, that Floria, as usual, was making things up, exaggerating what she had seen. But before I could say anything, Aunt Amalie spoke to me quietly.

"Go and ring the bell, please, Lacey. Let them know he has been found." She turned to the doctor with a warning look and then sent Richard into the house.

I went around the side veranda and found the great plantation bell that hung from a support. The rope I pulled sounded the clapper and the deep-throated voice of the bell boomed over the island. Someone shouted in response, and other voices answered. They were coming in now.

When I returned to the columned portico the doctor was getting into his car. Aunt Amalie stood at the front door and I ran to her quickly.

"Richard doesn't know," I said.

She nodded. "Yes. I heard him. I'll go in and get him upstairs to his room. It's best to keep what has happened from him for tonight."

I wanted to stop her, to plead with her to trust me, believe in me, but her face was a mask of restrained suffering, and whatever I could say would not matter. She was not thinking about me now.

I waited where I was to let the others know about Richard as they came in. The stable boys went back to bed, and Paul and Charles went into the house. Giles would be the last to come in because the top of the lighthouse was farthest away. I walked down to the edge of the beach and waited for him. My slippers lay where I had left them and I put them on.

The moon had dropped out of sight behind a clump of trees, and there was no longer a ladder of golden foil across the ocean. But the sky was still bright and I could see Giles's dark figure running along the sand, as he had run earlier that night. He did not cross by way of the sea wall, but took the steps that led up from the beach. I moved toward him and he saw me in my white dress, light against the darkness behind me.

"I found him," I said. "He was hiding in the live oak nearest the house, and I think he was glad to come in. He doesn't know that Elise is dead. Apparently the babble of voices, and the guests leaving early, didn't mean anything to him. It's something else that caused him to run away."

He took my hands and held them for a moment. "I'll go in and see him right away."

"Aunt Amalie has taken him up to bed," I said.

He drew me toward the house, hurrying to his son. For just a moment I held him back.

"She believes what Floria said," I told him. "Aunt Amalie has turned against me."

"She'll get over that." Giles was confident. "Come inside now, darling. This has been a hard night for all of us. And there may be more."

"Dr. Lane was here," I said.

"He's only the first. There are arrangements to make. And the police must be notified. I'm afraid you may have to stay up for a while longer, since you found her. But it will be only a formality."

"A formality?" I had forgotten the police. "A formality, when Floria—"

"She won't repeat what she said outside the family," Giles assured me. "I doubt that she believes it herself. She's bitter tonight. Because of Paul. Because Paul has been crushed by Elise's death. He's bearing up well, but you can see it in his face, in his eyes. Elise has kept it that way. Poor Floria."

I was feeling less charitable, and I said nothing. We walked to the house together and into its blaze of lights. Someone had turned on the floor lamps in the parlor again. The library was lighted, and chandeliers still burned in the wide hall where the dancing had been. The upstairs floor was alight too. It was as though the ball was still on, even though light flared upon emptiness.

"I'll wait in my room," I said to Giles, and went upstairs.

Aunt Amalie was coming out of Richard's room and she put a finger to her lips, drawing the door softly shut behind her. "He'll go to sleep now. He's warm and snug in bed, and I think he's tired and a little contrite about frightening us. Have you any idea what made him run away?"

I shook my head and went toward the door of my room. "I'll wait up here. Giles says the police may want to question me, since—since I was the first person to find her."

Aunt Amalie put a hand to her breast as though to still a sharpness of pain, and tears welled in her eyes. A few hours earlier, if I had seen her like this, I would have put my arms about her, tried to comfort her in her grief. But now I did not dare.

I turned away and walked toward the door of my room. When I'd crossed the threshold I felt for the light switch, and a lamp near the bed came on. But when I would have closed the door behind me, I found that Aunt Amalie had followed me. I moved away, and it was she who shut the door. We faced each other across the room.

"What are your plans?" she asked in the same cool voice she had used in speaking to me downstairs. The tears had been blinked away.

"I have no plans," I told her. "I'm still trying to catch my breath, trying to understand what has happened."

"The road is clear for you now," she said. "You can have Giles"—her voice broke—"and you can have your son. There's nothing to stop you."

I went to a window and opened it more widely upon the night. A wind had begun to blow outside, and the sound of the sea had risen.

"Floria can stop me," I said.

Aunt Amalie stood with her back to the door, watching me. "Floria will never cause a scandal. She will not hurt me that way."

"She may not mean to hurt you," I said, "but if I know Floria, she will talk. She has never kept a secret in her life. The time will come when she will whisper to some friend, who will whisper to another friend, and before long the matter will be open gossip. Giles could be hurt, perhaps even his business could be damaged by such rumors. People are always ready to believe the worst. Perhaps they'll even believe that he and I planned this together."

I could hear the hard, cold sound of my own voice as I flung my words in her face. "If *you* believe what Floria claims, anyone will believe it and there'll be no way to stop a scandal."

I had moved away from the window. Aunt Amalie went to it and threw back her head to breathe deeply of the wind from the ocean. She drank it in as if it revived her, gave her sustenance.

"Don't worry," I said. "I'll go away shortly. I'll go back to New York. Perhaps tomorrow or the next day. Unless the police choose to hold me under suspicion."

"I won't have that!" Aunt Amalie said, the words coming from her forcefully, as though she had suddenly made up her mind. "You must stay here for a while longer. You must stay and face down any talk there may be. The very fact that it was you who found her may cause whispering, but I'll see to it that Floria says nothing to anyone. And our support of you, our continuing hospitality should help."

"I don't think I want to stay, Aunt Amalie," I said miserably. "Not when I know you feel as you do. Not when I think you may believe what Floria claims."

There were tears in her eyes again, and this time she did not blink them away. She turned from the window, her hands held out to me, and I saw them trembling.

"Help me, Lacey," she said. "Help me to believe in you."

The coldness melted out of me. I felt tears burn my own eyes. Her hands clung to mine, and her cheek was soft against my own.

"I can't help you," I said. "I can only tell you that I had nothing to do with Elise's death. But you will have to choose which one of us you will believe. Floria or me."

"I want to believe you," Aunt Amalie said. "But why should Floria lie? What could she possibly have against you that would make her want to say what she did?"

I could only shake my head.

"All the more reason why you must stay," Aunt Amalie insisted. "We must get to the bottom of this. You should want to stay, Lacey—to—to prove your own innocence."

"If you want me, then I'll stay," I promised her. "For a little while longer, at least."

She stepped back from me, looking into my face. "I've lost so much tonight. I don't want to lose you, too, Lacey. I couldn't bear it if what Floria said was true. But I must go downstairs now. There's so much to be done. There are times when one wants to be weak and run away. But I dare not give in, even though Charles would encourage me to. Don't worry about the police questioning you, Lacey. We'll give you every support. I'll go and talk to Floria at once."

At the door she turned back, her eyes still wet, and made a last wordless gesture in my direction, as though she pleaded with me for patience, pleaded with me to give her time to right her own emotions.

When she had been gone for a few moments, I opened my door and looked toward the blankness of Richard's door. There was no one about and I went quietly across the hall. The knob turned beneath my hand and I pushed the door ajar, listening. I could hear Richard's soft breathing. I slipped into the room and went to stand beside his bed.

My son lay in shadow, sleeping. Tomorrow he would have to learn about Elise. Giles would tell him. Tomorrow held pain for him. Yet the pain would not be as disastrous as what Elise had planned. This was hurt he would learn to live with. What she had intended would have injured him for always. Now it could be more gently done. Some day, perhaps, he would know that I was his mother. I longed fiercely for that day to come.

When I bent to pull the sheet up over his shoulder and touched him lightly, he muttered and stirred, as if his dreams were restless and disturbing. I went softly out the door, and back to my own room.

The first early light of dawn pressed against my windows. I had slept very little and I awakened easily and lay for a moment listening to the first chirping of birds in the trees outside. Inside the house everything was still.

Memory came rushing back in a sickening flood. I remembered Elise being taken away last night. I remembered being questioned by a young, very serious police officer. I had told him everything that had happened, just as it had happened, though I held back our reasons for being on the beach. He did not think it strange that Elise had followed her husband there. Nor did he question my own claim that I had tired of the party, and that I often walked on the beach by moonlight. Nothing in particular came out about the stepping-stones across the wall, and I did not mention that I had found one stone loose. Let the police do their own sleuthing, if they wished. I was reluctant to connect myself with that stone.

The officer had written it all down, he had talked to everyone and then gone away. It was too dark to look at the sea wall at that time. This morning the police would probably return. But it was obvious that the case seemed a clear-cut accident. Elise had been foolish to cross the straggling, uneven line of stones by moonlight in her long dress. Anyone could have tripped on such a hem. Floria kept silent, and there was no reason for anyone to question my story of finding her sister.

We had all gone to bed very late, and if I had slept at all, my dreams were haunted. Now morning was breaking, and there was something I must do, something I must know.

I got out of bed and put on slacks and a windbreaker. Then

I hurried downstairs and out of the house. The sun was rising from the Atlantic, the sky streaked with rose and gold that tinted the water. Waves that curled in over gray sands had gilded edges. It was a beautiful morning, but my spirits could not rise to meet its beginning. As I ran across the sand to the sea wall, I saw the great splash of scarlet that was the cloak Giles had flung down on the rocks last night. It seemed to speak with eloquence of high tragedy, and I stood staring at it for a moment while the horror of memory engulfed me. But I must hurry—there was something I must do.

I did not take the stepping-stones to the far side, but climbed over at another place, and approached the far stones cautiously. It was the next to the top step on the ocean side that had rocked so treacherously last night. Carefully, I balanced on the steady step below it and reached out tentatively with my foot to test the rock above. It did not move at all. It seemed solidly wedged into a socket made by other rocks.

Yet I could remember the way it had tipped under my hand last night when I had got down upon my knees to bend over Elise. Now I put my foot upon it with more weight behind, and made a real effort to move the rock. It would not budge. It was as firmly lodged as it had always been. But how could I be wrong? Was it possible that in my fright last night, in the shock of finding Elise, I had been totally mistaken?

That was hard to believe. I knelt on the sand below the irregular stones of the wall and looked underneath the one I had tested. Several smaller stones seemed to be embedded beneath it, holding it steady. I reached out and prodded one of them. It did not move.

"What are you trying to do?" a voice said behind me.

I turned around, still crouching on the sand, and looked up at the broad, stocky figure of Hadley Rikers. He was no longer dressed as Robin Hood, yet the stamp of an audacious outlaw remained upon him as he watched me gravely, his eyes alight with the same challenge and suspicion I had sensed in them last night.

"That stone was loose," I said, touching it with my hand. "Now it's perfectly secure."

"I've no doubt," he said. "Perhaps you got up early to take care of it?"

I rose to my feet and faced him indignantly. "I came down to make sure of what I thought I had discovered last night."

"And to make sure that no one else would find the stone loose—is that it?"

His disbelief was frightening. More frightening than Floria's reckless words.

"Who stood most to win by Elise's death?" he demanded coldly.

I took a deep breath of the ocean-borne air. "You're leaping to a conclusion. How could I have known that Elise meant to come down to the beach last night? How could I have known she meant to go across this place in the wall?"

He was silent, still watching me, his eyes dark with ugly suspicion.

"I doubt that anyone knew she was going to indulge this whim," I said. "Except you, perhaps. But someone knew that *I* meant to meet Giles on the beach. Someone knew in time to come down here and loosen that stone. Anyone who stepped upon it confidently would have been thrown across the rocks. It was meant for that to happen to me. Not to Elise. It was sheer chance that brought her down here first, in my place. That's why I came this morning to examine the stone. I wanted to see what had been intended for me. But someone has already mended the damage. You can see the small stones that have been wedged under the big one to hold it solid."

Hadley Rikers bent to examine where I pointed. He tested the big stone himself, and I hoped he was beginning to believe me. Then something on the sand caught his eyes, and he reached out to pick up the small golden crown Elise had worn last night. Its make-believe gems winked emerald and ruby in the morning light, and he ran it around his fingers several times before he laid it almost ceremoniously upon the scarlet cloak.

"The end of Camelot," he said.

For a moment I felt drawn to him in unexpected pity. I did not think he would suffer for long, but in this instant the pain of Elise's loss had stabbed through him.

"What are you doing here?" I asked him. "How did you get here?"

He waved an arm toward the small motorboat drawn up on the beach some distance along. I had not seen it, had not troubled to look that way until now. All my attention had been given to the rocky wall. But I had heard no sound of a boat coming in and I did not know how long he had been about, watching me.

"I wanted to see for myself the place where she fell," he said. "She told me once or twice that she was afraid that someone might try to injure her. She was afraid of Giles, even though she went out of her way to anger him."

My brief pity for him vanished. "Giles wouldn't have loosened a stone for her to step on!" I cried. "That's ridiculous!"

"Until I saw your interest in that rock, I'd thought of something more direct," Hadley said. "In fact, I think it's more likely that she was given a rough, direct push from behind."

I remembered that he had been present last night when Floria had burst out with her accusation.

"But you can't really think—" I began.

He broke in on my words. "That you pushed her? No, I don't. There's a more likely possibility. After all, we have only your word for it that Giles was far down the beach, and nowhere near the wall at the time she fell. Of course you would lie to save him if it was necessary. You might easily invent a loose stone. That would be very neat, wouldn't it? Especially if you came down here early this morning when no one was up, and made sure that a stone was loose. The only trouble is that I found you too soon. And now I can swear that every stone in that wall is solid, and there was nothing to throw her off balance."

I could only stare at him in disbelief. "You're making every bit of this up. You haven't a particle of evidence—"

He caught me by the wrist, silencing me. "I have the evidence of your being here. I have the knowledge that you would try to save Giles if you possibly could."

"But there's Floria!" I protested. "Floria and Paul. They reached the wall soon after I did."

"So you claim," Hadley said. "Giles could have been well away by then, and Floria would prefer to blame you."

I put my free hand on his arm. "Oh, please!" I cried. "The truth is such a simple thing. No one has been trying to injure Elise, but someone has tried again and again to hurt me. I've thought all along that it was Elise doing these things. Elise trying to punish me because Giles—"

"What did she care about Giles?" he demanded angrily.

"She wouldn't divorce him to marry you," I said.

"We hadn't got to the point of talking marriage. I'm not sure I'm the marrying kind. But I know how Elise felt—about me."

What he believed was what Elise had wanted him to believe.

"What do you mean to do with this wild story of yours?" I asked.

He let my wrist drop. "I haven't decided yet."

I tried again to urge the truth upon him. "You've got to see that what you claim isn't what really happened! If you want to find out what happened, then you'll need to be open-minded. Perhaps you'll need to help me."

"Help you?"

"Help me find out who loosened that stone so that I might be badly hurt when I came over the wall last night. The same person who came down here later and wedged it solid again."

He shook his head, not believing me, and turned away. I watched as he went striding along the beach toward his boat. I watched as he shoved it into the water, got into it and started the motor. Not until he had roared away toward the entrance to Malvern River, did I start over the wall. That was when something caught my eye—something which stuck to a rock, dangling like a bit of seaweed. But it was not seaweed. Nor was it Spanish moss.

I bent and pulled the gray strands loose from a crevice of rock where they had lodged. What I held in my hand was Merlin's beard.

The thing looked somehow ghastly in the early morning light—a bit of gray and evil magic left over from the time of darkness last night. So Floria had been here, wearing her black costume, losing the beard on a spike of rock, not being able to find it among other shadows in the dark.

Or had it been Floria? She had left her Merlin things in a heap on a chair in the library. Anyone could have picked them up by way of a disguise and worn them to the beach. Whoever had put them on must be the one who had come back to make solid a stone that was loosened earlier last night.

The strands of gray clung to my fingers, and I ripped the beard away, rolled the beard into a wad and thrust it into a pocket of my slacks. Then I started back toward the house, leaving the scarlet cloak and golden circlet behind to play their last masquerade on the beach.

If Elise were alive I would have thought this sort of prank typical of her. But she had not loosened the stone that brought about her own death. Even if she had thrust that sand dollar into my napkin at the time of my last visit, even if she had closed the door of the freezing room upon me, even if she had hidden the less valuable brooch among the things in my room, and managed to shove a loose piece of masonry over upon me at the ruins of the hospital—even if she had done all these things, she had not done this. So now I must look elsewhere for someone who wished me harm. And in looking elsewhere, perhaps I would find—not Elise, but the author of all these other threats as well.

My feet were slow upon the path as I followed it toward Sea Oaks. I did not want to look into island faces, seeking for evil. Who could dislike me so much that my injury or death was intended?

The colors of dawn had faded by the time I went around to the front of the house, and the morning sun was up, touching everything with a warm and innocent light. As I started toward the steps, someone came from the path that led by way of the burying ground toward The Bitterns. It was Paul Courtney. He looked as though he had slept as little as I, and apparently he had not gone home to Malvern at all last night.

"Have you seen Floria?" he asked.

I shook my head. "Is she supposed to be here? Perhaps she's inside."

"She must have left the house before I was up," he said. "I'm worried about her."

I reached into my pocket and drew out the gray strands of Merlin's beard. "I found this clinging to a rock down on the sea wall," I told him.

He regarded the thing in my hand warily, as if it were something he had never seen before.

"Hadley Rikers was on the beach," I went on. "He said he wanted to have a look at the place where Elise fell. He thinks Giles was to blame and that I was lying when I said he was far down the beach when I found Elise."

"You'd lie for Giles if you had to," Paul said, still wary.

"But I'm not lying. And it would be dreadful if Hadley Rikers tried to make trouble for Giles."

"He won't," Paul said. "He'll want to keep out of trouble himself."

His words reassured me only a little. Hadley Rikers would be in character as a troublemaker. I knew that from reading his book. But there was nothing I could do about him now.

I looked up at the house from my place at the foot of the steps. I let my eyes follow the long, lovely lines of fluted columns, gleaming white in early morning beauty, and the impact of knowing Elise was gone struck me again.

"I keep expecting her to come out the door," I said. "I keep expecting her to come down the steps. I can almost hear her laughing."

"I know," Paul said dully. "There's a sense of unreality about everything that happened last night."

"I do believe," said a gently mocking voice above us, "that you are both hypocrites."

Charles Severn had stepped out from behind a pillar. His hands rested on the balustrade that rimmed the portico as he looked calmly down upon us. When we both stared up at him in astonishment, he came toward us down the right-hand steps. He was as neatly dressed as though he meant to go to the office, and he did not look in the least ravaged by the events of the night before, as both Paul and I did. When he reached our level he spoke to me directly.

"Do you mean to tell me, Lacey, that you miss Elise? Do you mean to tell me that you grieve for her?"

He was asking me for honesty, and I tried to shred away half-understood emotions and give it to him.

"I keep remembering her as a little girl—when I was a little girl. I admired her then, wanted to be like her. During the last few days perhaps I've hated her. With part of me I can't wish her alive again. Yet I can grieve for something that was needlessly lost and wasted."

"Lost a long time ago." He smiled at me benignly. "That's honest, at least. We need to clear the air after the turbulence of last night."

He turned questioningly to Paul, who looked at Charles as though he had not really seen him for a long while, as though he had not troubled to look at him closely. Looking now, he was forced to some answer.

"I was dancing with her only last night," Paul said.

"And forgetting Floria?" Charles asked in the same gentle manner that nevertheless cut deep.

"I don't ever forget Floria," Paul said, suddenly angry.

"Then you should be glad that something utterly evil has stopped living. *I* am glad."

Charles would have gone past us, leaving us to our astonishment, but he saw what I held in my hand, and reached out to touch the gray strands.

"Merlin's beard. So you found it. Where did she lose it, Lacey?"

"She?" I repeated. "Who do you mean?"

"Floria, of course. I saw her come into the house last night before the police arrived, wearing her black costume. But the beard was missing. Where were you, Paul?"

Paul seemed to hesitate, as if he might be trying to recall hazy details from a night of confusion. "I went looking for her. When I found her near the house she wasn't wearing the beard. Perhaps she never put it on at all."

"But why would she go out in costume at that hour?" I said.

"What else had she to wear? She couldn't run about outside looking for Richard in her long dress. And she must have changed her mind about putting on something that belonged to Elise."

Charles listened, still smiling gently, as though this were an ordinary conversation which rather amused him.

"How is Aunt Amalie?" I asked him.

"She's asleep," he said. "I persuaded her to take a pill last night. If it weren't for her shock over Elise's death, if it weren't for what Richard is going to feel, I would be quite content this morning. What has happened will be a load off Amalie's shoulders as well."

We watched in stunned silence as he turned away and followed the shell drive between the great trunks of the live oaks, walking along in as leisurely a manner as though he took one of his usual after-dinner strolls.

I looked after him dazedly. "I've known Charles all my life, yet I'd never have suspected that he could say such things."

"Charles has always looked after Charles," Paul said wryly. "Sometimes I feel a little sorry for Amalie."

"Aunt Amalie has found what she always wanted," I reminded him, repeating the phrase that everyone used.

Paul shrugged. "Elise told me he married her mother for comfort, not for love. But then—Elise never liked Charles, any more than he liked her. If he hadn't been Giles's father, she would never have stood for him living in the same house."

Once more I looked up at soaring pillars. "At least it's his house again. Elise always tried to make it hers."

Paul moved impatiently, as though tiring of our talk. "Sometimes I forget that it's his house. Let's go inside, Lacey. I want to look for Floria."

We climbed the steps together and stepped into the wide main hall. Sunlight could not reach into its depth, and it still looked empty and deserted. Scarlet and gold banners were a mockery this morning.

"I think there will never be another Camelot ball," I murmured. "All that belongs to a dream world. Just as the island itself is part of some sort of dream. I wish I could wake up."

"I wish we all could," Paul said. He crossed the hall beside me with so firm a step that I felt he was bracing himself against something. Perhaps against the memory of Elise.

Sounds came from the parlor—Vinnie's voice.

"Let me do that, Miss Floria. Why'n't you lie down there on the couch till breakfast time? You look awful this morning."

Floria and Vinnie were emptying ash trays, picking up glasses, straightening the room. They both looked around as we came in, and Vinnie said, "Good morning," to us each in turn. Floria dumped the contents of an ash tray into a plastic container and turned her back on us.

"You might have let me know you were coming over here," Paul said.

Floria did not glance his way. "I looked in on you, and you were sound asleep. I thought you'd prefer to rest. I couldn't sleep and I felt I might be useful over here."

Vinnie picked up a tray filled with glasses and started toward the door. "I'll go get breakfast started. Looks like everybody's going to be early this morning. Mr. Charles is already up."

When Vinnie had gone, Paul went to Floria, took an ash tray out of her hands and set it aside. Then he turned her toward the light that fell through one tall French door.

"Elise is dead," he said. "Perhaps it's a good thing. Charles thinks so. Maybe we'd better be as honest. Even though you were her sister, you never knew half what I knew about her. You never knew—"

"Oh, yes I did!" Floria cried. "I knew she had you hypnotized, for one thing. I knew—"

I did not want to listen. Whatever she had to say lay between her and Paul, and I left them to hurry across the hall. From upstairs came the sound of a door opening. I went to the foot of the stairs and looked up as Giles came out of his room. He wore a maroon-colored robe, and he had showered, so that his hair lay damply back from his forehead.

At the same moment Richard came running along the upstairs hall from the direction of Elise's room, still in his pajamas.

"Where is she?" he demanded of his father. "I've thought of something I have to ask her, but she's not in her room, and her bed hasn't been slept in. Was she really sick last night? Was that why Dr. Lane came—to send her away to the hospital?"

Giles went to his son and picked him up in his arms. "We'll have to talk about that. Let's go into my room and talk about it now."

I watched them disappear in the direction of Giles's room. My legs were uncertain under me and I let myself slide down along a baluster until I was sitting on the bottom step. The air seemed suddenly cold and I put both arms around my body and tried to hold myself still. Vinnie came into the hall and saw me there. In a moment she had gone to the coat rack near the door and pulled a jacket from a hook. She flung it around my shoulders and buttoned the top button under my chin. It was something she had done for me often as a child, and I accepted her kindly touch with gratitude.

"Richard is with his father," I said. "Giles is telling him now."

Vinnie stepped back to look at me. "Then I reckon you got to be brave, Miss Lacey. He's a tough little boy. More than you'd think. Sometimes kids come through better than grown-ups do. So don't you go all to pieces now."

"Thank you, Vinnie. Perhaps I'm a coward. I'm glad I don't have to tell him."

"Me neither," Vinnie agreed and went back to the business of getting breakfast.

Floria and Paul came out of the parlor looking thoroughly unstrung, and saw me sitting there.

I spoke before either could ask a question. "Giles is talking to Richard."

Floria stiffened. "Well—it has to be done."

"Floria," I said, "don't tell Richard that horrible accusation you made against me last night. Will you promise me that, at least?"

She stared at me, her expression stony with distrust.

Paul spoke to her curtly. "Give her your promise. Your mother would ask you the same thing."

"Oh, all right," Floria answered, with an edge to her voice. "I'll keep still for now. But you'd better leave the boy alone, Lacey. If you start making over him—" She broke off and turned away.

So one woman who threatened had been exchanged for another! It would seem that Floria meant to pick up where her sister had left off. But I could not worry about this now. I could only think of the ordeal that faced Giles in his bedroom upstairs, and of the suffering Richard must face at too young an age.

We did not hear Aunt Amalie as she came to the head of the stairs, and when I looked up and saw her there I was shocked. She looked frail and white and ill as she clung to the post, holding her rose-colored robe about her.

"Mother!" Floria cried. "You shouldn't be up! You belong in bed."

Aunt Amalie paid no attention. "Where is Charles?"

"He's gone for a walk," Paul said. "Just down the drive. Do you want me to get him for you?"

She drew a hand across her sleep-drugged eyes and tried to thrust back her shoulders in the old courageous way. "Never mind. Is Giles up yet?"

"He's with Richard in his room," Floria said. "He's telling the boy about Élise."

For a moment I thought Aunt Amalie would run along the hall toward Giles's room. Then she put a hand on the newel post and steadied herself.

"I mustn't," she said. "I must leave them alone. This is a task for his father to face."

"Perhaps we shouldn't all be here when they come out of Giles's room," I said. "We shouldn't stand here as if we were waiting to see what happens, waiting to see how he takes it."

Aunt Amalie looked down at me sadly. "You're quite right, Lacey. I'll come downstairs and perhaps Vinnie will give me a cup of coffee."

But she had no more than set her foot on the top step when the door of Giles's room opened and the boy and his father came into the hall. Richard walked ahead and Giles came after him. The boy's face was strangely blank, perhaps with shock or disbelief. He did not seem to see us, but walked past the head of the stairs. I thought he would go by Aunt Amalie without being aware that she was there. Giles looked worse than Richard did. His face was drawn, his eyes sick with pain.

It was Aunt Amalie who broke first. She ran to Richard and went down on her knees before him, her rosy gown flowing about her as she took him into her arms.

"It's all right to cry," she said. "Don't look like that! Let go, darling. Let go and let the tears come."

He thrust himself back from her with the touching dignity of the young. "I shan't cry," he said. "I'm going to go and get dressed now. After breakfast I am going into Malvern to see her."

Aunt Amalie sank back on her heels and covered her face with her hands. Richard paused to touch her lightly on one shoulder.

"It's all right if *you* cry," he said kindly, and went across the hallway to his room.

Tears were burning my own eyelids and I blinked them back. Floria ran to her mother and put an arm about her, drew her to her feet.

"Come along, dear. Come downstairs and I'll get you that coffee."

Aunt Amalie looked past her to Giles. "How did he take it? Why is he so stony cold?"

"I don't know." Giles shook his head unhappily. "He seems to be holding back something that troubles him. He listened to me with all his attention, and no show of emotion at all. Perhaps he's too shocked to understand what has happened."

Floria and her mother came down the stairs, and Paul went with them into the dining room. I left my post at the foot of the stairs and wandered into the library, where I could be alone. I felt shaken and inwardly torn. Richard must mourn for a mother who was not truly his mother, and I who was a mother by right of birth could not go to him as Aunt Amalie had done and try to comfort him. If he rejected her as his grandmother, how much more readily he would reject me. I could not even go upstairs and talk to Giles as I wanted so much to do.

In the library I dropped into Charles's big lounge chair and stared blankly at the painting of marsh fires burning. Outdoors birds were singing in the oleander bushes and the island was being reborn freshly beneath the early morning sun. But a new day brought no lessening of pain. Elise's death had ended her restless life, but it had ended nothing else. There was still the threat of Floria's words hanging over me. There was the threat Hadley Rikers had made against Giles. If there had been physical violence in the form of the unexpected thrust of an arm, or a blow in the darkness, then injury to Elise had been intended. If that stone in the wall had been deliberately loosened, then the injury must have been meant for me. In either case, the person who had done the harm was alive and very much among us.

Charles came into the room so quietly that I did not see him until he went to Giles's desk. Nor did he notice me in the dark shadow of the corner chair. He opened a drawer and stood looking down at something it contained. Tentatively, he reached in a hand as if he meant to take some object from the drawer. Then he closed it and stepped back. He saw me then, though he gave no start of surprise.

"Hello, Lacey. You look as though you've had very little sleep. Perhaps breakfast will help a little. Vinnie says it's nearly ready."

"I'm not hungry," I said.

He regarded me calmly. "It's natural to feel that way. But we must all eat to keep up our strength. There are difficult days ahead. For the sake of the outside world, we will have to play a role, however false. There are only two of us who will really grieve."

"Aunt Amalie," I said.

"Yes."

"And who else?"

"Paul, of course," he told me. "Didn't you feel it in him this morning when we met outside the house? Though he's trying to hide his feelings so that Floria won't guess. But she knows, naturally. Amalie is worried about Floria."

"And about Richard," I said, and told him of what had happened, and of the boy's curiously blank reaction.

"It will work out in time," Charles assured me. "Floria's our trouble spot now. But don't worry, my dear. In spite of the wild things she says, Amalie will control her. If only Amalie doesn't give way under the strain. If she's downstairs, I'll look for her."

Instead of going into the house, however, he went out upon the veranda by way of a French door. As soon as I was alone in the library I moved to Giles's desk and opened the drawer.

The gun lay half covered by a sheaf of papers, black and compact and deadly. I knew nothing about guns, but I felt about them somewhat the way I felt about snakes. It was not unusual for a weapon of this sort to be kept in a locked drawer in as lonely a place as Sea Oaks, but it filled me with a strange dread. It was as though the object in the drawer had the power to coil and strike out at me like a snake.

"I thought I heard Charles in here," said Aunt Amalie's voice from the doorway behind me.

"He went out on the veranda looking for you," I told her.

Aunt Amalie saw the gun. She reached past me to shut the drawer, and then looked about for the key.

"It's dangerous to leave it like that," she said. "You never know with a child about. I must ask Giles to keep the drawer locked. It's unlike him to forget."

"Are you feeling better?" I asked.

"I *must* feel better. There's so much to do. I'll go find Charles now. Do have some breakfast, Lacey."

She sounded brittle with tension and I knew that only her courage, her will, kept her going. It came to me that she was worried about more than Elise's death. She was worried about someone in this house who was close to her.

When she hurried out of the room, I followed more slowly.

Several days had gone by. Days of gray skies and a good deal of rain. Fortunately, the weather had cleared up in time for the funeral. All had gone smoothly, in so far as there had been no breakdowns, no explosions, no sudden outbursts of accusation. The police were long out of the affair. Hadley Rikers did not come to the funeral, and he had not been seen again about the island. Floria held her tongue. Charles was properly grave, yet I felt that a slight smile sometimes hovered at the corners of his lips. Of us all, only Charles seemed to hold the conviction that, granted healing time, all would be well.

Aunt Amalie managed to keep herself going, and at the proscribed hour Elise was put to rest in the small island cemetery which had superseded the old burying ground. All her wild restlessness lay forever quieted beneath a leaning pine tree, and at Sea Oaks and The Bitterns the effort to continue life in a new pattern had begun.

Richard remained the same strange little boy he had become after Elise's death, and there seemed nothing anyone could do for him. He was oddly polite to all of us, and there were no wild escapades. Yet I had the sense that some struggle went on within him. It was all wrong, of course. He should have let whatever he was feeling come through. He should have mourned openly for the woman he believed was his mother. Aunt Amalie did her best to break through the barrier Richard held against us all, but he avoided her, slipped away from her whenever it was possible. Neither she nor his father had been able to penetrate his new, strange guard. The same

cold blankness with which he had greeted the news of Elise's
death lay upon him, and he chose to go off by himself a great
deal of the time, refusing any offer of company or comrade-
ship. If anything, he was coolest of all toward his father.

I knew that the time had come for me to go home to New
York. There could be no point in my staying longer. The rain
was over, and this sunny Saturday afternoon I was in my
room packing. I had not yet told Aunt Amalie that I planned
to leave the next day. Nor had I told Giles. Aunt Amalie
would no longer try to hold me here, I felt sure. And between
Giles and me there was an artificial restraint put upon us by
Elise's death. Time must pass. A great deal of time must
pass before we could turn to each other. And during that time
the problem of Richard must be solved. The boy could not go
on like this. A breaking point would come. Perhaps it would
be better if I was away from Sea Oaks when it happened.
Better for me—since I could do nothing but stand by and
watch.

I had just folded a sweater listlessly and laid it in my suitcase, when a raised voice reached me from beyond my door—
Floria shouting in anger. There was no response that I could
hear on the part of another person.

I went to the door and opened it.

"Oh, how could you, how could you! You're a wicked
boy!" Floria's voice came from her sister's room, and this
time I heard an answer.

"She's gone," Richard said, his tone so soft and deadly that
it chilled me. "She's gone, and these things should be gone
too."

I ran down the hall to Elise's room and looked inside. Both
Floria and Richard were on their hands and knees beside a
great box of snapshots, photographs and papers that had
spilled out all over the floor. Richard held a long pair of
shears in one hand, and as I stepped into the room he
snatched up a photograph of Elise and slashed it in two with
the flashing blades.

Floria reached out to twist the scissors from his hand, and
shook him angrily by one shoulder. The boy's face was white
as he stumbled to his feet and stood looking at her.

"Don't do that," he said in the same low, deadly tone.
"Don't touch me like that, or maybe you'll be dead too."

Floria glared at him. "What you've got coming to you is a
good spanking, and if your father or grandmother won't give

it to you, then one of these days I will. You've no business destroying your mother's things. It's wicked of you!"

Richard returned her look insolently. "Why should you care? You didn't like her, did you? I should think you'd be glad I'm doing this."

His words must have taken her by surprise, for her face worked strangely, and I knew Richard had touched a point of new sensitivity in her. Perhaps there was a sense of guilt in Floria because of her feelings about her sister when she was alive. Perhaps that accounted for her over-reaction now.

An impasse had been reached between them. Richard broke it with another darting gesture, and came up from the box with a second photograph in his hand.

"Don't!" I said. "Richard, don't!"

My presence surprised him so that he hesitated, and Floria wrested the picture from him. For an instant I thought he might fly at her as she had done with him, then the gloom of despair seemed to come over him and he stood back from the wreckage on the floor, all the passion gone from him, and the dreadful blank look in place again.

I went directly to him and took him by the hand. "Come outside with me," I said. "Come for a walk with me."

"Good!" Floria cried. "Get him out of my sight while I put this mess of stuff back together again. He's only cut up a few things. I'll pack the rest away. But this isn't to be passed up lightly. His father will have to do something about it."

Richard's hand lay limply in mine, yet when I gave it a slight tug, he came with me. He would not stop of his own accord, but he was willing to be stopped from his destructive course by someone else. This was the time to talk to him.

We went downstairs in silence and saw no one on the way. I kept a firm hold on Richard's hand, lest he dart away from me, but he gave no sign of interest in making any sort of move. He came with me docilely, his face blank of all emotion.

"Let's go over near the marsh," I said. "Let's get away from the house."

He spoke only once on the way across the burying ground toward the open land near The Bitterns.

"I won't let him spank me," he said.

"Perhaps he won't want to, once he understands why you were cutting up Elise's pictures."

We reached the grassy bank just above where the marsh

began and I sat on the grass and drew Richard down beside me.

"This is a good place to come to when you're feeling stormy," I said. "Remember the time you found me here?"

"I don't feel stormy," he told me. "I don't feel anything."

I had released his hand, knowing that he would not run away from me now, but I took it again and held it lightly. He did not resist.

"Sometimes it helps to talk," I said. "It helps to release all the things that are bothering us. I don't believe that you aren't feeling anything. Perhaps it would be better if you could talk to your father—"

"He's not my father," Richard said.

I kept very still for a few moments, too shocked to speak. What had happened? What damage had Elise done before she died?

"Why do you say that?" I asked at last. "Of course he's your father."

Richard twined his fingers into a clump of long grass and pulled it out by the roots, flung it down the bank toward the marsh. Then he looked at me in a strange, frightened way, and when he spoke it was not about his father.

"I killed her, you know. It's my fault that she fell on those rocks and died."

"Oh, Richard," I said softly, "of course you didn't kill her. You were nowhere about. You were hiding in the oak tree. It doesn't help to make up things like that to torment yourself."

"I'm not making it up. I was in the oak tree, and I was wishing her dead. I was wishing it as hard as I could. And she fell and died. So it was my fault."

I looked into the small white face beside me and saw that his lips were working and his eyes had filled with tears. The blankness had dissolved, but this was a terrible thing he believed, and it was not to be lightly dismissed, however fantastic.

"Sometimes we all wish injury to someone else when we're angry and upset. But we don't really mean it when we're quiet again. And just wishing has never made it so."

He threw me a quick look, as though he wanted to reach for the hope I held out to him. Then he shook his head grimly in disbelief.

"Perhaps you can tell me about it," I said.

Silently he yanked up another handful of grass, and this

time he spread the blades out on the ground beside him, as
if he sorted them. I watched him at his concentrated, mean-
ingless work. A long time seemed to pass, and then suddenly,
in a burst of words which came out so quickly that I was
hard put to keep up with them, he began to tell me what had
happened.

After Elise had called him downstairs the night of the ball,
and sent him with a message to Hadley Rikers, Richard had
found him and told him that Elise was waiting in the trophy
room. Then, curious as any small boy, he had slipped outside
and gone along the veranda until he could hide himself in the
shadows just outside the French door to the room where they
were meeting.

From his words, I could reconstruct what he had seen, as
though I had been there. I could look into that small square
room with its lighted glass cases, its display of past equestrian
triumphs. I could see Hadley come into the room in his
hunter's dress, and take Guinevere in his arms.

Richard had watched in shock and indignation. He had a
sense of propriety toward Elise, and an utter loyalty to his
father. When Hadley began to kiss her intimately, Richard
had been possessed of a wild, thoroughly male anger. An
anger made up in good part, perhaps, of jealousy. He rushed
into the room and attacked Hadley with all the strength in
his slender body. He punched and kicked fiercely, while
Hadley held him off, laughing.

Elise did not laugh. She was as furious as Richard. She
jerked the boy away from his attack and slapped him full
across the face. At the moment, I think Richard hardly felt
the slap. All his attention was upon Hadley.

"I'm going to call my father!" he shouted. "He won't let
you kiss my mother!"

This fully intended threat must have been the last thing
Elise wanted. Her angers were uncontrollable, once risen, and
she gave full head to her own impulse. She put both hands on
Richard's shoulders and shook him until his head snapped
back.

"You listen to me!" she cried. "I'm not your mother. I
never have been. I'm not your mother at all!"

This time her words penetrated the red haze of his anger.
He stood suddenly quiet beneath her hands.

"What did you say?" he asked her.

This was not the way she had meant to tell him, but she
must have been beyond caring.

"I'm not your mother," she repeated. "I was going to tell you the truth tomorrow, but I've told you now instead. And I'll tell you something else you may not like—"

If he had stayed to listen, perhaps she would have blurted out the truth about me. But Richard had heard enough. He bolted from the room—out the French door and around the veranda to the wide portico at the front of the house. There he climbed into the first hiding place that offered—the low, strong branch of the live oak that overhung the balustrade.

Hadley came looking for him, and walked up and down the veranda calling to the boy. Richard kept very still in his hidden shelter. Elise did not look for him at all. Perhaps she was still beyond caring about what she had done. Perhaps she was already thinking of what she would say to Giles when she confronted him on the beach. Perhaps she even meant to tell him the truth about Richard that night.

Beside me now, my son huddled on the grass, rocking himself back and forth with his arms clasped about his knees. Before us, stretching endlessly along the river, the marshes lay dreaming in the sun, and a heron waded where the water was shallow.

Richard went on again, his voice low, with no longer any hurry in it. "She wasn't my mother at all. She only pretended to be my mother. Ever since I was a baby she pretended."

I spoke softly. "And because of that, for a little while you hated her?"

He nodded, ducking his head. "I wished she was dead. I wished she could be punished for fooling me."

"Feeling like that is understandable," I said. "But now you don't have to go on hating her. And you have to realize that whatever you thought you were wishing at the time, your thoughts couldn't hurt her. She fell because she tripped on her dress. Or because a stone was loose in the wall. Only because of something like that."

He looked at me with bleak hope, and I knew I must give him whatever I could.

"You have to remember that when she told you this, she was angry too. Like you, she said and thought things she didn't mean. But she raised you from the time when you were a baby. She loved you and you loved her. Which is what being a mother and son really means. Now that you're not angry any more, you can go on loving her."

There was a film of tears in his eyes, but he blinked it away before they could fall. "If she wasn't really my mother, then *he* isn't my father either. He—"

"That's not true," I said quickly. "That's not true at all. You have only to look at your own face in the mirror to know that you are Giles Severn's son. You've got his eyes—the very same green color. And you look alike around the mouth. Even your hair grows back in the same way, though yours is a different color."

This time the tears spilled over, and I let him cry. He sat looking away from me across the marsh, with tears streaming down his face, and now and then a small sob punctuating his weeping. After a time, I found a clean handkerchief in my slacks pocket and handed it to him.

He took it was a strange politeness. "Thank you, Cousin Lacey."

I wished that I could tell him to stop being grown up and brave. I wished I could hold out my arms to him, so that he would come into them and cry himself out. But he did not know me well enough. It had to be sufficient for me that I had offered him comfort, that I had been able to break through that cold, deadly guard he had held against the world to conceal not only his terrible hurt, but what he regarded as his own blame.

When there were only a few tears left, I stood up. "You must talk to your grandmother about this," I said. "She will help you to understand."

Once more he shook his head. "She isn't my grandmother. She is *her* mother—so she's not my grandmother at all."

"You mustn't look at it that way," I told him firmly. "My Aunt Amalie is as much your grandmother as a real grandmother could be. You know how much she loves you. You mustn't hurt her by saying things like that."

Again he seemed to take comfort from my words. He stood up beside me, the tear streaks drying on his cheeks, and we began to walk slowly back toward the burying ground. Under our feet the sandy soil was brown with puffy seed balls from the sweet gums, and the loblolly pines whispered high over our heads.

When we neared the old tombs, Richard seemed to come to himself, and to make an effort. "I haven't looked for the pirate brooch for a long time. Wait for me, Cousin Lacey, and I'll go down there now."

I waited in a place where sunlight fell through the trees and warmed me. My nerves felt as though they had been

pulled as tight as racket strings. I didn't know how I would
ever loosen them again. But at least I had given my son
what little I could. I seemed to have stopped wanting so much
so greedily. What I wanted now was Richard's well-being.
What I wanted was to see him grow up without the strains
that Elise had put upon him.

"Cousin Lacey! Cousin Lacey!" Richard came running up
into sunlight from the black cave of the big tomb. In his
hands he held the box that had once harbored the brooch.
"Cousin Lacey, the pirate brooch is here! Someone has put
it back!"

He opened the box for me to see, and there upon crumbling, yellowed tissue lay a great winking green gem. Sunlight
splintered in its faceted sides and shone from the gleaming
gold in which it was set. All around the central stone smaller
diamonds glittered, but the emerald held sway.

"Someone put it back," Richard repeated. "I must show
Grandfather Charles right away. Come with me, Cousin
Lacey."

I could have blessed the stone and whoever had slipped it
back into its hiding place. This was the final touch to make
Richard himself again. He would not be free from the pain
of losing Elise, but now he could permit himself to be distracted from pain, as a child should be.

When I would have started toward the house, however, he
drew back, suddenly hesitant, as though he had something
further on his mind.

"What is it?" I asked.

He looked at me almost shyly. "I'm sorry about that time
at the house."

"I don't know what you mean," I admitted.

"My moth—*she* wanted me to do it to upset you. So I hid
that other brooch in your things. I—I wouldn't do it now,
Cousin Lacey."

I gave him a quick hug. "I know you wouldn't. But thank
you for telling me, Richard."

His smile had a certain sweetness in it, and we walked back
to the house in comradely fashion. We were friends.

As we hurried up one curving flight of steps and went inside, Floria met us at the foot of the stairs. Her expression
was stiff with disapproval, but a lifetime of released emotion
had intervened with Richard since his Aunt Floria had shaken
him a little while ago. For the moment he had forgotten what
had happened.

"Look!" he cried, and held out the box to her. "Someone has put back the pirate brooch."

She had the intelligence to sense the change in him, and she did not mention his destructive actions of a little while before. She took the box and stared as I had stared at the fabulous green stone in the brooch. Then she gave the box back to him.

"Your grandfather and grandmother will be pleased. Let's go show it to them right away."

Aunt Amalie was upstairs, lying down. Her bedroom door was open, and Charles was standing near a window. Richard ran into the room, exclaiming in his excitement as he carried the box to his grandfather.

Charles turned from the window as Floria and I watched, and took the brooch carefully from the box, the smile breaking slowly across his face. He carried the brooch to Amalie and held it out to her.

"Look what Richard has brought us," he said.

Aunt Amalie turned her head listlessly upon the pillow. She looked at the brooch without interest and closed her eyes.

Charles seemed to understand. "Oh, I know it can't matter a great deal to you now, my dear. But it matters to me. Not merely because of its value, but because it is a symbol of the island and both our families. Besides, finding it clears the air. It doesn't matter who put it back, so long as it has been returned."

"I haven't looked out there for several days," Richard put in eagerly. "I just remembered this afternoon—and there it was."

Aunt Amalie was more interested in the boy than in the brooch. She held out her hand to him. "You're feeling better, aren't you, darling?"

He threw me a quick look. "I—I don't want to talk about it," he said.

I understood his look. There was a pleading in it. He did not want to face the emotional strain of telling his grandmother what he had told me. She would make over him, undoubtedly, and perhaps she would weaken his hard-won courage. The hurt and strain of readjustment still lay ahead of him, and he would need all the help he could get. I would talk to her myself. I would try to pave the way for the understanding and love that must now be given him by those he loved. It must not be an overwhelming, smothering affection, but a warmth that would both enfold him and leave him free. What was more, before I left the island tomorrow I must tell Giles what I had gone to the beach to tell him the night of the ball. I must tell him soon. I would tell him tonight. The things Richard had said had released me, as well.

Aunt Amalie accepted Richard's words without argument. Now that all the things which had been required of her were done, she had fallen into apathy. She, too, must be given time to recover.

Floria spoke from the doorway behind me, her interest still upon the emerald brooch. "Who could have put it back in that box? Who could have taken it in the first place—and why?"

"As I say, it doesn't matter so long as we've recovered it," Charles told her with a slight impatience in his tone.

"Elise put it back," Aunt Amalie said wearily from the bed.

We turned to stare at her, and she went on, her eyes closed again, as though she could barely summon strength to tell us what she knew.

"It was Elise who found the brooch in the first place," she went on in the same dry-as-dust voice. "She was keeping it for the night of the ball, though I didn't know she had it until she was in her costume. She wore it beneath the bodice of her gown. I saw it when she showed it to me. She told me that she would wear it for an hour and then put it back in the tomb and leave it for Richard to find. That's what she must have done. It wasn't on her later, and I haven't thought about it again till now."

"But—but why—?" Charles said blankly.

It was Floria who answered. "It's easy to guess that. She wanted it because of the legend. She always laughed at the story, but underneath she was superstitious enough. Don't you remember, Charles? Whoever wears that brooch secretly at the Camelot ball is supposed to be assured forever of her true love's love. Goodness knows who Elise wanted. Giles? Hadley? Someone else?"

"Please, Floria!" Aunt Amalie roused herself. "Remember the boy."

Richard had been listening and watching in silence, his eyes wide with too avid an interest.

"She didn't want my father," he told them in a voice as dry as his grandmother's, and I knew remembrance was upon him. He was thinking of Hadley Rikers holding Elise in his arms. I put a comforting hand on his shoulder.

"It doesn't matter now," Charles put in smoothly. "What I don't understand is how Elise could have found the brooch in the first place, without some clue. Richard might find such a spot by accident, but it's unlikely—"

Aunt Amalie broke in on his words and for once there was a note of impatience in her voice as she spoke to her husband.

"You've forgotten, Charles. You can be such an innocent. You told me where it might be hidden."

For an instant something like resentment flashed in Charles's eyes. Then he was his benign self again.

"I remember very well that I told only you what Lacey had said about the mailing place where Kitty might have left the brooch. I told only you that it was in the tomb and that Lacey and I meant to search for it the next morning."

Aunt Amalie sighed wearily. "And I told Elise. Later I suspected that she must have the brooch, but she only laughed at me when I asked her, and I didn't know for sure until the night of the ball."

"I see," Charles said. "Not that it wasn't your right to tell whom you pleased, since the brooch belongs to both our families. But I would have hoped—"

"I'm sorry," Amalie said. "It's too late, but I'm sorry."

"Much good it did her—wearing the brooch!" said Floria with scorn in her voice.

Charles looked at Richard. "Will you come and help me? I'm going to put the brooch back in its place of honor downstairs."

Again Richard was able to accept distraction, and he went willingly out the door with his grandfather.

"Is there anything I can do for you, Mother?" Floria said to the woman on the bed.

Aunt Amalie smiled at her half-heartedly. "No, dear. If you'll leave us alone, I'd like to talk with Lacey for a few moments."

Floria gave me a look that was faintly suspicious and went out of the room. I pulled a chair close to the bed and sat down in it. Aunt Amalie's eyes were open now, and when Floria had gone, she spoke to me.

"What has happened to Richard?"

I told her the full story. I began with the scene Floria had made when he was cutting up Elise's pictures. I told her how Richard and I had gone outside together and had our talk. She listened quietly, and only gasped softly when I related

how Richard had attacked Hadley Rikers when Elise went
into his arms.

"Elise lost her temper and told him he was not her son," I
finished. "She pulled everything down in an emotional crash,
so that he ran away and hid. The next thing he knew she was
dead, and he blamed himself because he had been wishing
that something terrible would happen to her."

Aunt Amalie sat up on the bed. "How dreadful! I must go
and have a talk with him at once. He'll need to be comforted,
and—"

"No!" I said. "Not right away. Let him be, for now. I've
already talked to him as well as I could."

"I suppose you told him that you—"

"Of course I didn't tell him. He needs to recover Elise
right now, not have someone else thrust upon him."

She lay back on the bed. "Thank you, Lacey. You've done
the right thing."

"Eventually he may ask about his real mother," I said.
"But perhaps not for a long time. He may not want to know.
He may be afraid to know. It's better to let him remember
his happier times with Elise for the present. He needs time
to grow strong by himself. Perhaps if you could lean on him
a little, let him comfort *you*—?"

"Yes," she said. "Yes, Lacey. I'll try. You're being wiser
than I ever thought you could be. Now tell me about your
plans."

"I'm going home tomorrow. I've stayed long enough."

"I suppose you must do that. What about Giles?"

"He seems a long way off," I confessed. "We can't run to
each other with Elise only just—gone."

"Yes, it will be best if you leave as soon as you can. It
isn't safe for you here any more."

I already knew that, but I was surprised that she would
admit it.

"Can you accept my word now?" I asked. "Accept my word
against Floria's?"

She closed her eyes briefly, as if in pain, and then looked
directly at me. "I think I always have accepted the truth,
Lacey. I fought against you because Floria is my daughter.
But I know her tendency toward exaggeration. And Paul was
there at the time to tell what he had seen. I'll be glad when
they are married. Perhaps it will be soon now, with Elise no
longer—" She broke off.

I was still for a few moments. I think she wanted me to leave her alone. I think my presence caused her to be restless and uneasy. But in a little while I would be gone, and I would not know any of the answers. Whether that would be for the best or not, I didn't know.

"I don't think anyone meant Elise's death," I told her. "No matter what anyone found the next day, there was a stone in the wall that was loose the night of the ball. It was loosened because *I* was going down to the beach that way. It was loosened because someone—"

Aunt Amalie came out of her apathy in a flash. All her normal energy flowed back into her body and she pulled herself into a sitting position on the edge of the bed.

"Hush, Lacey! Don't say anything more. I don't want to hear what you have to say. I only want the island to be peaceful and safe—the way it used to be. When you're gone from it, it will be quiet again. I know that now. I should never have let you come in the first place."

"Then you must feel sure that what happened to Elise was intended for me," I said mercilessly.

"I don't feel sure of anything!" Her denial was vehement. "But you mustn't stay any longer. You must get away before anything else happens. And you must never come back to the island."

I sat watching her quietly, appraising and measuring her. Of course it would be a mistake to appeal to Aunt Amalie. While Elise was alive she had been torn between the anguished love she felt for her unpredictable daughter, and her old affection for me, her sister's child. Now Elise had died because of something that had been intended for me—and it would be more than could be humanly expected to ask her to endure the sight of me any longer. Every time she looked at me she must suffer and remember. But there was more to it than that. Aunt Amalie belonged to the island. She belonged to those who lived here. And she would protect any one of them from the outsider who might come in to destroy. I could not bear to think who had loosened that stone, and perhaps she could not either. Or perhaps she knew very well, and would live in silence with that knowledge to the day of her death. She would know only that I must not be allowed to threaten those who remained.

I left my chair and put a light hand on her shoulder, bent to kiss her cheek. "Don't worry, dear. I won't come back. And I'll not ask any more questions."

She made an effort then. She touched my hand where it rested on her shoulder and looked up at me, her eyes tear-filled. But she could not speak. She could not find anything to say to me.

I left her there and went out of the room. From downstairs I could hear Charles's voice, and Richard's answering. They were discussing the proper way to display the recovered brooch, as though everything was perfectly normal. This was the beginning of the mending that must always take place after a death, when life begins to go on in the old way, with overtones of the new.

I did not go downstairs to join them. I went back to my room. There was still one person with whom I must talk. I would seek Giles out right after dinner tonight.

I did not go downstairs to dine with the others that night. I told Vinnie that I wasn't feeling very well—which was true enough—and she brought me a light supper on a tray in my room. An hour later I went down to the library to meet Giles. Vinnie had carried a message to him from me, and brought back word that he would see me there after dinner.

The others were gathered in the parlor and I could hear voices as I went past. Aunt Amalie had come downstairs, and Charles and Floria were with her. They did not see me as I went past the doors, and I was glad to step into the quiet of the library without being stopped.

A single lamp burned beside Charles's empty armchair. The rest of the room crowded dimly around that one focus of light, with springtime darkness pressing blue-gray beyond the open French doors to the veranda.

The library was empty—or so I thought—and I went directly to Giles's desk and pulled the knob of the upper right-hand drawer. To my relief, it was locked. If I had found it open, I would have called it to Giles's attention myself. The sight of that gun lying where Richard could so easily reach it, had left me unnerved.

"Are you looking for something, Lacey?" Paul's voice said from down the room.

I looked around, to see that he had emerged from shadows near the front windows, and I wondered why he was in here, and not with the others. Even by shaded lamplight he did not look well, and I knew that he must still be having a difficult time accepting Elise's death.

211

"I wanted to make sure that drawer was locked," I said. "It was open earlier in the day."

He seemed to make nothing of that. "I hear that you and Richard have recovered the missing brooch," Paul said. "The boy is full of the story. It seems to have brought him out of his state of apathy."

"Yes," I said. "Apparently Elise had it all along."

But my thoughts were no longer solely on the matter of the brooch. I was trying to formulate in my mind the things I must say to Giles, and I did not want to talk to Paul now. Like me, he was an outsider, and I was concerned tonight only with those who belonged to the island. I wished he would join the others and leave me to meet Giles alone.

"Floria doesn't know I'm here," he said unexpectedly.

"Weren't you with them for dinner?" I asked in surprise.

He shook his head. "I'm waiting for Charles to go for the evening walk he often takes. I can see him from the windows if he goes down the drive. I'll join them then."

My attention was still upon my own affairs and I was not particularly curious as to what Paul might want with Charles in a meeting that avoided Floria.

Paul moved back to his post at a front window and a moment later he said, "There's Charles now," and went quickly onto the veranda.

I found a place in a chair where the light would not fall upon me too brightly, and waited for Giles. I did not want to sit on the sofa, with him beside me tonight. I must have him well beyond arm's length when I talked to him.

But we were not at arm's length for long when he came into the room. He drew me out of my chair and into his arms at once, and I went to him gladly. For a few moments I could cling to him.

"Darling," he said, "We've been too far apart for the last few days. This is where you belong."

"I'm going back to New York tomorrow," I told him. He made a sound of protest, but I went on quickly. "You know I must. There's nothing to do but wait now—though not here on the island. Giles, when I go this time, I can never return."

He held me away where he could look into my face. "That's nonsense, of course. You'll come here to live, eventually. I'm afraid we must wait for a while. But in the long run Sea Oaks will be your home, as it is mine. You've always loved the island. Now you will live here for good."

I turned away from him and went to my chair. "I had to

talk to you tonight. I need to make you understand a number of things. Sit down and listen to me, Giles."

My tone arrested his attention. He went to the sofa and sat looking at me, suddenly grave.

Quickly I recalled to his mind the things that had happened to me since I had come to the island. For the first time I told him that I thought someone had tried to injure me deliberately that afternoon at Bellevue, when a great chunk of tabby had fallen upon me. I spoke of the loose stone in the sea wall, and of how I had gone to the beach the next morning, only to find it wedged firmly in place. Undoubtedly by someone who did not want it known that it had ever been loose. I told him of Hadley Rikers finding me there, and of the accusation he had made.

"I don't think he will try to do anything," I said. "But he's suspicious and it's best to quiet that suspicion by having me go away. In time perhaps all the talk will die down. Anyway, I must get away from the island and I must stay away. Someone here has a deep hatred for me, and I think it will be worse since Elise's death. I don't know why—or who it is. Perhaps it's best if I never know."

"Do you think I could live in peace with someone who wanted to harm you?" he said. "If this is really fact, and not just anxious fancy, then it should be uncovered. Whoever is behind such actions should be exposed, no matter what the consequences are. You must be able to come back here to live, Lacey. There's no other way."

I knew I could never come back. But there was more I had to tell him. There was the most difficult part of all. There was no immediate chance, however, because Floria burst into the room, looking thoroughly distraught.

"Vinnie said Paul was here," she announced, glancing quickly about. "Have you seen him?"

"He was in the room a few moments ago," I said. "He was waiting to see Charles, and I think he's gone for a walk with him."

"I'll go after them," Floria said. She started toward the door, and then swung about abruptly. "Are you leaving soon, Lacey?"

"Tomorrow," I said.

She gave me a look that was somehow spiteful. "And high time too!"

"But she'll be back," Giles put in. "She'll be back as soon as I'm able to bring her here."

Floria turned her look of spite on him for an instant, and then spoke to me again. "Have you told Giles your big secret yet?"

A chill touched me. I knew what she meant and I could not answer.

"Lacey has been telling me a number of things," Giles said.

"I mean about Richard," Floria went on deliberately. "Because it's time you knew, Giles, and if she hasn't told you, I will. Richard was not Elise's son. He belongs to Lacey. And you. She bore him, but they all took part in fooling you from the start. I didn't know the truth until recently, but Elise and Mother and Lacey conspired to deceive you very cleverly and cruelly. There isn't any doubt about it. You've only to ask my mother. She was the one who planned the whole thing in the beginning. But your worthy, honorable Lacey went along with her plan every step of the way."

Floria stood there looking at him, taunting and malicious, her hair upon her shoulders, fluffed and fiery. There was nothing I could say. It had all been done for me, crudely, and with none of the extenuation I believed had existed, and which I'd hoped to make Giles understand. If Floria wanted to drive me away from the island for good, she had chosen the best possible way to do it.

Out of his first shock, a deep anger was beginning to stir in Giles. I could see it in his eyes, in the tightness of his mouth, hear it in the coldness of his voice.

"Is this true, Lacey?"

"Yes," I said miserably, "it's true."

Floria understood fully what he was feeling, but she could not leave well enough alone. She flung me a quick, triumphant look.

"All those wasted years, Lacey! All those years with your son—thrown away! All those years when Giles felt he must hold an empty marriage together because of the son he shared with Elise. A boy who wasn't Elise's son at all!"

Giles made a sound of mingled pain and anger, and I could not bear any more. As I knew all too well, he hated dishonesty more than anything else. He could not bear anyone who cheated and deceived him. Near my chair a veranda door stood open. I jumped up and ran outside.

The night was cool, the stars bright in patches of sky above the live oaks. I could not fling myself into the branches of an oak tree to hide, as Richard had done, but the night waited for me, offered me concealment. I ran down the steps and along the path that led away from the white shell drive toward the burying ground. I could not bear the house for a moment longer. I could not bear the sound of Floria's spiteful voice. Above all, I could not endure the look on Giles's face. Only darkness and crowding trees could shelter me until I could gather my forces, summon a few last shreds of courage, and face what had to be faced. I had always known how angry he would be. I had always been afraid to tell him. What I had done so long ago would be, in his eyes, unforgivable.

In a few moments I had found my way into that dark place of sweet gums and pines and live oaks. The few tombs that stood among the trees were black solids, where starlight could not reach. The lights of the house were well behind me, and even the rhythmic beat of the Atlantic was hushed in this ancient place. But I was not to be allowed my dark solace for long. Through the night came the sound of footsteps following me, running in pursuit. Someone had come after me. I could not bear to face whoever it was, and I drew myself into the shadow of the largest tomb and stood waiting in utter silence.

"Lacey!" That was Floria's voice, but curiously hushed and coaxing. "Lacey, where are you? You mustn't run away from the house."

I pressed against the brick and tabby of the tomb's wall until rough shell cut into the palms of my hands.

"Are you there, Lacey?" The voice went on, false and coaxing. "I'm sorry, Lacey. I only did it for your own good. He had to know. Come with me back to the house."

Not for anything would I have stepped out of darkness into starlight. I could see her now, where she moved like a shadow among other night shadows, tall and slender and deadly.

Again and again she called me, always in that soft, whispery voice that frightened me—as though she did not want anyone else to know that she called. But she had no way of being sure that I was here, and I did not believe she had seen me.

Time seemed to stand still in the lonely grove. The night seemed no longer hushed. The very air hummed with the sounds of insects. The stars hung motionless in the dark blue sky, and no breeze stirred the leaves of the sweet gums. I dared not so much as shift my weight from one foot to another. I was desperately afraid. I could not outrun her, and I knew those strong hands which could conquer an unruly horse would hold me helpless if ever she found me. Why she hated me so much I didn't know, but her malevolence was something I could almost feel there in the darkness.

Then, quite suddenly, the tension eased. She seemed to give up. I could hear her moving away. Her tall shadow no longer stretched toward me over the ground, and I could hear a crackling under her feet as she went off in the direction of the house. I could shift my weight now, lessen the cramped pressure of my hands against the rough tabby behind me. But I still did not stir from my hiding place. I did not want to step into the open and have her come running back through the trees. For a little while I would wait where I was. I would wait until it was safe to return to the house and go upstairs to my room. The quiet of the burying ground no longer offered me the peace in which to recover a little from what Floria had done to both Giles and me.

"Lacey?"

The call came from not far away, and for an instant I stiffened again. Then the voice went on and I knew I was safe.

"You can come out now, Lacey," Aunt Amalie called. "She's gone. Come out quickly and we'll go back to the house together. She won't touch you as long as you're with me."

I pushed myself away from the cold solidity of the tomb and ran along its side and around the front.

"I'm here!" I cried. "You came just in time. I've never been so frightened—"

And then I saw her.

The whiteness of her dress stood out in a pale slash against black trees. Her face was a white oval in the starlight, and one hand was extended toward me. A lopsided moon was rising above the trees and its rays struck a glint from the thing Aunt Amalie held in her right hand. And I knew. It was not Floria I needed to fear. I knew fully and completely in a rush of acute awareness that needed no pause for reasoning. In the same instant I recognized that I stood entirely exposed only a little way from her, with fresh moonlight falling upon me, as it fell upon her.

There was just one thing to do. I stepped backward into the tomb. My foot missed the top step and I lost my balance. With my arms reaching futilely for the wall, I fell down three shallow steps and lay half stunned on the brick floor.

Her voice called to me matter-of-factly. "That was foolish, Lacey. Did you hurt yourself? Because I don't want you to hurt yourself. Not now. Not yet."

Painfully, I sat up on the cold brick floor and rubbed the
back of my head. I seemed to be all right. I seemed to be able
to move. And I was hidden by a dank and musty darkness.
From outside, she could not see me. I pulled myself up and
stepped silently toward a side wall and flattened myself against
it. She could not see me now, even if she came to the opening
to the tomb, but I was trapped here as thoroughly as it was
possible to be. There was no way out but one. The wide arch
of curving masonry rose over my head, shutting me in. The
distant back wall of the tomb was flat, without any opening.
I could creep back there into slimy darkness, but I could not
escape. For me, this might very well be my tomb.

Her voice reached me again. "Floria's gone now. She came
to rescue you from me, you know. And Paul has gone to talk
to Charles. He's been worried about Floria and me. He's
begun to suspect. Floria loves me, poor dear. She's tried to
protect me. She guessed that I'd loosened that rock the night
of the ball. She went down later that night to make sure that
it wouldn't move if anyone examined it. Not that I cared any
more. Not that I could care—when it was Elise who fell, and
not you, as I'd intended."

I had read a dreadfulness into Floria's voice, but this was
real. There was a cutting, matter-of-factness here that chilled
me inwardly, as the stones of the tomb chilled my flesh and
bones. I wanted to cry out to her. I wanted to ask her why—
why?

Without my asking, she was quite willing to tell me.

"I want you to know," she said. "This time there will be no
pranks to try to frighten you away. Like a sand dollar in your
napkin. There'll be no effort at injury that may fail—as it
failed that day at Bellevue, when I rode Mayfair around by
the wall and pushed over that block of tabby."

My breath was coming quickly, my heart pounding. Yet
there was nothing I could do. If I tried to storm out, if I
tried to rush her and get away, she would shoot me down
quite coldly. I knew that now. The gun from Giles's desk was
not locked safely away, as I had thought. It was there in Aunt
Amalie's hand.

As I waited, she ran on. "What happened at the freezing
plant that day puzzled you, didn't it? I'd warned you that you
must leave the island and never come back. That you must
never interfere when it came to Richard. But you were uncertain. You didn't know if you could keep your hands off
him. So I wanted to frighten you a little. Oh, I wouldn't have

left you inside the freezer for long. I didn't mean you serious harm. Not then. It was too bad that Richard saw me close the door. I was afraid he might say something about it. But instead, he decided that if I would do such a thing, then you must be an evil person to be punished, and he took his stand against you. It would have been better for you if he had held to that attitude."

Once she had loved me, I thought in fearful bewilderment. Once she had been kind to me, concerned about me, but at some time or other all that had changed. I had gone on seeing her as she once was, unaware of the inward change.

The light, calm voice had paused for breath. Now it went on as serenely as ever.

"Do you think I will allow the past to repeat itself? Do you think I loved my sister when she took Charles away from me? Do you think I ever forgave her? And did you think I would let *her* daughter take away *my* daughter's husband, take *my* daughter's son? Oh, of course I wanted you here. I wanted to learn what you were up to, and I wanted you to come to the island long enough to be thoroughly defeated, thoroughly frightened away. But you wouldn't accept that. You wouldn't take the sensible way out and give Giles up. You began to interfere with Richard. So now—there's only one ending. What happens to me afterward no longer matters. Not even Charles is really mine."

I wanted to cry out that there was still Richard, whom she loved. But I dared not speak and give away my position.

"You believed everything, didn't you?" she went on. "All my pretense of being so fond of you! Oh, it was true enough once, when you were younger. And I could be fond enough of you while you stayed away from the island. But after you became a threat to Elise as Richard's mother, pretending to love you turned into a role that nauseated me."

I listened to her, sick at heart to think how fondly and trustingly I had accepted her seeming affection.

"It gave me real pleasure to tell Elise where the emerald brooch was hidden," she went on almost conversationally. "I knew she would go and get it and defeat Kitty's intention of having Charles find it where she had left it. Though of course I'd foiled that intention the first time long ago. You said your mother must have left a letter for Charles when she went away. It's true—she did. But I found it first and hid it away all these years. I wanted Charles to think Kitty had kept the brooch deliberately. I didn't care whether it was ever found or not. Later I gave the letter to Elise, and she tried to find their mailing place. But she never could until you gave Charles the real clue as to where the brooch was hidden. Then she went and got it at once. Paul was coming across from The Bitterns that morning, and he almost caught her coming out of the tomb with it. She coaxed him away among the trees to talk to her, and while they were walking about, you and Charles went into the tomb. You heard them from there. Elise always wanted that brooch, and in the end she had it for a little while. Though only for—a little while."

The words choked off, and for an endless length of time the night was still. Nearby insects had hushed at the sound of a human voice, but now they took up their clatter again. My flesh crept at Aunt Amalie's words. I could see Elise wearing the brooch secretly, superstitiously, the night of the ball, conniving with her mother.

"Are you listening to me?" Aunt Amalie's voice sounded closer this time. "I've wanted you to understand fully why you must make a payment now. The past can't repeat itself, I tell you. Now you'll never have Giles or Richard."

Helplessly, I crept toward the back along the rough wall. She could not see me. She could not know where to aim. That was my only hope.

The first shot crashed into the long cave of the tomb and ricocheted against the arch of the roof. The explosion seemed to echo and re-echo forever in that dark and hollow place. I sobbed for breath and moved frantically away from the back wall.

"You can't escape," she called to me. "I've plenty of ammunition. And I can be a patient woman."

Once more she pulled the trigger. The awful crash of the explosion was repeated as the bullet splintered tabby and brick from the wall at the back.

Would it do any good to plead with her? Would it help to point out that if she killed me she would destroy her own life and injure Floria and Richard? But I knew it would not. She had crossed some invisible line into alien territory. Had she been in a passion of grief, or even a passion of hatred toward me, she might have been more approachable. But this was cold madness. The strain in her fabric had always been there, waiting, concealed because she was letter-perfect in the role she had chosen to play. She had called me to her, tested me out, and finally gone deliberately about her intention to destroy me. Until now she had failed. But now—

She had not fired again and I wondered what fearful strategy she meant to try now. I had not heard her move. I could not see her out there among a hundred other shadows. But she was there and she waited, perhaps moving nearer under the very sound of her firing.

Her voice cut suddenly through the stillness, chill with warning, and I realized the words were not addressed to me.

"Don't come any closer. Stay where you are, whoever you are! This is between Lacey and me."

"Mother!" Floria cried. "Mother, you can't do this. It will harm all of us tragically. Giles is here, and Charles, and Paul—"

My heart leaped with unexpected hope. Floria had gone for help. They had heard the shots. Giles was here.

Amalie did not raise her voice. "Stay your distance . . ."

I shrank against the wall and steeled myself to the inevitable roar of sound. There were cries outside in the grove and the running of feet. Then another shot, close at hand, but not directed at me. Floria screamed, and under cover of the confusion, I rushed up from the tomb and I tried to slip around behind it. The next bullet grazed my shoulder. I went stumbling to my knees with pain searing my upper arm as I tried to crawl away into shadow. I could see them now in the moonlight. Giles was struggling with Amalie, fighting to wrest the gun from her hand.

They seemed to move in a dreadful, endless dance, with Floria and Charles and Paul locked to the outskirts of a circle around them. Then Paul moved in and clasped Amalie by one arm. Giles tore the gun from her hand and flung it into the underbrush. A moment later he came running toward me and nearly stumbled over me. Then he knelt and touched me gently.

"It's my shoulder," I said.

He picked me up in his arms and carried me away from the burying ground. The others were gone, suddenly, strangely, and I heard a shouting, no longer near. Giles paid no attention. He carried me along the path and up the steps to the house. The servants had gathered about on the drive, and Vinnie came running toward us as Giles brought me inside. She gave me a single look, and fled away to fetch whatever was needed.

Upstairs in my room, the two of them worked over me quickly and efficiently, and I did not mind the pain, now that the nightmare was over. I lay quietly on my bed, and

from where I lay I could see my packed suitcase standing
near the closet door, my raincoat flung over a chair. The
sight of them reminded me.

"Tomorrow I'm going away," I told Giles again. "I won't
come back here any more."

"Don't talk foolishness," Vinnie said. "You ain't goin' no
place right away." Then she murmured, "Oh, poor Miss
Amalie," and went out of the room to hide her own emotion.

I tried desperately to sit up, and Giles pushed me back
with a firm hand. "Lie still. Give the bleeding a chance to
stop."

I had to talk to him. I had to try, but he hushed me at
once.

"I know there are things you want to tell me, but now
isn't the time. I know there's more to the story than Floria
blurted out, but I can wait for the rest."

I knew all the more why I loved him. He would be fair,
at least, and as generous as was possible.

He bent over me. "I will never forgive you, Lacey, for not
telling me at once. But I love you, and I will try to understand the rest of what you've done."

He kissed me almost angrily, and I knew he was angry
because of all those wasted years that lay behind us. Yet in
the same instant I remembered Elise. Remembered her as
she had been as a young girl. Would it ever have worked
out if I had gone to Giles with the truth at that time? Would
he not have felt bound to me because the baby was his, and
not because of the love he could feel for me now? I didn't
know.

When the others returned to the house and came upstairs,
he was sitting beside my bed holding my hand. They came
into the room, and Floria dropped into a chair nearby. She
looked quite dreadful, her face drawn and haggard. Charles
went to stand beside a window, to stare into the darkness
toward whatever nightmare now haunted him. It was Paul
who stood at the foot of my bed and told us what had
happened.

"Amalie broke away from us and ran toward the ruins
of the old fort. We went after her, but we were confused
about her direction, and she was well ahead of us when she
climbed up on the parapet and went over into the river. We
were too late. There's no way to find her until morning."

The room was quiet. I closed my eyes and thought of this
double loss. I had lost Amalie in life. Lost the loving aunt I

had believed in. Now we had all lost her in death. She had thrown everything away so needlessly. Even Elise's life had been thrown away because of Amalie's obsessive hatred of her sister's child. And now what of Richard, who must face another death? Where was he? I wondered. Why hadn't he heard the shots and the noise when we came back to the house? Why had he not come to this room?

Before I could ask about him, Charles turned from the window. I saw how white and old he looked. "It's better this way," he said. "Amalie couldn't face the aftermath of Elise's death—the aftermath of causing it. Paul has told me what she did. I've been worried about her for several days, but I was afraid to face the truth. Part of this is my fault."

Floria made a harsh sound of pain, but she did not repudiate Charles's words. "I knew! I knew the night of the ball. I saw her coming back from the beach, and I knew she was planning something dreadful—just as she had planned other attempts upon Lacey's life. That was why I had to accuse Lacey so recklessly—so I could hide my mother's actions. Later, after Lacey talked about the loose stone, I put on my Merlin cape and went down there to fix the rock so that Mother would not be blamed. The beard was in a pocket of the cape, and I must have lost it there among the rocks."

All the small details were coming clear now, and I felt sorry for Floria, who had never been her mother's favorite daughter.

She went on, still not through. "This afternoon, when I was putting Elise's photographs and letters back together after Richard spilled them out of their box, I found the letter Kitty wrote you many years ago, Charles, telling how she had left the emerald brooch for you to find."

"Aunt Amalie told me about that letter," I said to Floria. "It was she who gave it to Elise. Now it must be given to Charles."

"It doesn't matter any more," Charles said sadly.

"I still wanted to save her from herself," Floria ran on. "Tonight I tried as brutally as I could to send Lacey away under a cloud that would separate her from Giles forever. That was the only thing that would have satisfied my mother. But I knew quickly enough that it was the wrong thing to do. I'm sorry, Lacey. I almost cost you your life."

I had never seen Floria cry before. Paul went to her and put an arm about her. "Don't take so much blame on yourself. We're all partly at fault. For what we saw and didn't speak about. For the things each of us thought he wanted and couldn't have."

A silence lay upon the room as the truth of his words came home to us. A sound from the hallway caught my attention, and I turned my head as the others swung around. Richard stood in the bedroom doorway.

"What has happened?" he asked. "I was up in the lighthouse tonight when I heard the shooting. It took me a long time to get back here. Where is my grandmother?"

"There—there's been an accident," Floria said feebly.

Richard came past the others toward the bed and stood looking at me. "You've been hurt!" And then anxiously, "Cousin Lacey, are you all right?"

I held out a hand to him. "I'm fine. What happened to me isn't serious."

"I'm glad," he said with a relief that touched me. His gaze traveled from one to another of us around the room, and I think there was not a pair of eyes that could meet his own.

"He'll have to be told," Floria said harshly.

Richard threw her a quick look and then turned back to me. "My grandmother wanted to hurt you, didn't she, Cousin Lacey? She didn't like you. She tried all the time to make me hate you, just the way my—my mother did. But I never could. Tonight she tried to shoot you, didn't she?"

It was chilling to hear him. I had forgotten how calmly in our time the young can take the subject of violence. I had forgotten how they are so often bombarded with it on every side that horror can sometimes be accepted as we could never accept it when we were as young as Richard.

"Is she dead?" he asked us point-blank.

There was not one of us who could answer him easily. But I was his mother, and I had to try.

"We think she is," I told him. "She—fell into the river. We can't search for her until morning."

His long lashes came down over his eyes and then he opened them and looked steadily at his father. Giles went to him and put an arm about his shoulders.

"It got to be so I was afraid of her," Richard said.

"There was no need to be," Giles assured him. "She always loved you very much. And you must go on loving her. If you want to go to your room now, I'll come in later and say good night."

Floria jumped up from her chair. "I'll come with you, Richard."

They seemed to have forgiven each other for their earlier quarrel.

When they had left, Paul said, "I'd better go downstairs and phone the police."

Giles nodded, and Paul and Charles went out of the room together. Giles returned to his place beside my bed.

"Richard will be all right," I said to him in relief. "He has more strength in him than we give him credit for. I'm glad you gave his grandmother back to him. The truth needn't ever be known outside of this room."

He took my hand and held it against his cheek. "We'll tell him soon that you are his mother. We'll tell him that he's *our* son."

"No," I said. "Not for a long, long time. Not until he is older and can understand the reasons. Not until he is used to having me around and can perhaps love me as I hope he will someday. For now, let's leave him his happier memories of Elise. Too much has been taken away from him."

Giles slipped an arm beneath me, careful of my shoulder, and held me to him. "Lacey," he said. "Oh, Lacey!"

From the window I could hear the ocean sound forever rushing in upon the island. But it was of the river and the marshes that I thought. Tonight they held their tragic secret. Tomorrow they would give it up and a new peace would come to Hampton Island. Tomorrow we would begin again. The island was not lost to me any more.